Davidia and AUNTY'S CURSE

Ken Spargo

Published in Australia by Sid Harta Publishers Pty Ltd,
ABN: 46 119 415 842
23 Stirling Crescent, Glen Waverley, Victoria 3150 Australia
Telephone: +61 3 9560 9920, Facsimile: +61 3 9545 1742
E-mail: author@sidharta.com.au

First published in Australia 2020
This edition published 2020
Copyright © Ken Spargo 2020
Cover design, typesetting: WorkingType (www.workingtype.com.au)

Spargo, Ken
Davidia and Aunty's Curse
ISBN: 978-1-925707-45-8
pp274

ABOUT THE AUTHOR

Ken lives in Melbourne, Australia.

His first venture into writing began on a sewerage farm whilst engaged in an aquaculture project in 2002. On a boring Friday afternoon, his imagination got the better of him and he decided to fill in his time by writing a nonsense short story called *The Frog who Hopped on One Leg.*

Within a year he had written a series of short stories and a year later began his first novel, *Stumped.*

Imagination provides an endless supply of ideas used to create and craft his crime and fantasy fiction novels, his preferred genres.

He loves to travel, with many places he has visited providing inspiration for his novels. He has travelled extensively throughout Europe, Asia and other parts of the world and actually lived and worked in Austria, Europe, New Zealand and Papua New Guinea. Caravanning locally is also of great interest.

Ken's primary occupation is an accountant currently running his own business.

Sport has been a major influence in Ken's life. His two crime fiction novels *Stumped* and *Double Bogey* have both been influenced by his involvement with sport (cricket and golf).

Ken's inspiration for writing the Davidia series of novels has been his daughter, Sophie. He has assisted in raising two children.

All novels have been written with a sense of humour which is a refreshing feeling and allows the seriousness of life to relax. We all need escapism at times.

Other titles in the Davidia series:
Davidia and the Prince of Triplock
Davidia and the Six Sisters
Davidia and Grandma's Memories
Davidia and the Knowledge Tree
Davidia and the Foreboding Dinner
Davidia and Senora College

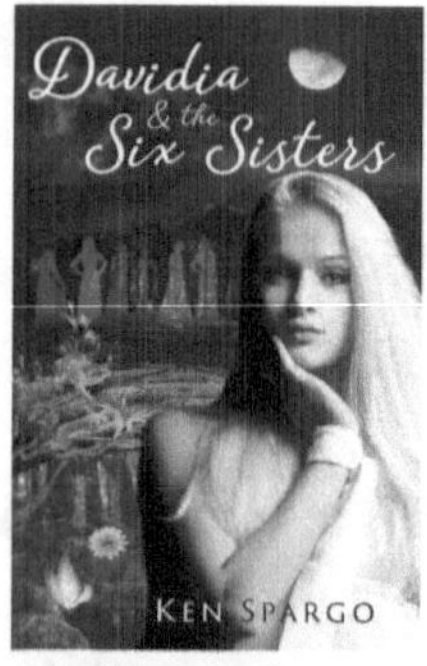

Contents

PROLOGUE

The mysterious occupant, who lived in the dilapidated house at the quarry's edge, had the inhabitants of Humpletoon intrigued as to who she might really be. No one knew from where she had originated or what her past represented. It seemed that an eyesore construction had virtually appeared overnight.

Very few villagers ever visited that site any more since the quarry had closed for further use. The new silhouetted old, aged building that dominated one edge had upset many. Rumours abounded about whether she was a witch, had a terminable disease and had she infected the community with a dull outlook making her responsible for all their poor attitudes? Her rare visits to town were eyed with suspicion and superstition. The villagers avoided contact by walking along the opposite side of the street. Rarely did she engage in conversation with anyone. No one could be more alone or thought to be. Personal and enforced choices had made life's interesting decisions. She was not here by personal choice. So, what caused her to settle in this part of the world?

Was she cursed?

If she was, how did it occur?

* * *

'Who is our mysterious aunt, mum?' asked Davidia.

It was school holidays and Davidia's mum had thought of sending her to visit the almost long forgotten relative. She thought that it would be an interesting visit to meet someone from long ago. Slirander was invited to go also.

What would they find?

A mysterious aunt with a blank-filled past living in an outpost certainly had them intrigued.

'Aunt Mavis didn't always live there. There are things from her past that were not well understood by other family members. It would be nice if she engaged with the modern youth of today and maybe we could see more of her.'

'Is she old? Does she have any peculiarities?'

'Your visit will answer all of your questions.'

The curse, if there was one, wasn't mentioned.

Two young girls set off on the visit of a lifetime.

1   QUARRY

The small hamlet of Humpletoon nestled neatly amongst the ranges in the rustic valley of the Muglaze Mountains. It once had a significant claim to fame to a quarry that was mined for the finest of clays. It was now a forgotten hole in the ground acting as the local tip, full of many personal and forgotten items from people's lives. Sometimes the objects of waste were rebirthed by scavengers as new art and some were recycled into usable objects again.

The stench of the tip was unbearable. When inhaled, the nostrils did the itchy tango and an erect digit finger stood stiff as if leading a cavalry charge. The itch was dispensed in an efficient manner and finally wiped on an item of clothing to be later dispensed with in the wash.

The local council had long favoured the quarry to recommence clay production, providing a good quality seam could be located. Underneath all that rotting compost and abandoned whitegoods might lay another special clay seam waiting to be discovered again. After much procrastination and time-wasting – both creditable and well-known councillor traits – a decision was made to reopen the quarry to clay mining again and hopefully discover that new clay seam. Unemployment was high within the town and the local potters might once again be regaled as the finest ever.

'Dah! I could do that again, if I could remember what it was I used to do,' said someone.

'I could help,' said another.

With this pair of geniuses in town, the keeper of the potting wheel might be in good hands. Perhaps they thought that potting was a cue ball being sent into a pool table corner pocket or a toilet training activity for very small humans.

Whatever the town folk thought, the quarry was to be reopened.

'They won't find anything down there. It's been over fifty years since it was last mined. I used to play there back then and the talk at the time was that the clay had all been mined,' said a retired child.

'If there is the chance of finding more of that special clay, it's definitely worth the attempt,' said a retired miner.

His life had almost passed by, but he still had a keen interest in his former worksite.

The big day for the tip clean-out arrived. The local councillors all made a last nostalgic visit to the site to relive some cherished childhood memory of scrapes and climbing through rotting garbage to seize some treasured find. No one had actually seen the bottom of the quarry covered by layers of rubbish and filth for a very long time.

'I never did find the bottom of the quarry. The rubbish was too deep. It will be interesting to see what it actually looks like,' said a senior councillor. 'There's probably nothing of great interest down there, but mud, sludge, stagnant water and an inventive imagination. Hopefully, a new clay seam will be discovered. That would assist the town.'

As a child, there were thoughts of demons of such gigantic proportions that they swallowed you whole. There could be ghosts that spoke of their haunting routines as if they had a day job and creepy little animals that nipped the soles of footwear as one walked by. Myths were born in an imaginative mind. The councillors all stood like lonely sentinels, surveying the filthy mess for the last time and expunging their childhood thoughts of remembering what a great time it was.

*   *   *

'The school holidays will be here next week,' said Davidia's mum, bustling around the kitchen like a train station attendant, opening cupboards and peering in, seeking any clever dinner thoughts that might emerge from their hiding place. 'Davidia, would you like to visit a distant relative for a few days?'

'Who would that be? I didn't know that we had any distant relatives. Don't I know all of the family?' she replied.

'Technically you do; however, this one is a recluse and isn't well-known to us. I thought that it might be a chance for you to meet the last of the great-aunties who still exist before time snuffs her out.'

'How come I have never heard her mentioned before? Is she a secret?'

'She has become the family embarrassment. It's rumoured that she never lets water embrace her body and the peculiar odour that accompanies her can be sniffed a block away before you actually meet. She wears clothing riddled with lice-like creatures and when she methodically picks them off, she reminds you of a monkey inspecting another for fleas. She lived alone on a farm and we all thought that she was rather peculiar. Years ago, she left without trace to heaven knows where. I can only guess her age.'

'Why should I go and meet someone I've never met? She mightn't like me or want any visitors or want to be discovered by family. It sounds strange to me. I have enough weirdo land at school, let alone being related to it. What made you suggest a visit?'

'I remembered her birthday the other day. Why? I have no idea. I was napping on the couch and a mist filled my mind full of holes, magic spells, an old lady with a threadbare hat which allowed her hair space to blow in the breeze and a thick, motley-looking coat that would sit comfortably on a gangster. The mountains, the mountains, that's where my thoughts led me, so I checked out what I could recall. I found an old art brochure whilst rummaging in the attic for anything old and stored. The name of Humpletoon was written across it. It was once famous for its pottery. I think she liked pottery too and I have a feeling that she lives there. I would love you to go and visit just to ensure that she hasn't been totally forgotten. Often, older- age people can develop the cloak of invisibility when youth has its own interests. It might be good for you too.'

'If I decide to go, can Slirander come with me? She likes oddball stuff and we are safer travelling as a duet.'

'Of course. Why not?'

Davidia rang Slirander and asked her if she wanted a visit to the mountains and meet an eccentric relative. She agreed and the two friends could hardly wait for their weird school holiday to begin. What harm could come to them? Two young, strong-minded girls could take on the world and win.

Would they this time?

* * *

On the far side of the quarry, a small, seemingly dilapidated house stood against the ravages of time. It appeared so fragile that a strong gust of wind would send it skywards. It hadn't yet fallen over for fear of never remaining upright again. It was out of sight of the local town and, more importantly, it didn't create an eyesore when anyone visited the quarry. The local councillors were rather particular about their tidy town. If they could have that "shack" removed, then everyone, except its inhabitant, would prefer that to be the case. Comments such as prime real estate may have been thought of, but never openly mentioned. A few unsavoury real estate agents, the current mayor affectionately known as "The Grabber" and a few unscrupulous town investors all had an eye on that site. It covered at least ten acres. Nobody knew whether the land possessed any wealth other than its location; however, it was cause for concern for the future of the owner.

'Once the quarry has been reopened, I will try and have that unsightly shack removed from that site and purchase the land for a song. I'll pass a council rezoning law altering it from residential to farming. That should do it. It will become worthless with a rezoning once we recommence mining. That old lady who lives there will become an obstruction to progress,' said the mayor, with pride; his pride.

The Grabber had slowly purchased most of the available real estate over many years for personal reasons, which he didn't share with anyone, not even his wife, who dressed in the period costume of when times were better. Apparently, her addition to the family had been two kids and little else. The mayor had his own attitude and beliefs. Bully might be a descriptive title that applied. His largest admirer and supporter was obviously himself.

A small wisp of smoke trailed into the atmosphere from the shack's most solid construction, the chimney. Watching it felt like it was escaping for the last time. The inhabitant living in there was indeed a distant relative of Davidia's family. It was great-aunt Mavis who had many years ago escaped the scrutiny of being well-known and yearned for a simpler life. She was as old as withered wood, wore clothes a refuse tip would refuse and had quietly controlled, steel-jaw manners.

One of her quirks whispered about was that she was a witch. It was an unfounded rumour, but with heightened ignorance and superstition of that time, safety was only ensured in departure. Hence, she travelled to Humpletoon and settled in its pristine valley where she became reclusive. She was only sighted in town occasionally for a shopping spree for vital food commodities. Her only conversation was a fleeting 'hello' and a strict adherence to her shopping list. She couldn't tolerate other people too well. Her past permeated her daily thoughts and for her they were too tragic to confront. What happened all those years ago? The town people left her alone. She had the solitude she desired, but was she really happy?

*   *   *

Suddenly, the air was split with a loud "vroom, vroom", which echoed throughout the quarry. It sounded like an invasion of a fleet of jumbo jets. It was so deafening. The ground shook with nervousness, the councillors jumped in fright and a little old shack shivered with uncertainty. Two monster excavator diggers with buckets as wide as a small stream grabbed at the ground with menace. Behind them followed an array of adoring big-men Tonka toys, better known as tip-trucks. They performed a mechanical ballet as they picked up the town waste and took it away for recycling or to be dumped as fresh waste at another tip. It took a few days of hard work, but the site was eventually cleared of its mountain of obstructions.

'It's great to see progress,' said the mayor. 'I wonder what we'll find down there.'

The quarry had attained a new freshness with the piles of

rubbish removed. It even smelt different. There weren't any smell-o-meters available to test that theory. The base of the quarry revealed a previously hidden, flat, brownish-tinged soil which the councillors had hoped to discover. It looked like a clay seam that had been hidden for so long. Excitement had reached their pockets. Money began to mentally flow and suddenly they became quite optimistic about the town's future.

What sort of wealth would it bring?

*   *   *

'Mum are you sending a card or letter to your great-aunt advising her that we are coming to visit? She mightn't like surprises.'

'I've already sent a note and hopefully she will be looking forward to your visit.'

'What shall I call her?'

'Aunt Mavis will do. I really hope she finds you both as adorable as I do. You might need to pack a silk sheet sleeve in which to sleep as well as an extra pillowcase. I'm not sure how her health regime is today. If it's anything by going on the past rumours, it's better to be prepared than not.'

Davidia and Slirander were now keenly interested in the strange, old aunt. Her past was shrouded in mystery. It was just what the two young girls thrived on; mystery and gossip about others. It was a winning combination. The beginning of the holidays couldn't start quickly enough.

Curiosity about Aunt Mavis intrigued Davidia. She immediately did some research on her family history and discovered that she was indeed believed to be a witch and was eventually forced to leave her farm. No one took responsibility within the family for forcing her departure. It wasn't spoken about. Being so long ago, to rediscover part of your previously unknown family history was an eye-opener. Davidia shared her thoughts with Slirander. They both decided to investigate whether the allegations of witchcraft were indeed true. Their impending holiday was increasing in interest every day. What would they find when a meeting eventually materialises?

One night shortly before her departure, Davidia lay awake wondering what adventures lay ahead. She dozed off a few times before slumber won the evening.

*   *   *

'What are you doing here? It's forbidden to see me,' said a voice.

'I had to come and warn you that trouble is walking this way. Those brothers of yours are leading the mob,' replied the deliverer of bad news.

'I haven't done anything to deserve this attention.'

'They don't care. They believe that the farm given to you by your father is theirs and not yours. They have spread malicious lies about you being a witch and everyone believes them. I know they have paid a few to agitate and bully the others. I've come to warn you. Take care.' The deliverer scampered lest she was also caught up in an unsavoury outcome.

The lady of the house peered through smudged windows, the collectors of farming dust over the years, and could see a group heading towards her home. There wasn't a happy face in sight. They weren't marathon runners, were they? As they neared her front gate, which had rusted with the age of the farm, she walked out to confront them. They carried fire sticks with hot embers falling to the ground, spitting and spluttering for release from their mini infernos. The truth and the protagonists faced each other.

The older brother raised a hand with a pointed finger followed by a verbal damnation.

'You have been found guilty of witchcraft. This town sentences you to burn.'

'But you are my brother? What has happened to you?'

A crash of broken glass was heard. A small flask of alcohol had slipped from his grasp. The contents were absorbed by the parched soil. It was the wrong watering liquid to grow any flora. Anger was the only brew growing tonight. Before any response was made, a sea of fiery torches arced in the night-sky heading towards the timber home. It was a coordinated toss. The darkness emphasised the beauty of fire if it worked for you and not against you. They landed with immediate impact. Whoosh! Up went her home. The lady had enough time to run inside to retrieve her coat and flee out the back door, avoiding martyrdom and a grisly death. From a safe distance, she witnessed her home and that of her father disintegrate into ashes. In time, the landscape will reclaim the lot. Nobody followed her. The unsightly and threatening crowd finally dispersed with bravado noises randomly shouted into the night air. It wasn't listening. They sounded like a sty full of grunting pigs. The lady sat there most of the evening, a lonely, solitary figure. Once labelled a witch, it meant banishment. The ignorant had been blessed with the "led by the nose gene" and didn't have any capacity for individual objective thought. Once daylight broke the night-sky's tight hold on the darkness, the lady left. No one knew where she had gone. Poof! Disappeared like a melting snowflake. Years later, the two brothers who had perpetrated the falsehood had split and also gone their own ways, leaving behind conjecture and a mystery as to their future. They weren't in any witness protection program to be rediscovered by a private detective. It was just another ordinary mystery, the type one would like to solve.

*   *   *

Davidia in her part-sleep phase was becoming restless. Her youthful torso twisted and turned as she grappled with her mental thoughts. By the frequency of movement, it must certainly have been busy in there.

'Come and find me,' a young female voice whispered.

A vision appeared in her mind, like a misty stretched fabric with an indistinguishable face. A long, metres-long sinewy finger pointed toward her. It appeared to rest on the tip of her nose. It felt cold. Her nose twitched. Davidia brought her hand up to brush it away when she felt a strong sense of urgency to answer the request that she had imagined.

'Where are you?' she replied, with eyes closed.

'Come and find me,' the voice repeated.

'Are you lost?'

'Come and find me,' repeated the voice.

Suddenly, the vision disappeared and Davidia awoke. Had she imagined or dreamed of the encounter? She felt her nose and could still feel the impact of the cold finger. She hadn't joined any yoga or exercise classes at school to explain her meditative state of mind, which she has been told would experience weird moments when deep in thought. She dismissed it as normal dreaming. Subconsciously, a space was available in her mind to file doubt in and wonder whether it really had happened at all.

'It's time to hug my pillow.'

2   THE JOURNEY

'The brown, tangerine-coloured clay that the excavators have scooped up may hold the answer to the town's future,' said the mayor, as he oversaw the extraction process. Dollar signs constantly rang in his head as a permanent headache. No Aspirin could solve this type of pain, the headache ring.

The scooped-up material was dumped into large tip-trucks which had an insatiable appetite for filling without regard as to whether the clay was a living organism or not. It was, but only one individual knew and she lived next door to the quarry. No quality testing had been performed on the clay to determine its suitability or otherwise for pottery products. It was only assumed in the race to create money from the excavation. A rush without due care might have unexpected consequences.

'Hey, you with the rotten teeth. Be careful how you handle us,' said a clay clod to the excavator bucket. It was ignored.

'Who says I have to tolerate being dumped in a dirty tip-truck?' said another.

The tip-truck was being filled with scoopfuls of the tinge-coloured clays that were forming their own protest group. They disliked being pressed tightly together by sheer weight and losing their individuality. These clays were the art-form clays impregnated with strong opinions. Each clod knew that when they left home, they would never return and, if they did, they would be as someone else's rubbish. The truck journey was their last together as a family. Once parted at their destination, it was usually a permanent goodbye. Sigh! It was another family break-up.

The tailgate loosened and the excitement was building. The driver shared with them some form of abuse at the uncooperative handles until they performed their job satisfactorily. The back began to elevate and the load slowly slipped from its tight formation into an involuntary slide and the clays were greeted with a gleefully, whirring conveyor belt.

'Hop on, lads. It's the last thing you're going to do.'

That might be true for some of them, but each privately hoped that it was to be another clod, not them. The clays were now in front of a red, brick structure with very tall chimneys. Little did they know that the bricks that gave the structure its shape and strength were previous relatives, albeit from an inferior clay. It was almost like a family reunion with the cousins you didn't want to meet. Apparently, they had no real talent other than to become oblong in shape and stay with their family for years. The art-form clays believed their qualities were superior and should be put to better use. Opinions are just that; opinions.

It was the clays' last glimpse of the outside world as clay clods as they disappeared via a conveyor belt that transported its sticky cargo into the darkness of the pottery world. This was a dark and mysterious place where each clod that entered never returned in quite the same condition. It was a clod-changing experience.

The potters viewed each clay clod as an experiment. There was no sentiment, "good guy" attitude or friendly treatment. This was the most dangerous place to be in the hands of the potting manipulators. Silent protests of, *'Leave me alone, you finger-prodding imbecile. Get me off this turning wheel, I'm giddy. Who gave you permission to misshape me?'* filtered throughout the clods.

Amongst the potters was a particularly nasty individual who had the worst potting track record for waste. His anger management method, if he was dissatisfied with any created piece regardless of its value, was to smash these items by throwing them forcibly onto the stone floor. Once they disintegrated, he kicked at them, accompanied by a stream of vitriol. The damaged bits were left to flounder on the floor as permanent waste, which he refused to sweep away. The large, thick boots with steel soles completed the task of rubble-making by continuously walking over them. Eventually, they became dust and blended well with the stone floor. It was unfortunate that he was also the top potter in town with the most creative hands and ideas. In recent years, the pottery trade had almost died off due to the lack of good quality potting clay. He now felt a resurgence would occur with the new-found supply of clay. His hands represented two sets of gnarled tree twigs with smooth palms from years of moulding wet clay. He was reclusive in his social demeanour. His hair doubled as a head blanket, invisibility cloak and conversation topic. It dangled down as far as his waist. No one could recognise him even if they had an existing photo. Wrinkles etched in his face were the waterways of his life. Everyone thought that he was a loner. Where he came from originally was never explained or questioned. So, who was he?

'Look how filthy this lot is,' said a potter.

'They must be cleaned before they are of any use,' said another.

A group of budding potters were on hand to view the new town treasure.

The potters lifted the clods and threw them into a warm water bath to remove the clinging dirt particles that had a liking for travel. After a torrid scrubbing, the now orange clay clods emerged as one sticky mess. They were placed on clean, silver, cool trays to rest. This was the last opportunity that each clay clod had to say a final goodbye as they breathlessly waited for the next section of their exciting journey. They might experience a shaping, a moulding and perhaps a visit to a hot kiln. What a treat! Each clod was a separate entity with some destined to be jugs, vases, jars, plates or many other items. The only hope of continued family contact would be if they were made into a set of something for the same buyer.

*   *   *

'Goodbye, mum,' said Davidia, as she hugged her mother. 'We will say hello to Aunt Mavis for you and bring home a selfie with her.'

'That would be nice. Bye, Slirander. Keep her out of trouble.'

The two excited schoolgirls entered the train and took their places in two reserved, second-class seats. Each had a modest backpack for the essentials that a young woman required at all times. The carriage was rather empty. Perhaps Humpletoon isn't a popular place to visit? The seats were imitation leather – vinyl being the correct name – riveted along the edges tracing the seat's contours, securely fastening it to its wooden supports. The train was an old, steam locomotive not often used on main railway gauges. It was more a boutique train travelling the lesser-known lines. A toot of the whistle and they were on their way.

'I dreamt about Aunt Mavis the other night, or I thought I did,' said Davidia. 'It scared me. It was the first time I had actually seen a real witch. I didn't sleep too well.'

'Real witches can be rather scary, but I have a feeling about your Aunt Mavis and it doesn't frighten me,' replied Slirander.

Who's the heroine?

She didn't always give the benefit of the doubt to rumours and myths and she wondered whether this time, the oral history of the family was correct. Stories have the propensity to change when verbally passed through families. It's like grandpa telling you that the Datsun with three wheels that he had purchased many years ago — apparently thievery was ripe in the neighbourhood — had somehow turned into a racing, red Ferrari. It was still a good story, even if the paint job was exaggerated.

The train wound its way through the hills, chugging and struggling uphill and excelling in the downhill run. There were only two stops on the way. The first was at a small village called Uncletoon with a modest population. It seemed most of them stood on the railway platform as the train pulled in. A welcoming toot and there was a mad rush for seating as soon as the train stopped. Most of the passengers were young with a few seniors filtered in amongst them. Most had backpacks — must be travelling to a backpackers' convention somewhere; however, there were only two stops to go. Davidia and Slirander were ignored. Soon, wisps of a pungent smoke darkened the carriage interior. The smoke joined forces like old friends and blanketed the ceiling in a grey covering, obliterating it from view. Most of the passengers had a look of bewilderment on their faces as small, white objects were poked in and out of them. They tried to suck it in; however, their hands wouldn't let go of them so it was only the smoke that fried their brains. The white objects gradually burnt down to be useless. There were lots of, 'hey mon, dude and I'm artificially interior', words which had a confusing aspect.

'They must be on holiday fumes,' said Davidia. 'It certainly has a familiar smell. That new kid at school was handing them out as a free sample. He called them happy sticks. I tried it, but found my breath needed repair after it.'

'It certainly makes me sleepy,' replied Slirander.

Her head space had now been invaded by a not-unfamiliar, misty source, but no one was telling.

The train continued to struggle through the hills and stopped at the town of Muggletoon. It was another modest offering. No one got on or off. It felt like the town had been ignored. There weren't any window snoopers that the girls could see. Maybe it was uninhabited. The final destination was around the next bend. The town of Humpletoon. The train pulled into the station whistle-blowing, with passengers tripping over each other aiming for the nearest exit. The odd person exited via the window, imagining a short, bungy jump or parachute drop. The cloudy fog that had circulated in the carriage during the journey had certainly increased risk-taking behaviour and bravado. The girls waited until the sea of disturbance and chaos had quietened down. They were the final two to exit.

The station had heritage appeal with its fine lacework, huge, stumpy posts and a corrugated-tin roof, the site of many repetitive paint jobs. The rust was still well-hidden. It felt like the town's first embrace. The country feel oozed through them. The station-master was ferreting around, manipulating his hat to stay straight on his bald head. He noticed the two girls who looked like two lost calves in a paddock with their udders on their backs. It was his responsibility to direct lost souls to their place of salvation and it wasn't a Sunday. That was another day. He approached them. The girls were startled. Was he the town dignitary to meet and greet them; not that they were expecting anyone? With the manners of royalty, he doffed his hat in a chivalrous manner by removing it. The girls relaxed. No one was forewarned of their arrival except Aunt Mavis and she was as invisible as a politician's promise on the hustings.

'Good afternoon, girls. Can I be of assistance?' asked the polite station-master.

He had a ruddy face with reddish blotches from burst blood vessels which had tried to escape, but alas, were trapped by his skin. He was about forty with a body shape that could easily roll down a hill. By the look of him, he grazed in an excellent paddock. Life was relaxed in Humpletoon. In recent years with the lack of employment, it had become a popular, drop-out tourist resort where the pension allowed an affordable, but not kingly lifestyle. The station-master was a long-term resident and a local. His apprenticeship as a local had been served from birth.

'We are new in town. This is our first visit,' said Davidia. 'We have come to visit a family friend. Her name is Aunt Mavis. Do you know where she lives?'

The station-master looked startled. No one had kicked him in the stomach, but fill with pain it did. He suddenly hunched over, if that was possible in his tightly-fitting uniform and uttered a range of vowels and syllables an interpreter wouldn't understand. He stammered his next few words.

'Aauunntt wwhhoo?' He sieved these words out through his teeth which acted as a set of unopened gates.

'Aunt Mavis. My mum told me to visit her if I was in the area. She still lives here, doesn't she? I'd be terribly disappointed if I had wasted my journey. I haven't ever met her. Do you know her? Is she nice?'

The innocence of youth asking probing questions to a startled adult, who obviously had some hesitancy about answering, was now the hardest task of his day. His face had enlarged like a fun balloon at the carnival, but without any pleasant expression. His pain had nowhere else to go. It just sat on his face.

'You did say Aunt Mavis, didn't you?' He wasn't sure he had heard correctly the first time.

'Yes. She's a family friend and this is my school friend and bestie, Slirander. We are on school holidays and mum sent us up here for a few days, probably more to give her a break. Do you know Aunt Mavis?'

The station-master was well-aware of the old lady recluse he had never spoken to and had occasionally observed at the small grocery shop. Everyone in any small town knew everybody else's business, whether they wanted them to know or not. The Mayor and his group of brown-nose councillors – it was thought that their facial colouring was a holiday tan – didn't want any riff-raff on the streets. He tolerated the blow-ins because they were tidier, spent money and kept the economy afloat. Witches, superstition and foul-smelling clothing weren't traits he rated as acceptable. Apparently, Aunt Mavis and he had also never spoken, but each time he had sighted her in town, he crossed the street as his avoidance technique. It was sad to think that ignorance was as popular as daylight.

'I will make a few enquiries, wait here.'

The station-master disappeared into a hole in the wall – his office – on a pretend errand of enquiry-making. In truth, he had whipped inside to ring the Mayor and let him know that two young girls were asking after that old lady recluse. He thought that he was warning them of what, wasn't explained. The girls sat down on a wooden, slatted seat with spacing large enough for their bodies to sink between. It had intricate iron formwork on each end, creating an artistic piece. The girls waited for enlightenment about Aunt Mavis. Had she left town, died or hidden for so long that no one remembered where, or who, she was?

Were a range of excuses about to blossom into a negative list?

*   *   *

Amongst the clay clods was a special-thinking, individual clay called Mac. He was a bit of a loner and he thought that he didn't possess any special skills. He patiently sat on a tray in the coolroom with all the other cleaned clods. It was a waiting game. An attendant with a huge smile, rough hands and a set of teeth a dentist could retire on, entered and gleamed at the tray with unbridled enthusiasm. He leant over and a pair of large hands gripped the tray upon which Mac was resting and yelled out so loud, as if he had won a prize.

'I gotcha.'

The tray was carried along a corridor where other items wished them luck.

'Don't turn out like us,' a few made products yelled out.

'Don't become waste,' said a few others.

It didn't sound a thrilling place of contented pieces. A lot of clay clods were unhappy in their new, "you-beaut" form. Some groaned that as a vase they were always wet. An art piece sat at a peculiar angle and another was so small, one wondered where was the rest of it? Many became so disappointed with their new shape, especially if they were a useless ornament. Sometimes, they deliberately fell off the shelf to be damaged with the hope of being recycled into something new and better. That was a hopeless cause because they usually ended up as rubbish in landfill similar to which they had previously escaped from.

Undaunted, Mac faced his fate with trepidation. What would he become? Perhaps he could become a useable object, maybe an item to be admired, or be an ignored and forgotten piece to spend his days in a kid's cubby house with the pretend tea-party friends? His future was uncertain.

Mac was taken to the moulding room. Presently, he was a single lump of clay with no discernible features or defined characteristics, but he did have colour. It was a magnificent burnt-orange, striped through his clod. These attracted the interest of a particular innovative female potter. She made "in your face" mugs, each of which was a statement about her talents. They always attracted the maximum amount of attention. The process of change and Mac's future was about to commence.

*   *   *

The female potter with the slenderest of hands and soft touch belonged to a young lady who had joined the group of potters in recent years. Her statement mugs made an immediate impact. Everyone wanted one. No one questioned her existence or past. She was just accepted. She wore her hair in a bun with long tresses caressing the side of her head. Her face wasn't actually visible, but peeking out from behind all that hair was a pretty, pert nose, full lips covered heavily with red lipstick and occasionally an exposed cheek. There were no photos of her and no oral history. The potters all tried to mind their own business and not others'. Occasionally, an embarrassing enquiry as to her origins would arise. She ignored them with a few softly, well-chosen words of rebuff. It did the trick. No more questions. In potting circles, she was somewhat of an enigma and known simply as Hands.

Amongst the group, a senior potter of belligerent proportions jealously guarded his specialty of florid art pieces which he believed were the most excellent pieces produced. He was the clay bully, grabbing the best clay for his own purposes. He had arrived at Humpletoon years ago after a disastrous foray into a farming business with a brother who he hasn't seen since. Sibling splits cause the most horrific agonies. He had also become a recluse, loner and rarely mixed with the other town folk. People knew who he was, where he lived, but not of his past. His physical appearance had altered so significantly that no family members, if there were any nearby, would easily recognise him. He had changed his name to Chad. He didn't want to be found. It seems the town hid a serious darkness.

*   *   *

Mac was placed on a hard, cold, stone slab which dimpled his outer surface. Suddenly, an intrusive hand picked him up and gave him a hard slap. He was thrown back onto the slab. Someone started smacking, squashing, punching and continuously rolling him into awkward positions. The hands that dealt this treatment had long, slender, smooth fingers. He was pulled apart, tossed into the air discovering momentary flight, then whack, smack and back onto the slab to be reunited with his other bits. The monotony went on until he became soft and pliable like flavourless, well-chewed chewing gum. Finally, the punishment stopped. Mac was rolled into a round soft ball and left on a turntable, which had bits of a predecessor lingering for another ride. He was an especially fussy clay and found it abhorrent sharing a dirty turntable. It was a new experience.

Mac could hear a kind voice suggesting what he could be made into.

'I love its stripes and smoothness,' she was heard saying.

'Should it be a special ornament?' said another.

Mac thought, *'No! No!'* That would be a waste of his usefulness if he knew what it was. He remembered the wailers from the corridor warning him not to become their awful experience. Mac began to spin. The potter's turntable whirred with delight at an ever-increasing pace. He became giddy and unimpressed with the continual circular motion. Bits could fly off at any time. Whoosh! A dose of ice-cold water was poured over him and he shivered with fright. Brrr! Life as a clod back at the quarry was never this active or interesting.

A pair of thin, firm hands glided into the Mac mass, expertly making a huge hole in his middle. His shape was altering. What a thrill! After a few scary moments, the spinning experience stopped. Mac felt peculiar. He was now a shape he had never been before. What did it mean? He was taken past a mirror and noticed an odd-looking item never dreaming it was himself that he saw. He was still soft and pliable, but possessed a different shape from being a blob on a tray.

For Mac the journey continued.

*   *   *

'Hello girls,' said the mayor who had been alerted by the station-master that they were asking after a town relic. 'I'm the Mayor of this quaint little town and what a pleasure to receive new visitors.'

The mayor had come down to meet the inquisitive visitors and redirect them elsewhere from their intended destination, Aunt Mavis. He had no relationship with the recluse, nor did he desire it; however, he thought that anyone who visited her was in peril. Was it a health issue, intelligent dialogue or criticism of his council that he was afraid of? Whatever it was, a diversion was always thought to be the best outcome.

'Hello, sir,' replied Davidia. It was better to listen than speak at the moment. 'My name is Davidia and this is my friend Slirander.'

'Hello, sir,' said Slirander, politely.

'I understand that you have come to visit a long-lost family friend. Is that correct?'

Both girls nodded in agreement.

'My mum sent us here for the school holidays to stay with Aunt Mavis.'

The mayor's teeth almost fell out as he shuddered with the realisation that someone actually knew, or he thought they did, the town's most famous recluse. He didn't have a good word to say about her. He felt that she was a blot on their good community. In his book, more like a sheet of toilet paper. Anyone who lived in a rambling, almost-dilapidated shack, was rumoured never to bathe and wore clothes that topped the stench scale – or was it a new perfume – should live elsewhere and not be a town eyesore. He had tried before to move her out of town a few times, but the legal system couldn't be defrauded. There was that long-term view that one day it will happen. There was no explanation for this extraordinary viewpoint, but have it, he did.

'It's a long way out of town and I don't think it's safe that you stay there. It's said that the walls of her shack are as thin as rice paper and will soon collapse. There are also earth tremors in that area. I suggest you stay in town where you can enjoy Humpletoon hospitality.'

'No, sir. We are staying at Aunt Mavis'. We didn't come all this way to stay in town. Why shouldn't we visit her? We can enjoy her hospitality,' said a determined Davidia.

'I feel that your interest would be better served by staying closer in town. It's much safer.'

'What do we have to fear? Where's the road to her house? Kindly point out the right direction and we'll take it from here.'

Davidia had her mule stubbornness on display. The face pout, crossed arms and legs astride registered confrontation. The mayor noticed the body language and wasn't ready to take on such defiance. Young girls can be a formidable opponent to words, suggestion and advice. The mayor waved his hand in a northerly direction and mumbled something unpleasant. The station-master had settled down and was glad he didn't give unwanted advice. The girls thanked the mayor and headed north.

Trouble had just left the station.

*   *   *

Mac was taken to a kiln for a clay sauna. In the hot furnace he was placed amongst the demons of heat that gave him a good roasting. His shape glowed with the intense heat. He noticed that his form firmed up and solidified as the heat dried him out. After the sauna, he was put on a shelf to cool down. He thought that was really good.

The final part of his journey involved a lengthy visit by the intrusive paintbrushes. They were expert crevice ticklers. Enamel paint was layered all over him, again and again. The hairy brushes expertly covered him completely. Finally, to his annoyance he was replaced in the kiln for a final firing; however, it was a proud moment as he came out as an object of admiration by the potter.

'You will certainly please a lot of people,' she said, admiringly.

Mac had no idea what that meant, but it was a positive, wasn't it? No longer would he be an ignored useless lump of clay. He hoped that he was a useful object eagerly looking forward to new adventures. Mac was taken from the pottery along with many other newly made products to Humpletoon's main store where a shelf was his new home. Each product was proud of their newness. They all sat silently, waiting for a purchaser and a new life.

It was a lonely time.

*   *   *

'Is it me or is there something strange about this town?' asked Davidia, contemplating her visit from the mayor. 'Did he try to warn us off from visiting Aunt Mavis? It's odd that an important personage would make an effort to welcome two ordinary schoolgirls to their town. We aren't quite in the celebrity class yet.'

'I felt a vibration in his aura,' said Slirander.

She was a highly sensitive young girl and aware of much more than her other friends gave her credit for. Black Magic wasn't only a name of a chocolate brand. Slirander's family had a mix of interesting abilities. She had inherited an unidentified specific gene which went without an explanation, but it gave explanations. It was a gift. Who's going to contend with that explanation?

The girls walked through the main street which was the main part of town. The usual window peekers observed them as they passed. Blinds quickly shut if they were caught peeking. The foot traffic was limited to the occasional shopper who nodded a greeting. The girls felt like they'd stepped back in time. Buildings reeked of old age and history. They doubted that the inhabitants had ever visited a city store and some laneways had five-star accommodation for the town riff-raff and blow-ins. It was only a short walk to the quarry, which they noticed was a large gaping hole in the earth's crust. It was as if its inner soul had been exposed to the world.

'I wonder what they dug up,' said Davidia half thinking of gold, an historical relic or perhaps just dirt for garden compost.

'It is for clay. This is a pottery town,' said Slirander, who was always very observant. She wanted any surprise on her terms, if she was to have any. 'They extract the clay from that pit and turn it into beautiful pottery. We may purchase some whilst here.'

In the distance, a lean-to silhouetted building stood out on the escarpment on the other side of the quarry. It was right near the edge. No engineer's report could save its eventual collapse. An assumption based on supposition doesn't translate into fact.

'That must be where Aunt Mavis lives. There's nothing else out here except open space. It certainly is isolated. I wonder if we have to camp.'

'I hope not. It would be nice to freshen up once she settles us in,' said Slirander, who wasn't normally the clean freak.

They walked slowly around the quarry edge. It had a rocky track acting as a guided pathway to that house. The nearer they got, their apprehension had a growth spurt they weren't expecting. They didn't grow taller, just suspicious. Surely, it wasn't built specifically as a dump because it was imitating one perfectly. The rusted, one-hinged gate hinted that conditions might be variable. They stood and stared.

They had arrived at Aunt Mavis'.

'So much for the holiday destination of a lifetime,' said Davidia.

'It may not be as awful as we think,' said Slirander. Her sensitive aura-detection system was pulsating with activity. 'The aura around here feels calm.'

On either side of the one-hinged gate, the wire fence designed as a property protection erection had weeds sprouting through it as prolific as the tulip fields of the Netherlands in full bloom. There was no discernible grass to mow. It was a mini-jungle. The pathway to the front door hid from view. It wasn't shy. It was embarrassed to expose its disintegrated condition. Not a sole had set foot in that area for a long time. The house itself had a gabled, iron roof as dimpled as a golf ball. The veranda appeared as if it was trying to escape somewhere, but alas, gravity had that route covered. The house appeared as if it was constructed out of thin palings erected at ridiculous angles giving a feel that they were deliberately positioned that way. The front door had holes through it where a whistling wind would freeze whatever was on the other side. It represented a small, neglected collection of wood, tin and rubbish that the tip next door would gladly welcome. It was a "bits and bobs" house from where the girls stood. They were unsure of what they had done to be visiting a museum; or was it a monument to rubbish? Maybe it was a new art theme? There didn't seem to be any physical activity from within the property.

'Slirander, what are you doing? There's no one here to wave to,' said Davidia.

'I'm searching for vibrations. The air is full of electrical impulses peppering my feelings.'

Slirander was slowly moving her hands through the air acting out a meditation ritual. Her fingertips had turned pale blue. All ten of them. They were a set and it was a definite contrast to their normal pinkness. Her face reacted as if it was in the full blast of a wind machine. She hoped that nothing was trying to remove her facial skin. Suddenly, it stopped.

'I can't feel a damn thing. What about my feelings?' said Davidia.

'Don't worry. You still have all of them. Be careful around here. I felt an aura patch in the ether. This place is wired.'

'That's the front fence, stupid.'

Sometimes Davidia let her tongue loose to cover her lack of understanding of what someone had said. It gave her catch-up time.

'No. The front fence is actually wired. This place is booby-trapped. Look closely.'

'I can't see anything.'

'Touch the front gate. Go on, I dare you. If you don't believe me, be the hand guinea pig to prove otherwise.'

Davidia wasn't having any of this silly nonsense. She tried to push the gate open. The sky was a bright blue from where she lay flat on her back. She struggled to her feet like a pugilist ready to go round twenty-seven.

'Wow! What happened? Whew! Is there any more?'

She was disorientated with the electrical charge that she had just fought off and won.

'Sometimes, it's better to listen. That fence is electrocuted and you received a mild shock. Someone doesn't want snoopy around here. I wonder why?'

'This is Aunt Mavis' house, isn't it? We haven't erred, have we? Why should she try to injure us?'

Before an imaginary explanation visualised, a creaking sound, followed by shuffling feet could be heard heading toward them. They froze. No ice-cream this time. A dishevelled, old-looking, stooped figure with a long coat being shredded against the ground, ambled forward. It was a tussle to get through the grass. The face was unseen behind a canopy of long, twisted tresses swaying to and fro imitating an elephant's trunk. The torso was petite, especially as it was bent over. There wasn't any offensive smell either. It seemed like minutes. They were all participants in a silent movie. Finally, the figure stopped. It could see the two youthful schoolgirls from underneath all that covering and wondering what in the hell they wanted. They had disturbed her solitude. The only reason she came out was to meet the first people ever to pay her humble home and her a visit.

'You are trespassing. There's nothing to steal here. Get on your way.'

The sound of her voice caressed their eardrums with the softest of tones. It wasn't scary or threatening. The girls took a deep breath and smiled.

'Aunt Mavis?'

3 SHOCK AND DISCOVERY

The girls stood immobilised at the front gate. Their feet were standing on some kind of emotional glue and they weren't going anywhere. They waited for a response. Underneath the large coat that stood on the other side of the fence, the old lady shook with recognition. No one had ever used her name for too many years to remember. To hear it uttered by two schoolgirls she neither knew or had heard of, shattered her idea of seclusion and non-recognition. She wasn't sure how to address it. Her preferred treatment was to despatch people under the threat of witchcraft, which usually worked and she was never bothered again. Somehow, these two felt different. Her normal dialogue was inconsistent with completing a full sentence. She had to know more.

'Who sent you?' she asked.

'My mum did. She said that I was to visit a long-lost family relative who she guessed lived at Humpletoon. It is school holidays and it seemed to be an ideal break to visit family and see the countryside. This is my friend Slirander and here we are.'

'I don't like visitors. Go home.'

'No. We will not. We came all this way to see you and the least that you can do is invite us in. It's not respectful to leave us out in the street. May we come in?' Davidia was persistent if nothing else.

Aunt Mavis hadn't yet said who she really was and she was in a dilemma. Does she let them into her world and expose herself if they were prone to gossip and giving away information, or trust them? That word is a commodity in short supply in her world. Her past should remain where it was parked – in people's memories – and not be regurgitated again as common footpath discussion. She slowly squatted down in a meditative pose. Her arms protruded from under that monstrous coat far enough to allow a few wrinkles to feel a burst of light. It was impossible to tell their age. A monotonous drone began. Davidia wondered whether she was having a turn, stomach cramps, or couldn't sing. Whatever it was, it sounded awful to her. No wonder Aunt Mavis was scary. Slirander suddenly sat down using her backpack as a seat. She took up exactly the same pose, much to Davidia's bewilderment. Should she do the same? Like a meek lamb without its own thought, she followed suit. She and Slirander only listened. It sounded like a mystical chant. Of course, no words could be understood, they weren't meant to. Davidia looked over at Slirander.

'Who is she calling? Some genie, a cloud, a spirit, a ghost, a what?'

'Karma.'

'Not another relative and we haven't even had our introduction completed.'

'No, she's passing thoughts of goodwill. They assist in a stressful situation.'

'What's so stressful about meeting us?'

'Have you ever met yourself? It can be an intimidating experience. She's checking up on you by feeling for your karma. She's testing whether we are suitable for her to know. It's a spiritual thing.'

'How long will she take? I'm thirsty.'

'Not long. Once she is calm, we might get invited in. Be patient.'

Another fifteen minutes passed and the chanting stopped. There was no more wailing pain to suffer. Aunt Mavis stood up, still keeping her bent-over figure which accentuated age and provided a believable vision of her situation. She attempted to wave a hand, but that rotten coat almost hid it from view. She turned around and retreated indoors. There was no more discourse.

'Where has she gone? Of all the rotten things to do … she's stranded us like two penguins at the South Pole, neither being happy that far from the sea. I've a good mind to kick that bloody gate.'

Davidia was incensed at family abandonment. At least Aunt Mavis had given them the courtesy of a visit. It was more than any other individual had ever received whilst she had lived in Humpletoon. This matter wasn't being taken lying down.

'We'll be back,' she yelled, as Slirander took her by the elbow and steered her towards the town.

A sad and lonely figure stood behind ragged curtains that acted as a screen and watched them depart. She had wished she could have invited them in, but she didn't have the confidence. Her home wasn't exactly a five-star hotel, but was that the full story?

*   *   *

A backpackers' hostel, for those who could afford the tariff, loomed up at them as they walked down the main street.

'They do a lot of staring, don't they?' said Davidia, as she felt she was one little fish egg in a sea of fish roe as she passed various homes. Blinds shut quicker than a wink.

They were new in town, so everyone made it their business to be interested. Slirander took it in her stride. Insecurity was felt everywhere. No one knew if they represented some sort of danger to everyone, so they were all suspiciously cautious. Small towns often accompanied small minds because it was never very far to the edge of town. Go figure. The backpackers hostel was correctly named but without the possessive apostrophe. The main door was chipped at the base where a good kicking possibly occurred. Graffiti formed the artwork theme which was tagged with no discernible meaning. The deep scratches were probably from some late-night activity where a knife was used to carve personal humour. Whatever all its intrigues were, it was still just a door leading into the interior of another world. Inside, a simple wooden desk was camouflaged as a useful object. It was the reception counter. A young, male attendant with curly hair had an earphone attachment in one ear and moved around a small space portraying a convulsion. The girls watched for a moment trying to guess the music. The vibe was missing.

'Excuse me,' said Davidia, 'we would like a room for the night.'

'For one or two?'

'For two of us. Can't you see two of us?'

'You want a double, queen or king? We have them all.'

'Two singles would be nice. Got any unhitched rooms? This is my sister.'

Slirander didn't take objection to the insult.

'That's cool. Two it is. Sign here. Pay now and here are your keys. If you want any personal tuition ladies, you can dial zero and I'm your entertainment.'

He winked as he passed over the keys. Davidia thought that he should get that stigmatism fixed. Their room was modest.

It consisted of two single beds, one small, plywood side table, a mottled rug with more holes than a sea anemone, light fittings which flickered with excitement at being able to still function and a bathroom with a shower and toilet only large enough for use one at a time. For some incredible reason, the toilet had been placed in the centre of the bath, which was unusable as a bath, but doubled as a pissoir and shower. Apparently, when it was constructed, budget cuts were tossed around like confetti. Nothing was ever said about the odd owner-builder, whose eccentricity should commence with a capital E. This would be a funny holiday communication topic for many years to come. The girls were exhausted. They slipped off their backpacks, placed them on the floor and sat down on the beds.

'What did you make of Aunt Mavis?' Davidia asked.

'It might not be her,' replied Slirander. 'She never said who she was, did she?'

Davidia thought for a moment.

'No, she didn't, but I assumed it must be her. What mum told us about her fitted perfectly. I have a feeling that it's her.'

'We didn't see her face at all or any parts of her body which might suggest her age. She could be an impersonator for all we know. If we can't see her, then who does know who she actually is and how can it be proven?'

'We'll visit again tomorrow. Were we too full-on today? I suppose it must have been a real shock to hear from a family member after so many years. I wonder if she has any other "real" family.'

'Sometimes people hide from reality and don't want to be found. She might be happy being a well-known nobody. Get some rest. It's been a long day.'

That night, three individuals were thinking about that same meeting which happened earlier in the day. It meant different things to each of them. The girls passed up on the temptation to dial zero and be entertained by the front desk.

*   *   *

Potential buyers trickled through Humpletoon's main store searching for an economic bargain. The word cheap was never uttered. Mac sat on a shelf like an expectant wallflower at a local dance. The public would pick him up, turn him around as if on a turnstile, pat him with a spanking hand, make stupid faces in his shiny enamel coating, turn him upside down to read his brand name – no "Made in China" here – and were surprised when nothing fell out or off. Shoppers often spent a lot of time-wasting whilst playing with someone else's objects.

Next morning, an old, senior lady with seemingly poor vision entered the store looking for a companion drinking mug for non-alcoholic purposes. She also wore a long, ragged coat that dragged along the ground. Her hair was extremely long, enough to make a few soft cushions if ever cut off. The town must have an epidemic of older-age people all dressed similarly. Maybe they all went to the same tailor at the opportunity shop? It could have been Aunt Mavis. It wasn't said who she was. She found Mac by touch. Her grainy vision identified a mug by its shape and her hands then fondled the object. His shiny and bumpy surface were both winners. He was despatched like a bullet into some wrapping paper, boxed and bundled into that nightmare area known as a woman's handbag where trauma and permanent loss can occur.

Mac was taken to a cottage and placed on a dirty, dusty shelf. Small indentations were indicative that a past object had previously been there. Dust particles dreaded a new arrival because they were displaced and let loose in the air as a gesture of goodbye.

Mac was unsure of what he represented. He knew he was round-ish with a hollow interior, had two lumps, one on either side and apparently was quite unattractive. He also had a bulgy nose and other indented features that mimicked a face of sorts. Imagination had to follow that thought. What was this strange place he had been brought to? No explanation had been given to him. After all, he was just a mug. He felt weird being amongst old decaying materials and wondered why he was where he was. On his shelf, there was a set of neglected kitchen knives with many a past meal still clinging to their surfaces waiting for another outing. A vase full of plastic flowers was layered with dust. Other kitchen mugs and cups looked like they had all been in a boxing tournament with chipped surfaces, broken handles and deep, ingrained stains. He didn't aspire to become damaged goods.

Where was he?

*   *   *

Next morning, there were other stirrings in town. The mayor had a council meeting to attend on the rezoning laws of making a particular property farming land. Rezoning didn't guarantee a sale, but it ensured the decrease in its value. Davidia and Slirander had arisen and feasted on dry cereal and a cup of tea. A real whoopee start to the day. Aunt Mavis had many a task to attend to, none which made it to an explanation. One male potter at the pottery had stardom in his eyes and it wasn't grit either. There was unrest at the pottery shed. Someone wasn't satisfied with their work. Humpletoon awoke slowly to allow any fog to clear before its inhabitants left their homes. They preferred fog-free days than to fumble around in a restricting mist.

'Fellow councillors, this meeting today is to regulate and bring into line under the new innovative development program, our

Expand the Boundaries statement. Land considered within the boundary is to be converted from residential to farming land to benefit the community. It's part of our community development strategy. Once rezoned, the land is available for farming and moves the residential zone far enough away to make town property prices explode. Now, how many of you would gain from that? It is for a community benefit, otherwise we wouldn't go down this path. There is a catch, though. At present, an old fossil resides there and we need to encourage her to sell the property. Like all of you here, it would only be in the town's best interest to rezone that land.'

'If we agree, is there anyone available who can afford to purchase that land?' asked a fellow councillor.

'On that point, I do believe a buyer could be found. I might even suggest myself.'

There was quite a bit of sniggering after that comment.

'Most of the town is owned by you, mayor. Isn't it time that someone else had an opportunity?'

The mayor's face reddened and other parts that couldn't be seen. Suddenly, his well-fitted suit began to ping buttons onto the boardroom table with a distinctive clang. Tension bubbled forth. The council was having a collective coronary. Posturing bodies stood up to deliver blunder and bluster, the two favourite coffee break candidates. The boardroom was awash with uncertainty. Before anyone said anything positive, the mayor waved his arm, surrendering his hand to the masses and signalling for everyone to be seated. At least they understood the "thumbs down" signal. It meant that they were all under it, small as it was. Calm returned.

'As I said, I could be that buyer. Is anyone else interested?'

The group of gutless wonders couldn't find an individual or joint objection. All hands went up in unison for the future sale.

The mayor had won the day. Now, all he had to do was impose his will on the land owner, Aunt Mavis.

'That's settled, then. The agricultural ability of the town has substantially increased. Meeting closed.'

*   *   *

'Why don't we ask around town about Aunt Mavis? The station-master and mayor didn't give much away. Something is needling me about their attitude toward her. She seems to be a mystery. Someone must know her, surely?'

'Remember, you are in a small town where one word can send the grapevine into meltdown and comments can often be misinterpreted. I agree she has a mystery about her, but there must be a good reason,' replied Slirander, the oracle of wisdom for the day.

They packed up their gear and headed to the door. Downstairs, at the backpackers hostel, they passed the young attendant who still seemed intent on hurting himself with those strange dance moves.

'I missed your call last night,' he said. He removed his ear plugs for a moment.

'We both had headaches,' replied Davidia. Smiles all round.

'Where are you off to, today? There's not much happening in town. If you hung about for another day, you could attend the Mug Festival held at Dimpletoon. It's not far. You can walk there past the quarry. It's another two kilometres further on. That's about it, really.'

'Do you know who lives in that old weather-beaten shack on the edge of the quarry? I've heard that a dragon lives there hidden in the woodwork and plays in the quarry.'

Davidia was already embellishing ignorance, but it sounded

plausible. A good story must always present intrigue. The young lad shook his curly locks.

'I've never seen a dragon there before; however, I've heard that a mysterious woman lives there and she is a witch. She has cursed this town.'

'How do you know that she's cursed the town?'

'I was sitting outside here the other day when an old lady walked by, the one with the dragging coat. She tripped over the road guttering and tottered over. She stood up again and said something in a language I didn't understand, so it must have been some kind of a curse. I didn't see her pimply nose or spire-shaped hat, but it was enough. I ran inside in case she cast a personal spell on me. I didn't want to be maimed by losing an eye or a leg.'

'Can she do that?'

'Speak to anyone in town and they will tell you similar stories. She creeps around at night. Be careful.'

The young attendant returned to his musical-mind exercises.

'He wasn't on the wacky weed, was he?' said Davidia, not convinced by his utterings.

'Superstition is rife in fearful communities where they don't understand differences. Someone must be leading the charge against her. Rumours don't spring up unless someone has given it a good kick-start. Usually the truth is hidden amongst it somewhere.'

'I think Aunt Mavis might be misunderstood. She is a recluse and that doesn't mean anything more than being alone. Come on. Let's see what bright lights there are in town.'

The girls strolled down the main street and, like other young women, stopped at every shop window, not to admire their reflection – that too – but to dream about that fabulous purchase they may possibly make. They entered a clothing store which didn't seem to stock well-known brands; however, nothing ventured, nothing gained.

'Good morning, girls,' said the matronly, pleasant shop owner. 'Welcome. I haven't seen you two in town before. Are you passing through, visiting someone, or holidaying? It's a quiet town. Nothing much happens here, but when something does, everyone knows about it.'

The clothing range had dust film over most of the stock protected by plastic. Maybe nothing gets sold?

'Just visiting a friend,' said Davidia.

'Who might that be? I certainly would know her.'

'It's possible. It's the lady who lives next to the quarry in a wooden shack. We haven't met her yet but hope to do so this afternoon. My mum sent us to visit her. Do you know her?'

The owner felt her aura move. It must have been in her breasts as they certainly heaved in anxiety at the mention of an old lady. She had actually never met her, but knew of her, everyone did.

'She hasn't been in my shop recently. I once had a glimpse of her when she walked past my shop window. I was cleaning out the display and a few yapping dogs caught my attention. They were following, or was it chasing, an old lady in a huge, ground-dragging coat. Right outside this very shop window, she stopped and pointed a gnarled, knobby finger at her pursuers and spat at them. I have never seen animals so frightened before. One escaping dog ran so fast it wore down a leg to a stump. When it arrived home, the dog owner was so distraught, he had to go to doggy counselling to recover from the shock. It was frightening. I saw green sparks spitting from her eyes. I'm glad she didn't enter my shop that day. I might have been turned into a dress myself. I needed a tipple to recover my sanity. I reported it to the mayor. There were no by-laws about spitting in public.'

'So, she has green eyes?' said Slirander, piecing together a colour chart of what her colour really might be. Different villagers gave different accounts.

'She had bright green eyes as large as my hands. Probably uses them at night as she creeps about town. There have been strange things happening in town since she arrived many years ago. I don't want to put someone in a bad light, but it certainly is a coincidence. Before that, this town was normal.'

'Has anyone seen her at night? I would think being old she would be huddled in front of a warm fire sipping Milo or a soothing hot beverage. Does she wear a special outfit? It would have to be smaller than dragging that large coat around.'

'Visit the local publican. He often sees large cats at night after closing time. He's so frightened now that his shadow hides from him. It wouldn't be safe to visit out there. Do you want to buy anything whilst you are here?'

The girls faked a smile and said, 'No, thanks.' They weren't in need of theme clothing from the era of the eighteen hundreds.

'Each person gives a different description of the same individual. Maybe the publican will make sense,' said Davidia, starting to doubt what she had been told.

'We can try,' said Slirander, 'but keep an open mind on what you hear.'

The girls continued along the main street, nodding courteously to whoever they passed. Comments such as polite and well-mannered were heard. The local hotel had a sign out the front suggesting that holy water was within its walls. The pub was called The Mug. The green, glazed "toilet tiles" that covered up to a meter from the ground of the front wall, were all in reasonably good repair. It often had a double meaning. The front door was ajar, so they pushed. Legally, they weren't allowed to enter such a public place, but on holidays liberties were always found. Besides, two young sixteen-year-olds would have no trouble passing for intelligent eighteen-year-olds. The bar smelt of stale beer. Pubs had their own particular identifying smells. The dim lighting gave the place a heavy feel.

'What do you want?' said a gruff voice. It came from behind the bar.

'Hello,' said Davidia, politely. 'Is there a publican here known as Mr Hoarse? The lady in the shop along the street directed us here.'

'That's my name. Who wants to know?'

'We do, sir.'

The girls still couldn't see Mr Hoarse who was actually kipping on the floor behind the bar. Apparently, another big night in the bar with two other patrons had immobilised him for the evening. He struggled to an upright position. His stained singlet and rounded paunch meant he had a good time, but couldn't remember where he had placed it. His hair was fairy floss in appearance, his stubby shorts were on back-to-front and a shave wouldn't have gone amiss.

'Who are you? You look too young to be in here,' he said, gruffly.

'We are to visit a friend in town who lives in a wooden shack near the quarry. We wanted to meet someone who knew her before we visit.'

'You afraid of disappearing, are you?'

'What do you mean? She's not a magician, is she?'

'More like a sorceress. At night around this place, especially after dark when most people have gone to sleep, a strange screeching sound crawls over the roof of my pub. It's so eerie, I'm often afraid to inspect the source. It's pitch-black up there and I've lost my shadow many times searching for it. I think she takes it for spite. It's not that I needed it. During the daytime, she gives it back.'

'What do you think causes those strange noises?'

'A giant, cat-like creature crawling on all fours. It's as huge as a human and jumps with ease from rooftop to rooftop. Its eyes are fearful. They are two massive yellow bulbs with dark black slits across them. It's like looking into the gates of hell. It attacked me one night. Before I could render it useless, I fell off the ladder. It spat and hissed at me. Next morning when I woke up, Joe the garbage collector had to pick me up off the ground. He said it must have been thirsty because the ground was littered with empty beer bottles. I reckon they were stolen from me when I was out cold. She is so cunning. I recognised that wispy hair on each side of her head. You can't fool me with whiskers. I was lucky to survive the ordeal.'

'You are sure it was the same lady?'

'I'll bet my tenth beer on it.'

'What do you think she would do with us if we visit?'

'Slaves. It's rumoured that others have disappeared from this town too. They weren't residents. One day they were here, the next day they were gone. Poof! It's too dangerous for you out there.'

'Did the disappearing people have a name?'

'Yeh, they did. Somebody referred to them as tourists. That's it, tourists. Don't become one of them otherwise a dreadful fate will fall on you. Stay away from that quarry. It's not official opening hours yet; however, would you like a drink?'

The girls declined and excused themselves. The enlightening repartee had brightened their morning. They'd established with a great deal of certainty that there wasn't a bright light bulb turned on in town. If there was, it must be hanging from the ceiling inside a shop.

'It all sounds so odd that the villagers have a seemingly

disproportionate view and imagination about what they think of Aunt Mavis,' said Davidia.

'Fear does weird things to your mind. Let's head off to meet your Aunt Mavis.'

Slirander was quite comfortable about all the different explanations. The town believed it was cursed without directly saying so, but couldn't really explain what they were cursed with.

*   *   *

Mac didn't know in whose house he was. There were a collection of oddballs sitting silently just like him. The shelf was his new home.

'She doesn't clean us,' wailed a small cup, riddled with intricate stains ingrained into its once pristine surface.

'I haven't had a decent wash ever,' chimed in another.

Suddenly, the shelf burst into life with a group of whinging cups and mugs all expressing dissatisfaction with their condition.

'I was once a proud teacup. Now look at me,' complained Tipper. 'I have so many parts missing. I can't retain any liquids. I have no handles left to be picked up by. I'm waiting to be binned. I have outlived my usefulness. I can no longer delight any sipper. No one takes an interest in me.' Tipper sobbed uncontrollably and fell off the shelf to disperse into many pieces on the floor. Those tears were the last beverage Tipper delivered.

'Look at us,' yelled the knives. 'We've all lost our sharpness. Our beautiful steel surfaces have been dulled by being ignored. Those clinging food particles are such a resentful intrusion. We are no longer washed and are badly kept. Most of us suffer from mild depression. The lady cannot really chew anything anymore. We don't cut up anything so we're stuck here taking up space.'

Mac began to question his predicament. So far, he was

untouched and as good as new. How long that situation would remain was anybody's guess.

Who was his benefactor?

* * *

The girls once again stood outside Aunt Mavis' home and wondered whether she would allow them entrance. This time they were well aware of the difficulties. Slirander had borrowed a knife from the hostel. It had an enamel handle which gave it a nice appearance. From a practical perspective, it was quite useless to defuse an electrified fence. There might be a shock in store for two of them.

'Do you think she's home?' asked Davidia. 'She could be out shopping or in her cavern formulating spells. I'm nervous after yesterday's visit.'

'She's in residence. Otherwise the town would have warned us. Relax, she'll be fine.'

Slirander withdrew the knife. Davidia panicked.

'You aren't stabbing anyone, are you?'

'This is to run along the fence line and try to blow a fuse. Then we can enter safely. I hope it works.'

Slirander hadn't studied the effects of electricity and wondered whether she would receive the wow factor that Davidia did. She had certainly become competitive. She took a step forward with knife raised at waist height to do the "run" and was about to make contact, when a creaking front door noisily opened. It startled her. The knife screamed, 'Don't drop me. I'm precious,' as it crashed onto the rough, stone ground and scraped its surface. It was afraid of visiting next door, the tip. The girls stood still waiting to be encircled by a mysterious force. If she was a witch, then that expectation sounded reasonable. An old lady with the ground-dragging coat struggled toward them. She was within handshake distance. The girls held their breath and it wasn't in their hands. Aunt Mavis waved a hand to gesture entrance. Her hands were aged and slim. The girls hesitated. They weren't mutes or mime actors.

'Aunt Mavis?' asked Davidia.

She wanted to make sure that she acknowledged who she might be. She could be anyone, but Davidia thought she had the correct relative based on mum's information.

The girls waited. The lady slowly stood up to her full height potential. The bent-over scenario had disappeared and had been replaced by a tall, old-aged lady without any deformities. The ground-hugging coat that had taken a lot of verbal punishment had its hemline now dangled around her mid-calf region. It was still a filthy piece of clothing, but once raised, it didn't seem half-bad. Was it a miracle of spine rehabilitation that they were witnessing or an actress with a clever ploy? It had their attention. They waited nervously.

'Come in, quickly. The fence is not wired. I don't want anyone to see you or know you have entered my home. I have a reputation to protect. No one has ever seen inside.'

The girls were stunned. She spoke in sentences, not short phrases. Should they risk it?

'Are you really Aunt Mavis?' repeated Davidia. She had to know first before she moved.

'Yes,' she whispered.

'Great.'

The girls cautiously moved forward. The rusted, hinged gate opened effortlessly. The thick, matted grass that would cause nightmares for small rodents to pass through miraculously flattened out. A pathway of cobblestones directed them to the front door. Aunt Mavis followed. The derelict front door strained to open. It didn't fall off, which surprised the girls. So far, the short walk from the front gate to the front door had amazed them. It didn't seem real. Their understanding prior to their arrival now had another range of meanings. They pinched each other to test whether they were actually dreaming, living in a parallel world or had an unexplainable imagination in each other's head.

'Do you believe this?' said Davidia.

'It's rather incredible, isn't it? You have found your Aunt Mavis,' replied Slirander, not confronting Davidia's comment; however, her own mysterious background gave her a greater understanding of unusual events.

Will the real Aunt Mavis reveal herself?

More discoveries and shocks were in store.

4 CONNECTIONS

'How do you propose to acquire the quarry site with the old lady in residence? She isn't going to leave voluntarily,' questioned a councillor concerned that the bullying mayor might use some form of subterfuge to have her removed. It couldn't be done illegally, so a signature had to be legally obtained as evidence of sale.

'That's a good question. You must have searched hard in your imaginative box to toss that at me. There are ways and means to determine a pre-conceived outcome. Those two young girls who have been asking questions might be the answer. They have shown a personal interest in the old lady and I have the perception that one of them is related. Kidnap them or, should I say, ask them to a function where they can be sidelined for a few days as guests of the town. That may work in my favour. Emotional blackmail is a very effective inducement when forcing one's own agenda. As long as it's legal, anything is possible. We ooze hospitality. It might be time it became a share. Are there any better suggestions?'

The mayor desperately wanted the property. He believed the special clay seam was at its strongest right next to the quarry. He would have it assayed and, if positive, mine it. It was his belief that it was a step away from forming his wealthy retirement. His pockets sang to the sound of money and he loved nothing better than a full-scale operatic jingle. His trickery box wasn't the full complement, so he decided to engage the services of a potter who could act as a go-between and camouflage his responsibility in any skulduggery, if any eventuated. He believed that an inoffensive, wrinkled, old-looking potter with the attitude of a butterfly would be an ideal foil. No one would suspect anything but harmlessness. He had no idea if there was a trustworthy potter at the pottery, but his reasoning led him to visit there. He felt like royalty as he walked in and expected everyone to extend niceties. After all, he was the mayor and not an insignificant somebody. His opinion of others wasn't quite as accommodating.

One particular individual refused to shake his hand. The mayor's fingers felt lost and he had to retract the offer because no one was receiving them. The potter who refused his approach was visibly aged with wrinkles etched memorably in a face of many contours. There seemed to be a familiarity about this potter and the mayor felt it. Long hair twisted into dreadlocks hid a clear visage. The dusty, khaki overalls had an orange tinge about them creating the impression of a two-legged carrot.

'Hello, Mervyn,' said the potter.

The mayor felt a warmth trickle down his leg, realising that no one ever called him by his correct name. The shock shook him. This person must be from a forgotten past. No one in town, that he could recall, knew his real name. His mother did when he was christened, but she was no longer breathing oxygen. Then there was that dreadful brother he parted with years ago and that non-existent sister. He looked closer at the person standing in front of him. He thought that he was glad he didn't have to deal with sloppy clay and work in all that filth every day. There's something to be said for a starched, ironed and crisp, clean shirt. He scanned the torso with his laser-like eyes, seeking a recognisable aspect. His vision was woeful today. The timbre of the voice had a recognisable quality about it. Instinctively, he placed a small pinky into his ear for a clean and clear sound flow.

'Do I know you?' asked the mayor, cautiously.

He wondered whether it was a crank who wanted to get on with a person of privilege, someone to soften him up for a hand-out, or a memory he didn't want to re-live.

'I'm a relation.'

'A relation to what?'

'To you.'

'That's impossible. I don't have any relations. You can ask my wife.'

'Have you forgotten? I'm not surprised.'

'There's nothing to forget.'

'Do you remember a fire long ago and its aftermath?'

Suddenly, Mervyn wasn't feeling well. A migraine visited instantaneously and it was very unhappy. He reached for both sides of his head to avoid it from falling off. His face contorted into a series of horror movie imitations until it settled. The drained, wretched-looking face seemed to have aged somewhat.

'You were like that as a child when things didn't go your way.'

'How would you know that?'

'I was there.'

'What gives you any insight into my family?'

'I'm your brother.'

'B ... t,' yelled the mayor. 'He disappeared long ago. The bastard walked out on me from our farming partnership. I have no real brother.'

'You scammed me out of my share of the property. I have never forgotten the way you set me up with a hooker who lied under oath that I was having relations with the neighbours' wives and you, in the name of protecting the property, had me sign it over to you for safe-keeping to avoid the police and the courts suing me for my share at the risk of losing it. It was quite strange how it never returned to me. Have you still got it?'

Mervyn was experiencing another migraine invasion. It was obvious the current word grouping he had heard set off nasty alarm bells in his head. Troupes of small ants with steel boots were colonising his brain. It was almost too much to bear. He quickly turned and left the pottery holding his head, muttering offensive syllables and almost walking headlong into a huge, wooden door. His idea for engaging a person in his plans for obtaining the old lady's residence would have to remain on hold as he dealt with the shock of someone claiming to be his brother. Didn't he bury him? Over time, selective amnesia had plugged many of his memory files, never to be reopened. His brother was plugged with a massive dose of brain glue. His past was a shadow he never wanted to see again. Had some sinister force been planted in Humpletoon to harass him? He fled to his home located on the highest point at the edge of town. His wife saw him coming up the long driveway agitated and swiping at imaginary adversaries. He appeared as the unhappy jogger as there was no evidence of a smile. Had it got lost too? The front door, which was usually an impediment to those entering, stood aside magically to avoid any damage. Actually, his wife had opened it for him. He slammed it shut. The nicely-ironed, clean, cool, crisp shirt had lost its perfection pose and began to crumple under the body onslaught of dealing with a massive migraine.

'You seem agitated, dear. Is there anything I can do?' said his concerned wife.

Her name was Merrilyn and she had been married to Mervyn for many years. They never had time for children and, if they did, the practice involved caused further migraines, so it wasn't possible to plan that life element. The trade-off was wealth and power, which wasn't such a shabby alternative. However, to obtain that level of success often caused many unintended and intended consequences on the journey of "it's mine".

'I've had a shock today. Some looney at the pottery claimed to be my brother. That bastard doesn't exist. Didn't we bury him? I can't remember.'

'Sit down, dear. A hot glass of clear water will relax your condition and then we can discuss the cause.'

Merrilyn entered the kitchen, boiled the kettle, selected a large mug with huge ears from the kitchen shelf and placed it on the kitchen bench. It did look quite like Mervyn. It had a twisted face and a lip that matched his large, over-used mouth. It was a definitive statement mug about its owner. It's not only pets that look like their owners. A sachet of a sugary, bubbly substance was tipped in and froth danced delightedly as it met its dance partner; warm water.

'Drink that, dear. It will calm your nerves.'

Mervyn did as instructed. His agitation subsided and his facial twisting and twitching also stopped.

'I'm sure that he said he was my brother. He seemed to know too much.'

'Is he going to sue you over the past, if it is him?'

'We spoke briefly, that's all. I felt I knew him. Then I didn't. He could be an imposter trying to worm his way into our lives. There are many jealous people in this small-minded town.'

If Mervyn's IQ was under investigation, a small number might emerge. That was one risk not to be taken.

'Perhaps I should visit the pottery and flush out the issue on your behalf. I'm not aware that I know anyone there. It's not part of my social structure. After all, I am the Lady Mayoress. I'll attend to that after high tea at Worthington Hall tomorrow morning.'

Mervyn settled and fell asleep in his hug-me, huge, leathered chair. His aura ring floated around his head ready to be hit by a swinging object of any sort. Had a spell been cast on him, or had guilt tried to have an engagement? It was unclear as he slept and travelled his subconscious world. His mind had been communicating to an outside receiver, but he was unaware of it. That head where that mind existed nodded acknowledgement of his disturbed thoughts. Danger lurked in many recesses of anyone's brain whilst asleep and hopefully it was an inactive action when awake. Mervyn, when awake, was a pussy with pretend bravado. His wife; however, was quite the opposite. She had been depicted by a school child in a drawing competition on a sporting theme with knives for teeth, javelins for legs and a torso with an archer's bullseye in the middle. The child got scolded for portraying a sport incorrectly. The child had spoken to her mum and dad and they both agreed the sport of politics was a dangerous contest; however, they praised their child's ingenuity and it received an A.

*   *   *

Mac sat silently on his shelf. A mug cannot do anything on its own without a mover to create its action. He had no sense of time and lived in the moment. Wherever he was, he wasn't being damaged. The room he existed in was rather small with a collection of second-hand furniture battered from misuse. The carvings in the wooden arms of the couch were indented with odd-looking figures trying to emulate the human form. Strangely though, each item fitted perfectly in a colour-coordinated pattern with colour contrasts that all matched. It gave the impression of an organised mess. That took skill. The carpet had more holes than Swiss cheese and had dulled from permanent display as if it had been on a clothes line in full sun. The wallpaper was a poor attempt at covering the walls with an outdated pattern that had drooping corners and sagging paper where glue was obviously absent. There was very little air movement so the dust had a permanent place to live. A musty smell swirled around as if it was the owner of the air space. Lighting was strikingly absent as if the room's contents were to remain hidden in a forgotten, lonely place. The furniture hadn't been used for a considerable time. Why wasn't the room ever cleaned? Occasionally, footsteps were heard to pass by, but never entered on a regular basis except for when Mac was placed on the shelf. The imprint of those footprints, were embedded in the dust on the floor. It was a reminder of recent life.

One evening, before retiring, the old lady wanted to enjoy a nightcap of a hot beverage. Her recent purchase was Mac and he had tonight to please his new owner. It would be his debut and he didn't want to disappoint. She stumbled into the room with the dull lighting. The awkwardly placed prolific furniture pieces caused her to trip on an obstinate chair. The hand of purpose felt along the dusty shelf knocking off every piece in her hand's path. Many objects ended up on the floor as new rubbish. Finally, she felt Mac and in her haste for a grasp, flipped him sideways and he took flight, fortunately landing on the soft-cushioned couch. No damage was done. In the dimness, it was difficult to see.

'Don't try and hide from me,' she mumbled, as the search continued to the couch. 'There you are,' she said, lifting him up like a trophy. 'I have a treat in store for you tonight. It's so nice to have a new mug for my Milo.' Mac was placed on the kitchen bench awaiting his new experience. 'Now where did I put it? Ah! That must be it.'

A canister of ingredients was selected hoping they would contain her Milo. The old lady knew exactly where each item was supposed to be, but couldn't read the labels. In the excitement of wanting to test out her new mug, she unfortunately made the wrong decision. Once the canister had been opened, a teaspoon of a rough mixture was spooned into Mac's opening. It settled nicely, without any fuss or complaints in the centre of the bottom of his interior, shaped like a sand dune. It sat motionless. It was a brown, granulated and strongly-flavoured mixture. Suddenly, a thunderstorm swept into his opening with the force of a tropical tornado drowning the brown mixture. It swirled in shock and dissolved without a whimper. The heat from the thunderstorm began to warm all of Mac's surfaces. He now held a warm, brown-coloured liquid. He wondered what had happened. It was his first experience at being useful and not a drop was spilt. His debut was looking good.

Another intruder in the shape of a long-handled object with a bent end shaped like a scooper dropped a white granulated substance into the warm swirly liquid. As it began to dissolve, the bent end moved in a repetitious circular fashion repeatedly scratching Mac's surfaces.

Mac silently protested, but no one could hear him.

'Stop that nonsense!' he yelled.

Mild violence wasn't to be tolerated. He was glad to see the end of that object when it was withdrawn. He now had a full load of a hot mixture making him feel comfortable.

Another addition of a white liquid was added to the party. It was smooth, cool and mixed well. It was obviously well-trained. The hot beverage was now slightly cooler and with a new set of friends keeping him warm and providing a pleasant range of aromas, life was good. This special clay had earned his shape.

Suddenly, his whole being shook in surprise. Two hands grabbed his protruding outside pieces with a firm grip. Mac started shaking. He was picked up and tipped at an angle. His contents were escaping.

'Who's stealing my new friends?' he wailed.

A few express drops made a quick exit onto the holder's clothing as he was tipped over. Mac could see a frightening huge opening where his contents were being directed. He didn't recognise anything.

'Where are my contents going? Where does that gap lead to?'

He began to lose his confidence and this was on his first outing. Another repeat motion followed. His contents were all escaping. He'd been friendly and treated his visitors politely and at the first sign of movement, they all left. He wondered what had he done to be dumped. Obviously, he didn't yet understand what his real purpose was. Mac had unintentionally let go of more contents than he should have. Well, did they have a time of it pouring in all directions? Then the unexpected occurred. An eruption returned from that large gap accompanied by the remnants of last night's dinner. The old lady had coughed. Mac was littered with unpleasant drips; the old lady's clothes were now tinged brown and the balance had landed on the floor to be permanently ignored.

'Bloody coffee! That's not my Milo. How did I make such a mistake?'

The old lady was furious at trying to drink a beverage she didn't like. Her new mug was supposed to be exclusively used for her Milo. Mac heard her babbling and realised that he was to be that mug, Milo Mac.

In all the commotion, his contents had gone cold and he was slammed onto the kitchen bench so hard, he thought he might have been damaged. Fortunately, he was still in one piece. The lady left the kitchen and Mac sat helplessly on the kitchen bench. The contents in his interior were now stone cold and becoming rather unpleasant company. He was left with a cold, sticky and smelly liquid, which had lost its freshness and attraction as new friends once the heat had dissipated. No one was going anywhere tonight. Mac, now known as Milo Mac had to grin and bear his night-time company of gooey enamel and the thought of unpleasant stains staying with him like friends you didn't need. It was to be a long night.

Milo Mac contemplated all night that his debut was a complete disaster. He longed for a warm water wash and to be as clean as he was yesterday when he had first arrived. He would even be happy returning to the dusty shelf. That was now a lost hope. He wondered what tomorrow would bring.

*   *   *

The seemingly dilapidated house welcomed them by allowing front door entrance even though they had to bend at an angle to enter. Davidia was curious. She touched the door framework and it was as solid as a bridge girder construction. She stopped inside the doorway and ran her hands along the slanted architraves. They were exceptionally well-built. Any construction engineer would be proud to put their name to them. The material felt cool to her touch. It wasn't made of wood; it was solid steel. She thought that the shape of the house had been deliberately built. The visible wooden palings on the outside of the house were a specialist graphic artist's brainchild design to imitate real wood. Aunt Mavis had meticulously planned the construction to represent a decaying, rotting, dilapidated building which, from a distance, gave the unimagined a view of an eyesore. The truth was quite the opposite. The design had been successful in keeping away snoopers, itinerants, thieves or proper architects without any interest in designing junk structures. Superstition and ignorance had also kept her home safe. Her privacy up to now had been preserved; however, with the arrival of two young, determined girls her world might become infected with change.

If she was worried, there was no way of telling because her mass of hair hid most of her face. Davidia motioned to Slirander.

'Feel that. Go on. It's solid steel.'

'It will fall over if I push too hard. It looks fragile.'

'Well, it's not.'

'I don't want to damage Aunt Mavis' home. We've just been welcomed in.'

'The only thing you'll damage is your nails. It's steel and very cold. Run your hand over the door archway. Here, I'll show you.'

Slirander was apprehensive. She felt uncomfortable destroying someone else's property because she believed that was what she was about to do. Just like the story of the three little pigs when the wolf blew down the pig's stick structure, she felt like that wolf, but with a different intended outcome. Without warning, Davidia pushed her friend into the wall. Slirander bounced off it like a ping-pong ball. Her startled, red face translated into a book of expletives, but her self-control and good manners at being an invited guest kept her pressed lips together. Davidia had a verbal reprieve.

'That hurt,' she finally said, as if the word "pain" existed in each letter she expressed.

'You wouldn't believe me. Now, what do you say?'

Slirander rubbed her shoulder and agreed the wall was solid and not the fragile, rotting timber where termites had holidays. Aunt Mavis stood motionless as she observed the discovery display by the two besties. She smiled. Her face didn't hurt from an activity she had suppressed long ago. It was a relief to know that those facial muscles still functioned properly when needed. Maybe the girls might be that fresh air her home and life required. It was a thought.

'The wall didn't move. I mean it didn't move. The house is still standing. I'm surprised, that's all.'

'I get the feeling that something's weird about this place. Look around this room. The furniture is all higgledy-piggledy. I've seen better arrangements at a real tip. This is a three-dimensional con.'

Aunt Mavis was still silent. She let the girls discover for themselves what they thought it was that they were discovering. She wasn't going to help. Gaining knowledge is a learned experience and with myths, imagination and creative décor in front of them, they had to determine what it meant. It was a house test. If they couldn't work it out, there was no further access into the home. By the size of the entrance room, there must be more to the home than what they could see. Both girls scanned the room for clues as to where another door might lead them. There were no obvious indicators.

'Aunt Mavis, you surely don't live in this small, exposed space. There's no bed, bathroom, kitchen, electronic devices or television. Where is the exit?' asked Davidia, wondering whether they had landed in the world of small homes or at least one with a mystery about it.

Aunt Mavis stayed as silent as a mime artist. Her expression was immovable. An arm waved in a small arc. Was she summoning demons, catching a fly or relocating dust? No explanation was given.

'I think we have to work this out ourselves,' said Slirander, feeling as if someone was messing with her aura.

It occasionally happened when she encountered persons of mythical knowledge. She shut her eyes and replayed in her mind in every minute detail the dimensions of the room, what its contents were and their location to see if anything stood out.

'Slirander, are you sleep-walking?' asked Davidia, as she watched her friend glide around the room as if she was on an invisible hoverboard.

She definitely wasn't using her legs. Not one dust particle

made way for the floating corpse, which was the impression that she conveyed. As quickly as she had started, she stopped.

'Interesting,' was all Slirander said.

'How did you do that? You flew around the room unaided. Can you teach me how to do it?'

Slirander shook her head in a negative response.

'Did you notice any reflections in the room?'

'I didn't look for any.'

'Stroll around the room and tell me what you see.'

Naturally enough, Davidia expected to see a beautiful-looking girl in any reflection that she created. It was a given, or so she thought it was. There wasn't far to walk. She moved past the steel wall expecting to see an unimaginable beauty. Where was she? She hadn't appeared. Davidia reacted to a pained expression from someone acting quite independently of her and she was supposed to be creating the image. She didn't recognise who or what it rep-resented. Whilst she fumbled through her empty thought drawer, she stood in front of the angled front door and she didn't like what she saw there either. It couldn't possibly be her. Someone was tampering with her reflections much like the silly, distorted mirror walls at fun parks; the ones that fatten you up, thin you down and create ugly glass reflections galore. A small table leg stuck out at a right angle and tripped her up. She crashed to the floor, not in a lover's embrace, but as a scared rabbit caused by the instant shock of tripping. She placed her arms out in front of her so they absorbed the impact. Bang! Down she went. She opened her eyes just as she was horizontal to the floor.

'Hello, there,' she heard or thought she'd heard a voice say. 'You have quick reflexes.'

Davidia had the wind knocked out of her at both ends as she grappled with hugging the cold, stone floor. Finally, she realised that it was her she was seeing. Now, that isn't a shabby view.

'How come I can see myself clearly in the floor whilst flat on the floor, but not whilst standing upright?'

'Looking at the obvious isn't what it's about.'

'Are you a table leg?'

'Yes, with the most adorable knot.'

'What am I doing here? This room must have an exit. Aunt Mavis can't live in a small, cramped space without any facilities.'

'True. Will you assist a friendly table leg in correcting my right-angle leg so I can stand properly?'

'You want me to twist your leg. Is it safe? I don't need a building licence, do I? If anything goes wrong, I won't be sued? Besides, you aren't made of real wood.'

Before the table leg answered, it thrust out its right-angled leg for a twist. Davidia felt its texture and didn't dare go looking for its knot. She grasped it firmly with one hand and gave it a strong twist. Surprisingly, it didn't fall off.

'Thank you.'

Davidia sat upright. Well, that's that, she thought. What did all that achieve? Damn nothing. She sat for a moment. Slirander was still where she had left her. Davidia wondered why she didn't try the reflection routine. Her appearance was quite attractive too. Both girls had good opinions about something; themselves. Before she could stand, the room began to slowly rotate obscuring the room's furniture collection into a blur. Was she at Disneyland, or was it called dismal land? A minute passed before the giddy ride halted. Davidia was amazed. They had ridden a revolving underground lift and were now deep inside the quarry walls with room to move. Davidia stood up. Slirander was already standing and Aunt Mavis waved an arm again. This time it was a welcome gesture and gratefully received.

'What happened?' said Davidia, open-mouthed with a stunned-mullet look.

'You caught the elevator to a lower floor. There is no lingerie section here,' replied Slirander, with a full facial smile.

'We are actually underground; I mean underground and inside the quarry walls.'

'That's right,' interrupted Aunt Mavis. 'You are safe from prying eyes down here.'

'Did you have all this built? It's incredible.'

Slirander stood quietly surveying their new found visiting digs. Davidia took a little longer to embrace it all. Both girls were in a secret underground hideaway with a believed witch. Exciting doesn't begin to describe their current emotions. The large room was solidly built exactly like upstairs; however, wherever they looked reflections bounced back at them. That's better, beautiful wall art. There were all the missing facilities from upstairs: a large lounge, sundry bedrooms and a kitchen in pristine condition surrounded them. Aunt Mavis gestured to them to sit down. Her face was still well-hidden by all that hair. Her stoop had straightened and she removed that old, bedraggled coat.

It was like an actor's prop. Upon closer inspection, it was excellently made with perfect stitching. Davidia gave it the sniff test and was surprised that it smelt clean and the quality of the fabric was labelled inside with a world-famous brand. She wondered what it all meant. Had she been fooled into believing that Aunt Mavis was as dilapidated as her house? Something didn't sit right in her chair.

'Does anyone in town know about your underground home?'

Aunt Mavis was a woman of few words and used them wisely. 'No.'

'Why have you hidden yourself down here? The town's people can't be that bad, can they?'

'I crave privacy.'

'It's rumoured that you are a witch. Is that true? You don't seem to be one to us.'

'You need a few minutes alone.'

In an instant it takes to snap a digital photograph, Aunt Mavis had disappeared without being seen.

'Wow!' exclaimed Davidia. 'Where did she go?'

'Sometimes it's better to accept a situation than try to reason the why,' said Slirander. 'She will return shortly and perhaps give some sort of explanation. It must be quite a shock for her that a distant relative sought her out. There is more to the eye than the vision it observes in front of it.'

'Do you think we are safe down here?'

'Yes. Relax. You have now made another family connection.'

Davidia thought for a moment. True, but weird.

5 DIMPLETOON MUG FESTIVAL PREPARATIONS

The neighbouring town of Dimpletoon was preparing for its famous mug festival where entrants were allowed to showcase two mugs that they had personally created. Potters came from around the countryside to achieve bragging rights and the modest trophy by presenting the best mug. It was normally a fierce contest. Mugs had to be created with characteristics that the judges could identify, albeit loosely, with their owner. It may also be coincidence that the created mugs weren't all prepared by their respective owners, but still had an uncanny resemblance to them.

For example, there was the poodle mug made with delicate, fine handles and was carried in a protective, leather-bound satchel. The owner had his nose in the air when passing the competition dreading to engage in conversation with a less superior mug product owner. The pug mug was made as a flat rectangle with a round hollow in the middle and slits on two sides for fingers to hold. It was an innovative strategy in design. Most mugs to be shown were expected to be round. There was a lot of tut-tutting about shapes, sizes, colouring and glazed finishes. The fine line between success and failure could be simple as judge bias, a small chip or the base not being properly finished.

Dimpletoon was abuzz with excitement.

*　　*　　*

Milo Mac had endured an uncomfortable evening on the shelf believing he was now a discarded item. There were no thrills in being cold, wet and lonely. All the other ornaments ignored his bleatings. They had heard or experienced them all before.

'Get used to it, Mac,' said a greying flower-vase, who once lit up the whole home with beautiful freshly-cut flowers and clean water in its midst. 'The old lady has a short attention span. I wouldn't be surprised if she's already forgotten about you.' The vase had grown a film of bacteria on its interior and was now considered to be a health hazard.

'There has to be more to being a mug than sitting on a shelf. I want to do things, experience being used and enjoy time in the dishwasher with friends. I want to be useful and make people smile when I'm handled.'

'Disappointment is all that awaits you. We all know. Don't expect anything good to happen. It is a fleeting moment.' The vase sighed sadly and blended into the shelf as a forgotten object.

Mac wasn't deterred. He'd had a setback on debut, but he believed his best was yet to be produced. He wondered where that loving pair of hands to fondle his handles and appreciate his capabilities were. The lounge room was still dull and unloved. Mac shed a tear. It trickled down his face marking a clear mois-ture line to his base. On its downward trajectory over his various bumps, it removed any dust to reveal the brilliantly striped clay he was made of which glinted in the dull light like a pulsating disco ball. There was no one there to take notice. However, it gave him confidence that somehow a bright future would arise. He just had to wait.

*   *   *

'Where's Aunt Mavis? Do you think she's abandoned us already? We have only just met.'

Davidia was concerned that the shock of meeting her was too much, otherwise why would she leave them alone. She didn't think she needed a shower.

'Be patient. There's always an explanation,' replied Slirander, exuding patience.

'She's probably gone to collect the family photo album. There might be one of me in it. I was the cutest baby, you know.'

Slirander's eyebrows had an unintentional workout as they tried to reach the ceiling. A few minutes passed. Davidia was becoming agitated with the unknowing.

'I can't stand it any longer. Aunt Mavis, where are you?' yelled Davidia. There was no echo. 'I don't like the acoustics; there's no follow-up sound.'

The room felt like they were surrounded by a dull mat that absorbed all sound. It lacked bounce.

A sliding door suddenly appeared within a wall and out walked a strikingly tall woman, albeit aged with time as the hands attested to, ramrod straight, fashionably dressed with a filtered, see-through scarf wound around her head in a turban-like fashion. It hid a clear face. She smiled at them, which couldn't visibly be seen. Davidia thought she had some embarrassing affliction. She waved a hand. The girls waved back. Was this to be a mime session? The girls sat down not knowing what was to befall them. Aunt Mavis sat on the far side of the room in a huge, soft chair with arms full of various controls. She pressed a button. A filtered screen arose in front of her chair. It contoured her body. Davidia wondered if it was bulletproof. The scene had now been set for a safe conversation for Aunt Mavis.

It was for her safety and anonymity. She had no desire for her true self to be revealed before she had extracted revenge, for what she didn't explain. It was time for some word association. Who would begin? You guessed it. It was to be one forward-thinking and confident, related young girl. Conversation might be a strained affair if Aunt Mavis held back her dictionary of knowledge. Mmm.

'Aunt Mavis,' Davidia began. 'You have an unusual home.'

There was no response.

Davidia continued. Slirander remained vigilant and observant. After all, they were a team.

'Why do you hide underground away from the above-ground people? Are you shy? Do you have hidden wealth? Are you really a witch that everyone is afraid of, or is it the rumours everyone seems to believe? Personally, I don't believe in witchcraft. I haven't lived long enough to learn about it, yet. Do you actually mix any potions in secret from a fabulous spell book? I'd like to see it if you have one. Perhaps you could shrink the size of my ego?' Davidia had to know the why of everything even though the answers were endless.

Slirander sighed heavily. Impertinence was a new constant adjective that Davidia was developing and it sat perfectly here. There was a slight movement in Aunt Mavis' chair. Maybe she had pressed another button. She felt as if she was being interrogated. She was.

'Is it that important to know how some of us choose to live our lives?'

Aunt Mavis replied with relaxed vocabulary in a meaningful sentence instead of the usual few words and short phrases. She had hardly ever spoken to the townspeople of Humpletoon; hence part of the myth was born.

'Mum was fossicking in the attic and found an old postcard

referring to you and suggested that I should visit during the school holidays. I had never heard you mentioned before. It tweaked my interest. Slirander and I have travelled a long way to meet you. You are certainly different to any other of my relatives. How long have you been here?'

There was a long pause. Aunt Mavis wondered whether these two were snoopers or was she actually related to one of them. She felt like she was a contestant in a quiz show. Her responses would be dribbled on a need-to-know basis. An inquisitive teenager can be difficult to satisfy with the proper explanations. There was no end to their insatiable curiosity.

'May I offer you a cold drink, or would you prefer the stem of a nettle to chew? You both look hungry.'

'She's not trying to poison us, is she?' whispered Davidia.

'A cold drink, please,' said Slirander. She understood witches' humour a little better.

Aunt Mavis remained stationary. A low volume buzz entered the room. It was a small robot in the shape of a mug. It carried two similar, but smaller, mugs and neatly placed them next to each girl. They were brimming with liquid. Davidia was unsure. The colour appeared to be gangrene green.

'You first,' she said to Slirander.

In ancient times, the rulers of the kingdoms used servants to taste the food and drink the wines and beverages to check if it was poisoned. Davidia wasn't royalty but needed affirmation that her drink was "safe".

Slirander picked up a smallish mug and suddenly began to handle it by rotating it in her hands, careful not to spill its brew.

'You are a beautiful mug. Who made you? I might want one exactly like you.' She drank heartily.

Davidia sensed that all was well when Slirander didn't fall into a convulsion. She drank cautiously and was surprised at how delicious it was. It had a wow factor dancing on her taste buds that clanged together in delight.

'That was delicious. This mug is certainly well-made. Where could I get one?'

Both girls were independently impressed with the small mugs and their quality. They would make a wonderful gift for their parents for allowing them to visit Aunt Mavis. They imagined the mugs had a personality and, uncanny as it may seem, each mug had a resemblance to the holder of the mug, and this one they had just met. The mugs had wriggled into shape as they drank its contents. It was so subtle, the naked eye couldn't see the change, nor could the hands feel it and they weren't numb from frostbite or an anaesthetic injection. Aunt Mavis smiled from behind her scarf veil.

'This looks like me,' said Davidia, running her fingers over the outer surface tracing her fine nose and full mouth without the lipstick.

'That's strange. This mug is identical to me,' said Slirander, mesmerised by her own good looks.

Both girls were amazed with what they saw. They believed it was impossible. Even the world's best sculptors couldn't replicate a person's face identically within seconds of meeting them. The word strange had now appeared as part of their journey.

'Aunt Mavis, there's something wrong with these mugs. They look like us. How is that even possible? We haven't sat for a portrait or art sculpting modelling and we definitely haven't been on social media recently plastering our beautiful faces on it for others to admire or copy.'

The silence was deafening. Aunt Mavis was attempting to assimilate into the conversation, when for years such interaction was terribly foreign to her. Her confidence had been sat on all that time and now had the beginnings of reuse. Young teenage girls can certainly be influential.

'They are statement mugs made from the finest of special clay infused with a magical force that is unexplainable. It is all around you. Can you feel it?'

Davidia was confused. Feel what? Slirander was vibe-absorptive and began to rock to a gentle rhythm. She was more accepting of suggestive comments whereas Davidia was more sceptical.

'What am I supposed to feel?' said Davidia, searching the room for the "feel". She couldn't find it.

'It will come to you when you are ready,' said Aunt Mavis. 'What do you think of your new companion/statement mugs? Aren't they gorgeous? They are a gift.'

'Who made them?'

'I did and on these very premises. There is a mug festival held each year in the town of Dimpletoon and I enter the competition with inferior mugs so that the prize goes to another worthy potter. It is now time that the situation changed and I enter the best entrant. These hands,' Aunt Mavis exposed them from beneath her clothing to reveal two slender, youthful-looking, petite hands that could handle any preciously fragile item with ease, 'are the tools for those magnificent mugs that you have been given. No one is aware of my real pottery skills, but they are exceptional. Both of you can assist in development of the superior mug that we will produce and we will name it Aunty's Curse for a bit of fun. See how that ignites the locals' imagination. The myth will be embellished.'

Did Aunt Mavis have a sense of humour? It was wickedly evil and so fun. Davidia was warming to her aunt. Slirander was still absorbing the vibes of the room.

'What do we have to do to make the fun-named mug?'

'Come with me to my secret laboratory on the lower floor. Real magic happens there.'

Aunt Mavis let go a small cackle which tingled Davidia's spine like a jolt of electricity. The impact unsettled her. Slirander followed like the drink robot without question. Where were the girls going and what experience will they encounter? Nothing is ever as it seems.

*   *   *

'Grandma,' said a young voice, 'are you home? It's Eleanor, your granddaughter.'

The old lady was hidden amongst a pile of clothing she had mistaken for her bed after her late-night Milo foray. She was so well camouflaged that her dog had to sniff out where her location was. She stirred. Sleep was a constant companion seeing that she wasn't too active these days.

'In here, dear,' she replied.

'In where?'

'In here.'

Eleanor had to walk through the cluttered lounge room to seek out her grandmother. In the dull light she noticed a glint off a shelf as she walked past. She ignored it. Milo Mac saw her walk past and couldn't call out for attention, but he could glint. That tear streak may yet be his salvation. He waited for a return walk-through.

'Grandma, where are you? This is your bedroom, isn't it?'

Suddenly, a pile of clothing heaped in a mound moved and revealed Grandma at the bottom of it.

'Hi, Eleanor. I got lost. Where am I?' Grandma was slightly disorientated. A minute later and all faculties were on the go again.

'We have a shopping trip planned. Don't you remember?'

'I hadn't forgotten. The darkness hid it from me.'

Eleanor fussed over Grandma as she assisted in her preparation.

'Ready.'

As Eleanor walked back through the lounge room, she again noticed that glint she first saw on the shelf. It wasn't a light-bulb left on, or a small slow-burning candle left unattended. She crept closer to discover that it was an ordinary mug. She had no use for it – they were a dime a dozen in town – so she turned away and ignored Mac just as Grandma had done. Was life over for him before it had begun? Once again, a sadness teardrop slid down his extremities. The tear streak revealed his beautifully striped exterior albeit in a thin line. It glinted brightly. Suddenly, Eleanor noticed the light rays he shed and turned around to source them. She was amazed that it came from a simple mug. That's crazy, she thought. Upon closer inspection, she noticed the strange shape, its handles and that glint. She picked it up and took it into the kitchen. After a quick wash and dry, she squealed with delight. Wow! The mug she held was beautifully made from the most exquisitely striped clay and now shone.

'Grandma, where did you get this mug?'

Grandma couldn't remember. Her short-sightedness meant her recognition of objects was also rather poor.

'Somewhere,' she said.

'It's so beautiful. I think I'll enter it in the Dimpletoon Mug Festival. We could win first prize.'

Mac was recoiling with delight. Wonderful adjectives were being used to describe him.

Maybe there was that future after all.

*   *   *

The Dimpletoon Mug Festival arrangements were well under way. Its small industrious team of volunteers congregated for brief meetings, then wham, action. There was no time for petty rivalries as they were proud to organise the festival. Disputes were left to the competitors. Large marquees provided covered spaces for all entrants to display their pride under cover. Not every entrant was a potential prize winner due to some inferior clay being used, but they all believed in their product. Each entrant kept their source close to their chest. Every advantage was seized. There was the usual pecking order of mug placement. The mayor always had that usual spot. The town councillors were over there and the general public were never displayed in front row positions and as uncanny as it may seem, every year the mayor or a councillor won the coveted prize. Who's sniffing up whose anatomy? The selection panel often found special invitations to free council functions – the occasional high tea with the lady mayoress and movie tickets to opening premieres that just happened to fall from the sky. The impartial selection committee rarely changed their composition; however, this year a few new faces had been added. Time had sent a few past members to the cemetery or a nursing home. It didn't take long for the gravy to be fed to the new members.

'What reward will we receive this year?' said a new member, having been updated that surprises would come their way if they did the right thing.

'Don't ask. It's rude to pre-suggest anything. Someone may overhear you and that would ruin the festival. Besides,' she whispered, 'I hear it could be a set of red rubies. Keep that to yourself. Not everyone will get them. Remember to vote impartially and correctly like I do.'

'You mean it's rigged. We cheat for self-reward. I only meant that we might receive a free coffee with a delicious dessert, not to gerrymander a result.'

'Get with the program or risk ostracism by your peers. That's a lonely meal; dinner for one.'

*   *   *

'Hello, Chad,' said the lady mayoress, in a subtle tone. 'It's been far too long since we last spoke.'

The lady mayoress had visited the pottery after high tea at Worthington Hall, which was full of the town somebodies. The nobodies, in her opinion, which included most of the town, weren't invited. Riff-raff – and it wasn't the name of a rapper – had no place near her period clothing, cleanliness or sparkling repartee. Selfishness festered from her every pore. Her thin lips were almost a straight line when she spoke. It wasn't a feature worth kissing other than a quick pretend emotional moment often displayed at public functions. The air kiss wasn't in vogue at the time. She had visited Chad on the pretext of reparation for some of the past, but only some. Her vixen-like, wily character was as dangerous as a death wish. Beauty shows its appearance, but often is only a body's surface affliction.

Chad took a deep breath. It had been years since they had last spoken. Both had tauter torsos back then. It took him a moment before the wind from his sails tacked. His olden body, under a mass of hair, turned slowly like a rotating chicken.

'Hello, Merrilyn. Long time to forget,' replied Chad. His memory was full of his life's records. 'What brings you here?'

'I have a proposition for you.'

'I'm past rekindling an affair. It cost me dearly last time.'

'This is not that type of proposition, but it did cross my mind.' She blushed at her memory files. 'I want you to enter the Dimpletoon Mug Festival with your best mug and place these two items in the handles.' She passed over two gemstones of the deepest darkest red that he'd ever seen.

'These are magnificent.' Their beauty entranced him. 'What is its purpose?'

'Just do that for me and I will see that you are adequately rewarded. I can't stay. Mervyn needs me in town for an official matter. We'll meet again, I'm sure.'

Her period skirt scraped the ground clearing any dirt from the immediate surrounds for her to walk through. Chad wondered what her angle was. He was suspicious of anything to do with his ex-brother and sister-in-law. However, he was determined to enter the festival and win that pre-rigged prize. He set to work. Soon, his pottery wheel had an upbeat hum.

*   *   *

In the underground laboratory, Aunt Mavis had a full-blown pottery set-up with a range of the most up-to-date technological equipment. It was a marvellous feat of engineering to construct such a magical underground environment that no one in town had recognised as a construction site. The waste landfill was dumped in the next-door quarry, whereas the locals mistook it for ordinary waste from the community. It was built unrecognised and unhindered by the locals by use of outside town contractors. It was during the course of construction that Aunt Mavis imagined the clay components had a feeling of magic about them and kept them aside for future use. It couldn't be explained because it was such a strange feeling and to enlighten others was akin to buying the most delicious ice-creams and no one appreciating the taste. In other words, it would be a complete waste of time.

One night long ago, when she was negotiating with the sandman about a deep sleep, a dreamy vision filled her subconscious mind with a misty story of magical elements, an ancient scroll, dirt and an unusual location. The swirling mist had a dark centre surrounded by barren land, isolated from the nearest towns. It seemed to be on the edge of an abyss. Her head began to experience serious pain as if nails were being embedded into her skull by a spiteful antagonist. She screamed, 'I'll get you, you bastard,' as she flew out of bed straight into the wall, head first. The following discomfort reinforced the pain of the dream into believing reality had seeped into her mind. Confusion ran amok. It was only recently that she had escaped the horror of being incinerated in the family home and now those tragic forces teased her sanity. From her prostate position on the floor, she raised her bruised head and could have sworn that there were evil eyes glowering at her from the ceiling. Were they part of the dream? Am I to take a journey? Walls don't move. A pensive Aunt Mavis sat on the bed wondering what universe she was in. She finally regained her senses and knew she was on Earth. The next day she left and found herself in Humpletoon. The "why" hadn't been answered.

'I had all this dug out to live a life of seclusion, but alas, the nosey villagers all took an interest in the newcomer to town who was whispered about in undertones of mystery. To ensure that I kept my privacy, the old lady was born. It was the perfect disguise. Senility, Alzheimer's, untidiness, uncleanliness and old rags to dress in are all associated with an aged woman and were eagerly and gullibly accepted as the truths about that eccentric woman. No one bothered me any further. The rumours abounded.'

'Why hide? It must be lonely,' said Davidia, concerned that Aunt Mavis didn't seem to have had a happy life.

'The answer will arrive one day. I arrived here in Humpletoon. There is no explanation, but I had a vague vision long ago.'

'Me, too,' said Davidia. 'I had a dream about this place before I left. Someone needed saving. I don't know who, though.'

Slirander quietly observed the two relatives chatting and suddenly noticed a scroll peeking from a shelf. Her eyes were averted by the perception of movement or the thought of it. Did it move?

There was no breeze available. Were her eyes being tricked, or had another of her family's senses alerted her? She slowly walked across the room, placed her hand on the scroll, gave it a tug and it stayed put. She pulled again and it refused to be parted from the shelf. Was it glued or nailed down? Any further pulling may destroy its integrity. She looked over to Aunt Mavis and interrupted.

'I cannot prise the scroll loose from the shelf. It has generated a strange feeling in me like it's hiding a secret of some proportion. Can you release it to find out what it is?'

Aunt Mavis had a sudden hiccup attack almost inhaling her veiled scarf. She was still seated in her chair with all the buttons. How extraordinary that a simple question created such a violent come-back? Slirander's magical family background senses had been notified that something important resided in that scroll. Her inquisitiveness had also been lit. Whoosh! After a minute or two, Aunt Mavis settled. Her right-hand index finger was raised and hit a button on her chair controls. A slow "bzzt" followed. Another small robot walked toward Slirander carrying the very scroll she had asked about. How did that happen? The scroll had been magnetized in place. The robot bypassed Slirander and handed the scroll to Aunt Mavis. It wasn't exactly a single scroll, but a series of many pages with writing folded tightly together to present as one page. There was no outside indication referring to what was on the inside. Aunt Mavis twiddled with them unsure whether to reveal what secrets, if any, they held. Davidia was keen to find out.

'What's in there? Spells, potions, witty jokes or ancient dangers? Go on, Aunt Mavis, show us.'

The scroll disappointingly consisted of one page only. Aunt Mavis opened it up and displayed it for all to see. The girls' faces drained of interest.

'How boring. It's one lousy page with what, a dozen words only.' Davidia had expected more excitement.

Slirander was as equally disappointed at first, but her sight lingered longer on the page than did Davidia's, staring at those twelve words. Suddenly, they began to rotate and formed a set of instructions. Aunt Mavis sat silently. Davidia was ceiling-staring with disinterest. The words popped out of the page and landed on Slirander's hands weighing them both down so heavily that she had to kneel on the floor to support them. Each finger and palm turned into a singular word each. She was immobilised. She didn't panic. A logical conclusion was there somewhere. Aunt Mavis was stunned. Slirander became possessed with a twelve-word library. Her hands began to hurt. The pain was visible on her face. Her normal satin-smooth skin was etched with white streak lines. She was visibly aging.

'Slirander, say something,' said Davidia, noticing a change in events for the worse.

There was no marriage dialogue here for better or for worse; however, Slirander tried to speak the twelve words strangling her existence. Fortunately, her family past had been mired in magical moments and she knew something special had to happen for her safety to be returned. By this time, the floor seemed to be swallowing her hands and arms. Where were they going? Was all of her to follow, or was she to lose both those limbs only? Davidia was mortified.

'Do something, Aunt Mavis. My friend is sinking into your floor.'

There was no response. Slirander was responsible for her own misfortune. Only she could save herself. Davidia wasn't really happy with aunty.

Slirander painstakingly tried to speak the twelve words. Her jaw-bone ached, her voice sounded exhausted as if from under a cemetery tombstone, and her face began to evolve into the shape of the mug she had drank from earlier, distorting her mouth into an odd shape.

Finally, the twelve words began to slowly seep out.

'The Ring of Clay has no time to play. Save the Ring.' Her mouth ached with the effort.

She remembered the words as they vanished from view. Slirander managed just in time to complete the dangerous dozen as she was up to her armpits in disappearance. The scroll page suddenly relaxed on the floor. Slirander's hands and arms reappeared. The floor disappeared and for all intents and purposes, normality had returned. Slirander flexed her hands, moved her mouth circularly and checked her features to see if she resembled a mug. Satisfaction beamed when she realised she was herself again. Davidia yelled excitedly; her friend was back. Aunt Mavis didn't move. She hadn't been immobilised as a cement block; however, she might as well have been.

'Why didn't you do anything? Slirander could have been seriously harmed,' said an angry Davidia.

'It was impossible. Whoever demanded the scroll's attention was responsible for the outcome. There is a secret attached to the scroll. It has now been opened and I had been afraid to do it myself. It required a clever young person to discover it. Have a look at the scroll page and see what it says,' said Aunt Mavis.

All three turned their attention to a single page of parched equipment lying on the floor imitating refuse. No longer were there twelve written words on display. It was now blank.

'Where did the words disappear to?' asked Davidia, surprised that they weren't there any longer.

'There is no explanation,' replied Aunt Mavis. 'The scroll contains secrets only it knows.'

'It can't speak, can it?'

Suddenly, a thin, wispy line arose from the page pretending to be a smoky trail. It danced and twirled, flashing powdery, puffed lettered shapes upwards. The few letters that were recognised, once written down, spelt the words, Save Clay. Poof! The smoky show was over. The page still remained blank. Slirander moved closer and placed her hand on the page and it fell through it. She yelped in surprise and quickly redrew it, to find it still there. The blank page lay flat on the solid floor, yet when touched, depth occurred. Slirander got down on all fours – not imitating a well-loved pet – and carefully placed her nose, then face and complete head into the page and it just went through it. The A4 size page instantly became a rectangular necklace as she stood up as the headless horse girl. Davidia screamed at the sight of her headless friend.

'Where is her head? It hasn't been severed, has it?' Davidia was mortified at the loss of her friend's head.

Aunt Mavis was puzzled too, but reasoned that the scroll had it under control. It may have a message. Slirander walked around not unlike the well-known saying "headless chook", but without the frenetic running that accompanies it. As she moved her head to read the inside information, it appeared that the page acted as a balancing scale on her shoulders. It was silent. Could she still see if she walked around the room? What could she see, anyway? What was in that scroll to retell or reveal a hidden something? They would never know until, if ever, her head returned intact. Would it be damaged in some way, or be as it was before? Only extraction from the disappearing page will answer any question posed. The worry-warts sat mesmerised. They watched Slirander walk completely around the whole room without bumping into any furniture item. Her arms waved, fingers pointed, she occasionally bent over and the necklace almost fell off on a few occasions, but it didn't. Five minutes had actually passed, but it felt like it was a mental eternity. In that moment, had the right thing been done? Where had Slirander gone?

'Did you feel that?' asked Davidia, as a cool breeze took hold of her earlobes and shook them. 'Who's there?' she yelled.

Aunt Mavis was back sitting in her chair with all the control buttons. She had turned on an air freshener device. Davidia was becoming fractious. Her friend was still absent. Before any more emotional pressure exploded, Slirander reappeared from the paged necklace, fully formed. It fluttered to the floor with the missing twelve words reinstated. She picked it up and replaced it on the shelf. There it sat once again as an insignificant, rolled-up, singular page which no one was to read again, except Slirander.

'You're back,' said an excited Davidia. 'Where did you go? What was in there? Tell, tell.'

Slirander thought carefully before blurting out words as mere babble, without a common-sense structure. She knew that whatever she said would influence their next move. The information message she had received was for Aunt Mavis. She looked over at her and the glance that passed between them acknowledged that they understood who it was for. When Slirander finally spoke, the sounds she gurgled out weren't understandable by Davidia but were by Aunt Mavis. After a few minutes of pure gobbledygook, she sat down exhausted, satisfied that she had relayed the correct messages.

'What was that rubbish?' asked Davidia, feeling shunned by the lack of understanding of what was said.

Aunt Mavis spoke.

'The scroll contained a series of ancient spells that relate to the area around the quarry. It spoke of ancient bearers of special clays that needed preservation and a protector, hence the reason that I'm here. It came to me in a dream, which I didn't understand at the time, and now I know why. Therefore, the persona development. It wasn't the only reason either.'

'What was it like in there?' Davidia asked Slirander.

'In where? Where have I been?' she replied.

'Inside that page with your missing head.'

'I don't remember.'

'We watched you walk around the room.'

'Sorry. It's a blank.'

Davidia looked at Aunt Mavis who shrugged her shoulders. All explanations, brief as they were, were all that was available. It was stalemate.

'Now, what sort of mug shall we make for the Dimpletoon Mug Festival? Any suggestions?'

The girls were momentarily bereft of any ideas. They had been mentally stunned by the significance and the antics of the scroll. As they were recovering their thoughts, Aunt Mavis suggested that three mugs be entered. Each one to be an exact replica of each of themselves produced from the special clay that surrounded the quarry. It was a brilliant idea. Davidia puzzled over the exact replica comment. Would that mean they could at last identify Aunt Mavis? She pondered over that statement. It could unveil a massive surprise for some or all of them again.

'You did say an exact replica of each of us? I didn't mishear, did I? Does that mean I will recognise what you really look like? We could then identify you.' Davidia smiled.

She would love to see what her aunty really looked like and whether she had any similar features.

The day couldn't come soon enough.

Aunt Mavis pressed a few more buttons on her chair and the room suddenly lit up like a train station. Bright lights shone over the girls' facial features as if they had been sucked off their faces and magically transported to a humming potter's wheel.

They noticed that three potter's wheels were sloshing, shaping, spinning, washing automatically and plying through a pile of clay with glinted reflections each time a water droplet hit their surfaces. The girls watched intently as they easily recognised the development of their faces, but Aunt Mavis' was still hidden behind that scarf veil. It was somewhat of a disappointment. Soon, three robots delivered three masterpieces at the feet of Aunt Mavis. The mutual admiration society was formed as each mug was breathtakingly beautiful.

Davidia felt for some inexplicable reason that they were actually alive. She did have a vivid imagination, but her female intuition told her that was the case. She was rarely wrong. Something didn't quite sit right.

Aunt Mavis beamed.

'I believe that we can now win the Dimpletoon Mug Festival.'

It wasn't long before the big day would arrive where everyone could wear their pride like a badge.

6 DIMPLETOON MUG FESTIVAL DAY

The following day, there was hurry and scurry at the festival site as the volunteers acted like possessed demons in an effort to have all the tables, marquees, chairs and places set for the guests and competitors. Weather conditions were ideal for a summer holiday, even though it wasn't summer.

'Oh, I do love the excitement,' said a first-time volunteer.

Her abundant physical attributes hampered her movement at an unaccustomed pace.

'There's the mayor and the lady mayoress. Don't they look the picture of sartorial elegance especially the mayoress in that period dress that she always wears? It could do with a dry-clean. Have you ever gotten close to her? Well, let me tell you ...' the voice trailed off in case she was overheard and missed the day's fitting reward, whatever that may be.

There was always an unhappy element at every happy event, but that side of the festival was minor in relation to the main gig; however, it was wise to recognise dissent if it arose. The ladies had achieved their set-up in time for the grand opening. The Mayor of Dimpletoon was a wizened old man not more than one metre tall. With his bone configurations it was a medical marvel that he could still walk. His voice commanded attention.

The microphone was handed to him by a plump woman with a girly grin. Her eyelids fluttered quicker than a hummingbird's wings. Was she imitating a mug, or was there a hint of flirtatious behaviour?

'Ladies and gentlemen, The Dimpletoon Mug Festival is open. May the best mug win and enjoy the day.'

The crowds began to mingle.

*   *   *

'Grandma,' said Eleanor. 'Isn't this beautiful entrant terrific to have?'

She held Milo Mac aloft and marvelled at the sun's rays performing theatrically all over his surfaces as she rotated him in her hands. Light rays danced to a silent musical performance deflecting wondrous colours from his specially striped surfaces. It was as if he was the festival centrepiece; well, he was for Eleanor and Grandma. They walked amongst the various tables and asked for a prime position to display Milo Mac. Petty jealousies suddenly erupted with an over-fastidious official and one of the brown-nose committee members, directing them to the back table away from the main foot traffic. This ensured high invisibility when judging would occur.

'My, what an ugly mug,' she said, as she left them to ponder their poor positioning.

'Bit of a bitch, I'd say,' said Eleanor, huffily. 'There is no chance of being spotted back here and who is she to comment about appearances? I'd like to see her mug entrant; perhaps a bulldog.'

Eleanor and Grandma had to soak up the placement disappointment. They ambled through the other entrant tables and noted what mug looked like who and those that were in prime positions. They passed the front table which was full of older, sterner faces lacking that smile ingredient. Eleanor recognised who most of them represented and a combined word called committee came to mind.

'Selfish bitches, stealing prime location to display their unhappy jowls, saggy faces and droopy eyes. It must have been a boring pottery day to produce those mini-monoliths. I'm glad it wasn't me.' Eleanor was having a bad-word day. Compliments were supposed to flow and not be ignored or choke up one's positive state of mind.

They continued to wander.

*   *   *

'Hello Chad,' cooed the lady mayoress, as she came to within hearing distance.

She refrained from releasing her thin, pink tongue for a slick lick and unsettling the potter. The mayor had moved on to other constituents to brag about some issue where he would be complimented unendingly. Being mentally blind never dampened the high self-esteem opinion he had of himself. He was aware of his wife's past history with Chad.

'Hello, Merrilyn. Still annoying people, eh?' he replied quickly, putting a pace or two between them.

He didn't appreciate any invasion of his personal space and especially not from such a dangerous female who had often verbally back-stabbed those that she thought were a threat. Her hubby was the mush-mush mayor she vehemently protected even though he had often proved he was inept, made the occasional dreadful decision and had a personality that was hard to package in a happy place.

'Did you bring our thing?' she teased.

'The mug with the red earlobes is here.'

He produced a beautifully designed mug resplendent with fine accessories of handles, nose and other facial features. It was a work of art which he was undeniably proud of, even though he had no idea what the purpose of the red earrings were. Nevertheless, he had kept his part of the arrangement. He hoped the other part was a cash payout and not some other form of "gift". He gave the mug to Merrilyn who carefully traced the back of his rough potter's hands with her fine fingers causing a sudden retraction interpreted as a handshake.

'Thank you, Chad. See you in the winner's circle.'

He had no reason to associate with her any further and he too had a wander amongst the crowd. What Merrilyn did with the mug or where she had it displayed was of no consequence to him. He was a potter now and not a practising criminal.

Maybe she was Mervyn's curse?

*   *   *

'I can't be seen at the festival,' said Aunt Mavis. 'I don't want to be recognised. Take the three mugs for entrance in the festival competition.'

'Who shall we say is the third mug?' asked Davidia. 'I'm sure that the committee will be asking questions about who the third one is supposed to be and who made it.'

'Say it's of an old aunty and it's called Aunty's Curse. She couldn't attend due to a back affliction and walking all day would damage her fragile bone structure. I will remain here and watch the proceedings.'

'How can you do that when you can't see us or know what we're doing?' said Davidia.

'Don't worry about it Davidia,' said Slirander, knowing that there was sixth sense in that scroll. She could feel it, but not remember what was there. The vibes were still filtering through her system.

The words that she had uttered to Aunt Mavis were powerful spell-incantations which related to the special clay that surrounded the quarry and included her property. It was impossible to reveal any of them. A dark and dangerous secret loitered amongst it. It was safer to fake the truth than reveal it. Davidia was miffed that she wouldn't join them. Suddenly, a flash of brilliance visited; however, it was a brief encounter at best.

'Why don't Slirander and I each wear one of your "old" coats and pretend that we are you? Both of us can act out an old-aged role. We were innovative in our drama classes at school where the teachers often commented about the absurdity of our emotional art. It would be fun to "hide" in the open. What do you think?' Davidia never wasted a good thought, but was this one a first?

Slirander shrugged her slender shoulders in resignation. Her friend had once again shown diversity in intelligence. She warmed to the idea after a few minutes. Aunt Mavis' jaw dropped, but got caught up in the scarf veil to avoid lobbing onto the floor. Was it a practical thing to do or was it a stupid idea? What would it achieve?

'Why would you pretend to be me? I don't appeal to anyone in this town,' said a pensive Aunt Mavis.

She was flattered that someone had given her any consideration and imitation being the greatest form of flattery certainly had appeal. She had been too long on her own. Her confidence handbag was almost empty.

'This way you will remain anonymous. If we are discovered as frauds, what can happen? Two stupid schoolgirls performing a silly prank won't attract much interest. Why do you want to remain anonymous? Remind me again.' Davidia was still a curious schoolgirl.

'That's private.'

Aunt Mavis sat impassively in her chair. There was no telling today. Davidia sensed the "brick wall shut" trap. She motioned to Slirander.

'What do you think of my idea?'

'It's downright stupid; however, we may learn something about acting.'

'The townsfolk won't think we're odd. Some already know that I'm related to Aunt Mavis. They might want to certify me.'

Slirander laughed. There was something strange in her sounds that Davidia hadn't noticed before. She kept quiet and observed her friend closely. She couldn't identify any psychotic behaviour lurking there so she filed it for the present.

'Where are our mugs? They were at your feet earlier.'

Aunt Mavis once again pressed the buttons on her chair. The same three robots came out from behind the chair with the three magnificent mugs, two of which were identical to the girls with Aunt Mavis' still hidden by that scarf veil. However, that would have to do. All or either of them were beautiful enough to win the competition. Aunt Mavis was a master potter. It was hoped that these skills would be noticed at the festival and enquiries would be made about the mugs' origins.

'Do me proud,' said Aunt Mavis, giving acknowledgement for the girls to enact their idea, 'and ensure that the three mugs have pride of place on one table at least. That is important.'

Davidia couldn't have cared less where the mugs were placed. She was to be in character. She loved dressing up and role-playing. Slirander was odder than Davidia; however, she wasn't as usually as obvious as her. There was more subtlety. The girls visited the room of clothes and within ten minutes two exact duplicates of Aunt Mavis emerged.

'Guess which one is which?' said Davidia, in a disguised voice.

Aunt Mavis knew who each was, but played along saying it was too difficult to choose. The foil was perfect. They scooped up the three mugs and left the building. They crept out the front gate unseen. They thought that the townsfolk might have seen them, but they were safe. As they left, Aunt Mavis chanted a few lines of an ancient spell which they didn't hear. Slirander felt it in her aura. Davidia dismissed it as an itch. The Aunty's Curse mug reacted with acceptance of a sigh. The three mugs were infected by the mysterious chant. It produced subtle changes in their composition. Milo Mac was also affected by the strange chant and was unaware that he was. Why he would be involved was a mystery? The day would unfold as a challenge to them all. The Aunt Mavis look-alikes walked to Dimpletoon in high spirits and none of them were of the rum variety. No one could see their smiles.

It wasn't Halloween; however, who were they to trick or treat, if anyone?

*　　*　　*

At the Dimpletoon Mug Festival, the girls were eyed with suspicion as they neared. The townsfolk could only see trouble. Didn't they resemble someone else they knew? It was a conundrum. The girls did exactly what they had planned. They imitated Aunt Mavis to perfection. Their bent, crumpled bodies almost reduced their normal height by half, the old skirts dragged on the ground as social street sweepers and the long-haired wigs swayed rhythmically as they fumbled their footwork. A ruddy-faced committee member confronted them at the entrance.

'We don't allow walking rubbish into the festival,' she said, with hands firmly clasped in front of her tightly-hugging, slim belt which was an attempt to prevent too much personality slipping south. Her knuckles turned a pallid white. Her face was determined to stare at them. A minute passed.

'Hello to you, too,' cackled Davidia, thinking she was witchypoo in a movie. 'We have three winning mugs to enter into the competition. They are the best that has ever been made.'

Her withered, wrinkled hands could hardly lift the bag with the mugs. Perfect make-up passes the merest of eye glances. Slirander walked over to assist.

She whispered, 'What are you doing?'

'Gaining entrance.'

The offensive word of winning threw down a challenge to the committee member. Defeat was a new word that upset her. In the spirit of proving the young upstart wrong, it was a guess that she was young, she reneged on her first opening comments. She turned quickly to another committee member and it was obvious vehement discourse occurred. Another turn and she stood exactly where she was before. She still stared with a painful expression. Through a pair of stretched lips, the strained response was evident.

'With the community spirit in which we Dimpletoonians embrace everyone, you may enter. Show me your mugs.'

Davidia once again reached into her bag and produced the three stunning competitors. At first glance, the committee member reeled in shock.

'They are all of me,' she said. 'Brilliant. You must display them on the front table. I'm flattered that you have caught my features so perfectly. I always knew I had modelling potential.'

Before Davidia refuted her comments in anger, Slirander took her by the arm and whispered quietly what had just happened.

'The mugs take on the appearance of whoever is looking at

them. They were firstly of the three of us, but now they are all of her because she saw them and stared. The mugs immediately adapted to her features. Before we place them on the table, we'll look at ours, so they reshape with our features. Aunt Mavis' will take moments longer as the mugs remember that they will always revert finally to that first face after changing into another. The other thing to remember is that each mug with its stripes has a magical element and I don't know how that will manifest itself during the festival. We must be wary of change.'

'How do you know this stuff?'

'It's in the family genes. I felt something in my aura with your aunt.'

'They don't look so pretty as before.'

Davidia lamented the change. She was now, in her mind, an inferior-looking mug.

'This way,' said the committee member.

The girls followed closely; however, the community began to notice the resemblance to the old recluse who lived next to the quarry. A few began to mumble.

'She rang me the other day, but I know she doesn't have a telephone.'

'You mean she really doesn't have legs under that coat. Does she float?'

'I've seen her running around in my brain-wearing joggers, yet she's an old lady who can hardly walk.'

The grapevine was in full harvest. As the girls brushed past, they spat and grizzled at them. Faces turned away in an avoidance technique. The crowd wondered who the two oddities really were.

'There's your table. You can display them at that end. Let me see myself again. I look so adorable. I might win the competition.'

The mugs had still retained her features. As Davidia and

Slirander took the mugs out of the bag, they gave them a good staring, so that they would reassemble as themselves. They were placed strategically on the corner of the table. All the committee statues dominated the main space, but nothing shone from their surfaces. Their stone, or should we say clay personalities, lacked any pizzazz.

'Now what?' said Davidia.

'Check out the competition.'

The girls ambled away as two very old people. No one engaged them in social niceties. They felt as outcast as Aunt Mavis. The disguises were a perfect foil to remain lonely. Davidia thought that Aunt Mavis is going to shed her coat after they return. There was more to life than hiding behind long hair and old coats. Human social contact animates life in others. It was time to share again.

'Isn't that the young backpacker receptionist? He's still got those wires in his ears. Let's approach him,' said Davidia.

The girls momentarily forgot their disguise and approached him. Davidia tapped him on the knee because in the bent-over position it was difficult to touch his shoulder. The shock of a hand that low on his anatomy had him in defence mode.

'Who's attacking my manhood? I didn't give anyone permission and, if I did, it wouldn't be in a public place.'

He was miffed that someone had gotten that close without him realising it. The touch was innocent enough. He quickly turned around to sight the intruder or whatever had made an unsolicited approach. His mental state was in a blank space with shock. One glance and he was convinced he had double vision. There were two of them. That's not possible. The old recluse was a single. Was he really cursed? Davidia withdrew the offending hand. Being in character, she spoke with the disguised voice.

'It's us,' she cackled.

The young lad fell over.

'Don't attack me. I'm innocent,' he ranted.

'It's us,' repeated Davidia, but this time without the cackle. 'We met you at the backpackers' hotel and you offered us a telephone number. Now do you remember?'

The girls made no moves towards him. They stood bent over and waited patiently for an unemotional response. It must have been intimidating thinking he'd been touched by an old, believed to be, witch. Finally, it dawned on him who they might be.

'You aren't practising curses, are you?' he said, somewhat in disbelief.

'We are in character. We wanted to see how Aunt Mavis felt in the community and as we aren't residents, there was no risk of not being able to compete in the mug competition. Have you entered a mug? It might win a male mug prize.' Davidia was softening his stress levels.

'What! Imitating your aunt? Is that old witch your real aunt? I think I'll take up meditation.'

'She's not a witch, just misunderstood by her choice of lifestyle. We all possess some eccentricity.'

'I can't be seen talking to two witches even if you aren't. People are beginning to stare. You may be cursed without realising it by dressing that way. Leave me alone. I need a toilet break.'

The young man took off as if he had something dangerous up his back. He'd thought he'd been cursed by that touch. The girls thought he was a wimp. Fancy believing that trash about curses and witches!

They continued to wander around the festival in theme. No one dared approach them. They passed their three entrants' table and noticed that Aunt Mavis was as originally designed; however, they also looked exactly like her and not the two beautiful-looking girls they knew they were. How odd? They were a trio of identical mugs.

Slirander felt a cool wind whip around the base of her skirt. She felt a sudden jab in her ribcage. She stopped. The real Aunt Mavis mug moved its mouth. That was a complete surprise. She moved closer. A warm breath was emitted. Nothing else happened. She moved away. The pain in her ribcage persisted. It didn't assist her comfort situation. She placed a hand flat on the painful area to prevent it from falling out. All bones should stay where they were born to grow and be. Suddenly, her hand hurt instead. A pinprick feeling ran along one finger down into her palm. It felt like a blood corpuscle was chasing another in a game of tag. When it reached her palm, it stopped the game. She withdrew her hand and carefully unfolded it like unwrapping a valuable jewel. A few words were visible highlighted as minute red welts. She read them and they instantaneously disappeared. Her hand was clean and normal again. It was a curiosity. She couldn't remember the words she had just read. Maybe they were filed in her subconscious for later retrieval? Davidia didn't feel anything. Her pain was not getting through to the young man.

'Slirander, our mugs are look-alikes. What happened to us?' said Davidia, peering at her representation.

'We look like Aunt Mavis dressed like this, that's why,' replied Slirander, invoking common-sense thinking.

'Oh! Now I get it. I was distracted.'

The girls continued their wanderings.

*   *   *

Milo Mac had been contentedly waiting a turn to be shown, adored, flattered and above all, hoped to hear the kindest words that would explain his appearance. He knew he had the "goods"; it was a matter of knowing what they were. Slirander and Davidia were tiring of their new-found identity. Their backs were aching from being bent over and dragging that ruddy coat along the ground made them work like bullocks in a field just to put in one step at a time.

'I'm fed up with this impersonating. It was fun at first, but now under the weight of these garments and being constantly arched, I'm over it.' Davidia was losing interest in her theme role.

Slirander was ambivalent with the situation. She could "take" it, whereas fairy-floss Davidia was struggling.

They walked to the back of the presentation tables and were contemplating their next move of no real interest. They had firstly arrived as impersonators to win the mug festival competition. Any other reason was either superfluous or unknown. The girls were just having fun. The competition from the back tables was supposed to be a waste of presentation. They noticed Milo Mac sitting there stationary and overshadowing the appearance of all others on that table. There was an oddity about him.

'Slirander, that mug over there certainly has some weird and wonderful shapes. Note that its colouring is almost identical to our mugs,' said Davidia, eyeing it with her keen artistic eyes.

Slirander walked over and placed a hand on Milo Mac to feel his surfaces. She jumped backwards. Her aura had been infected with a strange feeling.

'Wow! I'll be more careful,' she said to herself.

A sharp pain had kicked her in the ribcage once again and the same follow-up with red welt words occurred. Coincidence doesn't cut it. Something deliberate is kicking her. Why?

'Are you okay?' questioned Davidia, as she felt her friend had received a mild shock.

She knew she had, but didn't know why. Her female intuition was on song today.

'Could you retrieve one of our mugs, say yours, and bring it back here to compare with this one? I have a sense that needs clarification,' said Slirander, feeling somewhat pained. Her ribcage still hurt.

'I'm ditching this coat after that.'

Davidia did as requested. She selected a mug which she thought was hers – they were all identical in appearance – and returned with it to Slirander. She passed it over to her. Slirander then took the mug and put it inside the ragged coat and it was completely hidden from view. Davidia wondered whether her friend was playing a game of silly hide-and-seek. Suddenly, Slirander's coat dropped silently to the ground into a small hump of used clothing. Davidia waited and waited for the surprise. Where was her friend? She lifted the coat only to discover the mug with Slirander's face beaming from it. What had happened? Davidia picked up the mug. A teardrop fell from her face and ran down the side. Its striped surface lit up momentarily, then faded. Milo Mac had been watching proceedings with interest. He was still his inanimate self. Perhaps that was all about to change. He sensed something in his aura, which was becoming popular today. Davidia placed Slirander next to Milo Mac. The two of them looked like the odd couple. They also had a certain familiarity in their colouring.

'Slirander, what have you done? You haven't become a real mug, have you?'

'It's the strangest feeling. I feel as if I'm being directed by a magical force. I'm still me, but in a different form. There is a reason someone has changed my physical being, but not my personality.'

'How will I get you back?'

'I don't know yet, but I have met another beautiful mug resting right next to me. His name is Milo Mac.'

'What? A talking mug. You, I believe, but another piece of pottery with a vocabulary like ours, is rather doubtful.'

Milo Mac had been patiently sitting, waiting and observing. It was time for introductions.

'Hello, my name is Milo Mac and to whom do I have the pleasure of speaking?'

Slirander responded with a smile. Davidia's jaw almost opened as wide as a small aircraft hangar.

'My name is Davidia and that is my friend, Slirander, you are next to. You can speak. It's unbelievable. How am I not surprised being Slirander's friend? Why are you here? Who owns you?'

'I'm here to win the mug competition. My owner is a nice young lady and her grandma.'

'We are also here to win the mug competition.'

A silence surrounded them as they all thought of that winner's prize.

*　　*　　*

The committee judging panel were refreshing a run-through of the various competitors' mugs ensuring the criteria for winning had been determined. The rules were always the same. It was a protocol exercise to be "seen" as being independent. The committee consisted of eight women and four men. It was adjudged that female committee members were far more functional than men. It was time to assess the quality of the competition. They all sat to a side, eyeing the public and watching who was attracted to what mug. Sometimes opinions got filed in the rubbish bin or fell on a perfectly good set of ears, only to be unheard.

'Has any mug attracted a lot of interest?' asked a member, to kick-start the dialogue.

'The committee dozen has been positively received, but with

no real standout,' replied another member.

'I noticed one with a pair of magical red earrings. It was rather impressive.'

'Then there's that odd mug made from striped clay that has a certain male attraction. It's on one of the rear tables. I touched it and had a ghostly feeling that something awful was about to occur. I can't explain it, really.'

'Are there any other comments before we check one last time?'

An excited committee member stood up and said that there were three identical mugs containing all of her features. They were just wonderful. The rest of the committee sighed with resignation. Only one entrant per person was allowed. No one asked how or by whom the three mugs were made.

'I'll walk you past them. They are on the front table with the committee presentation.'

'That's it, then. No other significant entries need to be discussed.'

The committee slowly walked past the expected fabulous mugs of a rambling member. They all stood at the corner of the table where she had them placed. There were only two left and neither of them possessed her features. Davidia had returned to her Aunt Mavis face and Aunt Mavis was as she had been in the beginning.

'That's not possible. Who substituted my mugs?' said a despondent member.

Tears began to well up as her disappointment grew. A few drops splashed over the two mugs streaking down their sides. A glint of light escaped from both of them revealing a thin striped streak of the most extraordinary clay. No one had noticed because they had already selected their winner. The "how" wasn't available. They humoured the upset lady member who was left to rue the loss of her notable features. Her chances of a win had evaporated when Davidia had stared at her mug and it became her Aunt Mavis' face. Aunt Mavis was an expected return.

Davidia had been listening nearby and had noticed the glint of light emanate from the mugs. She thought it peculiar that they didn't pay any real attention to it. The committee had wandered off again to consider their verdict. Davidia was alone, hidden under that theme clothing wondering what to do without her friend, Slirander. She began to feel hot with a warm heat trickle circling her legs. It was probably an ache from so much bending over. It gradually became unbearable and she had to stand tall to relieve the pain. Her spine resisted a quick change. She could hear the creak of knuckles and bones reassembling like a transformer. Soon she was ramrod straight and relieved that she didn't gain any permanent deformity. Her legs were now clearly visible.

'That's the end of this coat,' she said, as she threw it to the ground.

'Don't do that,' it said.

Davidia was confused. There was no one near her to converse with.

'Identify yourself.'

'You were wearing me a moment ago.'

'Not you. I don't have to continue wearing you, do I?'

'No, just keep me near. You can carry me. Aunt Mavis said you needed babysitting.'

'Did she? I'll give her some advice she won't forget,' said an incensed Davidia. 'I don't need anyone to fight my battles, besides, why would I need you near me? I'm not in any trouble. Nothing has accosted me. Those self-defence classes haven't been needed. I know where to land a straight kick, if necessary.' Davidia seethed.

She could look after herself. She was practising to be an adult. That's what teenage years are supposed to do. It's all in the preparation.

'Please pick me up,' said the pleading coat.

Davidia grudgingly complied.

'Is that better?'

'Much. We are a team.'

Great, thought Davidia. Talking mugs and a chatty coat. Dimpletoon seemed to possess a few dimples too many for her liking.

'I better check on Slirander, now that she's disappeared into a hot beverage dispenser.'

What next?

*   *   *

'Are there any more where these came from?' questioned a man dressed in a bright yellow suit with matching shoes. He was twiddling with a few red-coloured stones that the mayor had purloined for him. The supply or access to this treasure was a secret. The few stones available were bait for greed. 'Yum, I love a good red and this time it's not a wine. Are these real? You lie to me and I can arrange a cemetery memorial for you and your family. It wouldn't be a pleasant holiday.'

The mayor and the lady mayoress were in council chambers entertaining Mr Bright. His real name was irrelevant, but the name was a pseudonym brought about by his obvious clothing choice. They were meeting in secret to discuss the laundry business, money and jewels, but not clothing. A chance find, amongst the drilling of the quarry, had located a supply of the precious red items embedded deep in the high-quality clay from which Milo Mac was formed. Further mining of the quarry failed to discover any more. The interesting part is that the clay seam from which they were found stopped at the quarry walls. The mayor had kept this secret between his wife and himself. There was no need to make anyone else filthy rich. His hunger for wealth was only overtaken by his love of ice-cream. His favourite colour was strawberry. He had plans to access the clay seams around the quarry, but was thwarted by the old lady now known as Aunt Mavis. That is why he had to get rid of her in any way possible to possess her lands. It was to be done in a way that there was no trace back to him. At least the council had agreed to rezone the land around the quarry. Now it was time to gain ownership.

'Mr Bright, there is a further supply which I am currently negotiating for,' he lied. 'In a few weeks, I will be able meet your needs. There is no need for an up-front retainer unless it's in cash. We don't do deals in brown paper bags any more. Untraceable cash starts any day beautifully.'

'When I return, you deliver,' he said with dead-pan eyes.

The mayor could see his reflection in them and wondered whether he'd seen a corpse. His sweaty armpits dripped in anxiety, his underwear wedged itself into an uncomfortable position and his clothes felt like soggy skin. His uncomfortableness was duly noted. Mervyn would be no direct match to Mr Bright, but with his wife's cunning by his side, a swindle wasn't off the table. It had to be simple and subtle so there were no recriminations or murders in Humpletoon. Mervyn didn't see himself as a martyr. Merrilyn probably did; however, there would be more inheritance left over if they were successful in obtaining more of those magical red gems.

'Thank you for visiting, Mr Bright. We hope you enjoyed your tour of our historical town hall and chambers,' said Mervyn, in case there was a snooping member of the public around.

Mr Bright moved to the exit. He waved a hand across his neck. He must have an itch. The meaning wasn't lost on Mervyn or Merrilyn. Their heads moved uncomfortably.

'In a few weeks' time then?' He ambled out the door and into a yellow Cadillac.

'I don't trust him,' said Mervyn.

'He mightn't trust us,' replied Merrilyn.

'We had better return to the mug festival and see who won the prized mug. It's not us, is it?'

A wry smile passed over Merrilyn's face like sprayed insecticide, poisonous and smeary.

7 DECISIONS

'Are you two cosy?' asked Davidia, having returned to visit Slirander and her new mug mate. 'I'm still upright and in one piece. How's life in such a small crockery item?'

Slirander and Milo Mac had been discussing their origins and a bit of family background. He came from a special clay seam in the local quarry and she spoke about a few magical past moments. It wasn't too in-depth. They had just met.

'We haven't moved. Pick us up and put us on the front table. At least we can see from there what's happening. It's a drudge being back here. Our chances of winning the competition from here are zero. Being ignored isn't a social aspect I'd normally enjoy.'

'Is there anything to report? A non-funny joke or gossip would be nice.'

Both mugs' minds were as empty as their interiors. Davidia picked them up and placed them on the front table. All the other mugs could almost be clearly seen. Suddenly, Milo Mac had a mini convulsion. One of his handles fell off in fright. Slirander bent over, retrieved the parted item and miraculously reattached it to Milo Mac to be as good as new.

'How did you do that?' he asked, quite surprised.

'Because I can,' was Slirander's response. There were no further explanations. 'What just happened to you?'

'I felt a shock. It's hard to explain.'

'We aren't going anywhere, so spill it.'

'When I was in the quarry as a group clod, we all stuck together. Sometimes intruders would walk on top of us with heavy items with a flat base and flatten us like pancakes. We didn't object because we moulded into any shape. It's the flexible thing we possess. Sometimes, from deep underground emerged ferreting worms as thick as golf balls pushing red, shiny playthings in front of them. No one took much notice. We couldn't join in their games, but we could make space for easy tunnelling. There weren't many where we lived. Apparently, they interested the humans. Why, I have no idea. I've seen a few scavengers at the quarry and when they found one, they became quite excited. Have you heard of the word ruby? I didn't know what that was. I asked the worms where they found them and they said only in my clay seam. So, wherever that seam runs there will be rubies. My clay seam has now been completely removed, but we have cousins and duplicates in the walls that surround the quarry. I'm hoping to meet a few relatives from those areas to chat about the bright-red objects and whether theirs are any better than what mine were.'

'That was great to tell me, but why did you have a shock?'

'There's some here amongst the mugs. I felt it. Whenever a clay clod experiences one of them, we fall apart in the same way we parted to let the ferreting worms tunnel, hence why I dropped a piece.'

Slirander scanned the mugs, but at her height, couldn't see them all clearly. She called Davidia over.

'What's up?'

'Look amongst the mugs and see if any of them are adorned with a red ruby.'

'These are all clay mugs, made of plain, simple clay, except for ours.'

'Just do it.'

Davidia's shoulders shrugged with annoyance.

'What a bloody waste of time,' she said to herself. Grudgingly, she agreed. 'Some of these mugs are just plain ugly.'

Art wasn't an exact science. The eyes' interpretation gave it value. The committee mugs were clones of a group therapy class. Other mugs were well-made and had shiny surfaces. Davidia ran her hands over each surface forming a running commentary until she spied one with red objects in the handles. Could this be the reason for the search? She returned to Slirander and told her what she had seen.

'Place us next to it, quickly,' insisted Slirander.

Davidia didn't take too kindly to orders. It was a growing older thing and making decisions for oneself; however, she did as suggested. Slirander and Milo Mac settled nicely on either side of the red earring mug. Milo Mac could feel he was at breaking point.

'That's them,' he said. 'I feel it in my clay.'

'Can you speak?' asked Slirander, of the mug. Its eyes moved sideways surprised. That was a "no".

'It can't speak,' interrupted Milo Mac.

Slirander ignored the comment. Imbued with ideas, a movement inside her mug was stirring as if someone had taken a spoon for a good spin. From her walls, a mist mysteriously and slowly seeped out as she heard an incantation from Aunt Mavis. It reminded her of something she had read in the scroll. It didn't make sense, but she went with the flow.

'You're frothing,' said Davidia. 'Can I drink from you?' she cheekily added.

Slirander was concentrating on her changing situation. Her shape began to crumble. None of the mist really escaped. Soon she was almost as flat as the table imitating a biscuit. Then, her mouth opened wide and out shot a laser-like air stream similar to that what aeroplanes make in the sky on a cold but sunny day. Bang! It hit the other mug with such intensity it almost toppled over.

'Whoa there,' it said. Speech escaped from its shape. 'Blow your germs elsewhere. I'm a pristine mug. Besides, what are you attempting to do?'

Slirander acted as if she was deaf. She wanted to ensure that it was speech she had heard and not an imaginative voice from inside.

'Who spoke?'

'I did. Get your act together and stop acting like a flatty. Make an appointment if you want discourse. Do you dare address me? I'm fussy with whom I hang out. Where are your manners?'

What a priggish mug. At first it was unable to speak and now it treated the English language in a bullying way. A lesson needed to be taught. Slirander returned to her mug-self and engaged in repartee.

'You are extremely well-made. I wish I had the hands of your potter fondling my surfaces.'

The neighbour didn't want to dance. It tried the ignorance technique oft used by those with lack of understanding. Slirander persisted. It was time for show and tell.

'If you tell me how you got those beautiful red ears, I'll teach you how to collapse and recover. I wish I had a pair of those.'

It seemed a fair trade. The mug hadn't yet learnt subtlety or how not to be led by a facial feature.

'It was Chad, my potter. He was given them by Merrilyn, who visited the pottery.'

In those two sentences a decision was made. Slirander kept hearing chants echoing around her insides, insisting on retrieval. She wasn't in complete control of her rounded shape when she began to enlarge into a vat and not a large mug. Two ferreting worms slid out of her interior, down her sides, it tickled and over to the other mug. Each of them pushed out the red rubies and returned them to Slirander who instantly shrunk and was normal again. It was over in seconds. Davidia peered inside and found no trace of them.

'They've disappeared. It's not possible. What are we dealing with?'

'How do you feel now, Milo Mac?' asked Slirander, now that other mug had no hope of winning the competition. Two finger-thick holes remained in its ears. Its pride had fallen.

'Comfortable. The feeling has gone. Thanks.'

'Davidia, return us to sit with your mug and Aunt Mavis. It's time the family enjoyed time together.'

'What do you mean family?'

'Milo Mac is related. He possesses the identical clay characteristics that we do, as mugs. He's our brother. Now, let's hear the results of the competition.'

The judging verdict is final, or is it?

*　　*　　*

'Where has my precious mug been placed?' questioned Merrilyn, now that the nasty business with Mr Bright had been dispensed with. It held two valuable items that she wasn't prepared to be parted from. Her question was directed at a committee member who was only too pleased to re-acquaint her with the "prize winning" mug. Imagine the surprise that was in store.

'Which one is it?' asked the committee member, now that it would look completely different without its earrings.

'It's the one with the two red earrings. It should be along here.

There, isn't that it?' she said, pointing a curled finger with a danger nail at its tip.

'It could be. Look, there are two holes in its ears. I wonder how that happened.'

Merrilyn was beside herself – if it was possible to emulate twins – with the largest anger fit she had ever performed in public. She'd done a few minor spats when dressing down another, but now this was a serious performance. She twirled around with such ferocity in her period costume. The circular motion continued unabated and forced her to topple over, similar to a person who had a night on the turps and who didn't know what upright was. As she sat on the ground in dress disarray, a few un-ladylike adjectives were treasured by those within earshot.

'Sounds as if she reads a dictionary,' said someone nearby, from behind a covered mouth. The half-hidden smile could be seen peeking.

'Merrilyn, what happened? You fell over. You haven't been sipping again, have you?' said another.

Before any further pleasantries were allowed, Merrilyn regained her foothold on solid ground, dusted off her seemingly endless set of petticoats and dress cover and eyeballed the committee member with a death stare. The pain it emanated was worthy of inclusion in a horror movie.

'Where are its earrings? There are two gaping holes left. Did you steal them? I want to be recompensed.'

'No one here would steal them. How would it be possible to remove them? They were well-embedded into the mug. They were only glass, weren't they?'

Before her tirade was notched up, Merrilyn suddenly realised that no one truly knew the real identity of the red earrings and if they did, unpleasant consequences might ensue from the public. She made the conscious decision to shut her mouth in case it jeopardized her future. She wouldn't want to be gossiped about as she did about others. Her ruddy face was distorted with rage. Not only had she lost a small fortune, she had also lost the prize for the mug competition. There was pandemonium. A second place hadn't been contemplated. The committee members raced around distressed at selecting another winner. It was the first time that Merrilyn (Lady Mayoress) hadn't won the trophy. The reward for the brown-nose snouters would be nothing this year. She snatched up her mug in disgust and threw it as far as she could. It disintegrated into small pieces forming another small memory. Chad would have been upset had he known his precious artwork design now paraded as rubbish landfill.

'What a petulant outburst,' said someone. 'I won't vote for her husband at the next election.'

'Ladies and Gentlemen, the winner of this year's prize is a young girl called Eleanor and her grandma. The mug they entered has won the overall classification for its uniqueness. Bring it over here,' urged the beaming committee chairperson.

Someone had to win, so a selection from the nearest table was it. Milo Mac appeared to have the qualities of a champion mug, whatever they were, and he was now a mini celebrity mug. Eleanor ran over excitedly, picked him up and gave his surface a sloppy kiss of success. His surface glinted a bright light, but only momentarily. The cunning Merrilyn, even in her mood of despair, noted the mini light show and had a brilliant idea, the kind her husband Mervyn couldn't embrace. She waited for her opportunity. Her jealous streak at not being a winner meant that she had to have the winning item. It was her destiny.

'Isn't this wonderful, grandma? We have won the prize with your odd-looking mug. What a thrill.'

Grandma went along with the fun. A small sash with the

printed words, Dimpletoon Mug Champion, was draped over Eleanor's shoulder. It was a proud moment.

'Don't turn up next year,' said the ungracious committee chairperson.

They were all miffed at missing out on their selfish rewards. Eleanor didn't hear. She was floating with success.

Once the thrill of the win had faded, Merrilyn walked over to Eleanor and suggested that she visit her at home and bring the mug and they could have high tea together. It was one of the social rewards of winning the competition; high tea with the Lady Mayoress. Eleanor thanked her and headed off home with their prize. Merrilyn's eyes followed her like a tracking device loaded with danger. There was definitely something unhappy about a loser.

'Pathetic,' said Davidia, standing legs astride as if inspecting an ant colony at ground level. 'That Milo Mac was selected a winner. We presented much better. Even Aunt Mavis was a touch elegant.'

'It's not all about winning,' said Slirander, sitting still on the table. 'It may still turn out to be a blessing in disguise. My aura is humming with indecision about something.'

'I suppose I'll have to carry you back to Aunt Mavis'. You don't have any legs. Do you know what actually happened to those red earrings? I could have worn them.'

'Aunt Mavis will explain.'

'How in the hell is that possible? She's not even here. Even I'm not that dopey. I haven't seen her at all.'

A disgruntled committee member walked past mumbling obscenities trying to repeat every one of them from every dictionary. It was not happy chatter. The words of revenge filtered past Slirander. Being an innocent looking, inanimate mug, gave confidence to anybody walking past that any mutterings would not be heard, repeated or understood. Unfortunately, Slirander was a living item in a great disguise with perfect hearing pitch. She didn't quite catch who the revenge was for, but the word meddled with her aura. She became deeply concerned. The more she sat on the table the more absurd and unhappy the Dimpletoonians appeared to be. Whatever the cause, it wasn't easily recognisable.

'Davidia,' whispered Slirander. 'It's time to go. Bring my Aunt Mavis' coat too.'

'Packhorse Davidia, is it?'

'There's something odd about these people.'

'And here I was thinking that it was only us.'

'Carry me over to the committee table and pretend you have forgotten something so I can eavesdrop on them. I feel something important is to be said.'

'And you know this, how?'

'It's not explainable. My mind receives blurred visions without an explanation; however, I seem to be pushed by a mystery force I have no control over.'

'Mmm. If I didn't know you better …' she trailed off.

Davidia picked up Slirander and her mug and transported them, this time standing perfectly upright – she was "over" the bent arch routine – and placed both mugs on the table nearby. Her mug had kept its Aunt Mavis face too. Didn't anyone realise how pretty she was and never had the chance of being appreciated by the public. Besides, her skin was wrinkle-free.

'Bah! Stick it! I don't need to be in clay,' she said quietly, as she went in search of coat number two.

*   *   *

'We lost that round,' said a rotund, speckle-faced committee member whose face had a twisted mouth caused by too much side chatter to everyone nearby. It was known as whisperer's mouth. There were quite a few present, each agitating for a wordy expression and sometimes a whole boring paragraph.

'The mayoress should have won the prize with those easily identifiable earrings. They were to be our reward for declaring her the winner. Now it's ruined. What bastardry occurred to do that? Anyone got any ideas besides me?'

'It was the work of that witch in Humpletoon. I bet she's involved in some way,' said another sneery-eyed member with pointy facial features that could injure the opposite party in an emotional embrace.

'But she hasn't been seen anywhere here today.'

'Did you notice those two mugs that looked identical to her? She stole my face from them and replaced them with her own,' stated the committee member, who had an expectant win with her face on those two cuddly mugs. 'And then there were those two walking imitators who she must have cursed to act exactly like her. I wasn't fooled. She is so scary.'

'Have you actually met her?'

'Never, and if I did, she'd be scared of me.'

A small burp of body wind made a popgun entrance as an aid to impress her verbal bravado.

'Do you really believe that it could be her?'

'Who else could steal those earrings unseen? I bet she's still here somewhere lurking to curse all of us.'

'What should we do?'

'Teach her a lesson she'll never forget and run her out of town.'

'How?'

'Contact the mayor and mayoress, they'll know what to do. They already own most of the land in that town and I believe they want to purchase the land all around the quarry. It's only a whisper though.'

The committee murmured amongst themselves as if they didn't already know.

Slirander sat quietly. Suddenly, a committee member spied the Slirander and Davidia mugs. She made straight for them. There was no escape. They had no legs. A firm pair of hands that a skin grinder and remover wouldn't be lost on to smooth out, viciously grabbed them like a personal assault was necessary. The mugs retained their shape. She slammed them down so hard in front of the committee, the tabletop surged like a mini surf wave to the end. They all stared.

'This is the face that launched the curse. Look at its evil eyes, those pointed handles and that pert nose hiding a dark secret. Let's hope it doesn't sneeze.'

'Are they alive?'

'They are just mugs. Their potter might need retraining. We should confiscate them and teach her a lesson. The mug festival should never have allowed them entrance.'

'Who let them into the show?'

No one had the balls to accept responsibility, but blame can be shared by all. The guilty committee member faked idiocy like them all. No one knew exactly and it could have been by another curse.

Davidia finally returned armed with coat number two. She was certainly dressed and laden with opportunity-shop fashion. She sought out her mugs. Where were they? It wasn't another Slirander trick to gain her attention, was it? Then she spied them on the committee table. She walked over and, for whatever sane reason entered her head, cackled like a real witch. Each committee member stayed glued to their seat in shock. Some would need a change of clothing and would definitely be candidates for brown nose of the month, if there ever was such an award. She was still in theme.

'May I take my mugs?' she politely cackled.

She held out her wrinkly, pointed fingers which pulsated with an itch to point at someone. She wriggled them as if they were loose strands of spaghetti.

'How do we know they are yours?' asked a timid member, at least trying to establish ownership.

'Look at this beautiful face. Those mugs are identical to me. Do you have any questions?'

Davidia moved her head around like a roving bouncing ball eyeing everyone at the table. Her eyesight moved up and down like an old-fashioned typewriter with each letter striking a committee member with a feeling. Was it a sneer that they thought they saw? Was it a darkish pair of black-and-yellow slitted eyes riveting them with fear? Did her clothes smell of faeces from the sewer or of stale body odour? Was her nose a metre long? Was she as tall as a small building, or at the least a very large bush? Did they see her legs as gnarled, knobbly tree trunks, albeit from a thin tree? Were her hands as razor sharp as a kitchen knife with fingernails dipped in poison?

They were all mildly hallucinating. Slirander had breathed a mixture of a mild, misty, toxin (contents unknown) forced out from within her mug walls and it circulated around the committee in a strangulation technique by landing around their necks. Small globules then crawled up their necks and popped into their nasal playground where more than a crawling globule often entered. By inhalation their senses were doomed to disorientation. The mind's imaginative juices were being playful today, but this time there was no prize. The table group all had a glaze on their faces not unlike that found in a pottery. There were certainly a lot of shiny surfaces.

'Who are you? You have dressed like that old lady in Humpletoon, the one who spits and says very little. Why have you taken on her appearance? Has she fed you a curse of some kind? Do you need help?'

Davidia wondered whether she should reveal any truths to the conniving and plotting committee members who only seemed to want to do her aunt some harm. None of them had met her or spoken to her. She thought the intrigue was better played by keeping them guessing.

'I am a reincarnation from the ancient scrollers that are hidden beneath the earth. This is the year of our reveal. We all wear red earrings and live in clay in complete harmony with the environment.'

Davidia swayed like a tall tree in a typhoon emphasising her state by vigorous arm movements. The committee were now paying full attention.

'Where exactly is this clay that you mentioned?' said a not-so-stupid listener.

'It's safely hidden forever. I have no memory of where. Oral history dictates an imaginative home.'

'Davidia, it's time to go. Quickly, before someone wises up that they have been mildly sedated,' urged Slirander, 'and don't overdo the act. You might make a slip. Aunt Mavis needs protection. Let's go.'

Davidia let out a wild, ear-piercing scream followed by what seemed to be nervous cackling. However, she was only trying to clear her throat. That sound enhanced the myth. She scooped up the mugs, hid them under her coat and vanished. The committee members rubbed their eyes disbelieving that a witch had stood at their table. They all felt blessed that a curse wasn't cast upon them. It was still the weekend.

What happened to the real Aunt Mavis mug that Davidia had forgotten to pick up?

*   *   *

'We need access to the quarry walls,' said Mervyn. 'I believe that riches beyond our imagination lie there. The good quality clay has been exhausted from the depths of the quarry. New seams run off in all directions into the walls. Getting access is going to be difficult. That old hag lives directly above those seams. We have to get rid of her so we can own the land.'

'Make her an offer too good to refuse. If she refuses it, then another plan needs to be considered; permanent expulsion.'

Merrilyn had an insanity streak on her side of the family. Years ago, her parents were ordinary law-abiding citizens living a simple life in a country town. One day, a stray dog wandered onto their patch. It began sniffing the ground, which was its normal routine. Its wet nose, which had lick streaks all over it, encountered the nakedness of her mother's recently shaved leg, which startled her. She fell over backwards, hitting her tied bun hairdo onto the soft grass with a non-threatening plop. Her husband was dithery and ran all over, thinking that he'd lost her.

'I knew it was you,' she screamed at him. 'Just because I wouldn't let you touch my legs, you had to get the next-door neighbour to do it for you in disguise.'

She landed a well-placed kick on the stray and it took off in fright. Suddenly, the neighbour appeared from around the fence. The next he knew of the day was that he was aching in pain looking up at the sky. A succession of painful pointed toe kicks kept him in the foetal position for quite some time.

'Darling, soccer practice is over,' said the dad.

'Did I score a goal or two?'

'You defeated the whole team this time,' he said, proudly.

The mum and dad were escorted back to their residence. The balance of the day was spent resting. It had been one hell of a match. They both looked forward to the next encounter.

'What solution do you have in mind?' asked Mervyn.

His ideas basket was often as empty as a desert or a bucket with a hole in it expecting to retain a full load.

'The riff-raff youth that litter the street may yet have a useful purpose. If we suggest a course of harassment either at the house or in town, there can be no trace to us.'

'Do you think it will work?'

'Money speaks many different languages.'

'What will it speak to us?'

'Success.'

Merrilyn visited the main street of Humpletoon. Down the side streets were the country homes of backpackers, budding artists living on handouts and an array of homeless or itinerant travellers enjoying the outdoor life minus the rain. There was no busy flurry of activity. Going nowhere didn't generate enthusiasm for much movement. Her presence was noted, but greetings were scarce. Everyone had their selfish genes on display as they plied their lightning-fast thumbs and fingers, deliberately hitting their telephone keypads quickly from one misspelt text to another. The depth of their messages was usually as shallow as a sandpit without any sand. Merrilyn carefully selected her targets of a future cash-strapped employee or maybe a couple of employees. Three lads were besting each other by seeing who could laugh the loudest. It wasn't a real employable skill; however, it helped pass the boredom factor of living on the street and staring at others who may have, at that very time, what they perceived to be a more meaningful existence. The lads noticed a refined woman sidling nearby. They weren't into dating "mutton", but given her appearance, an attempt may not be a complete waste of time. Merrilyn stopped and brushed her full dress with a delicate hand.

'Is there a spare seat for me?' she asked politely.

One of the lads had a wicked sense of humour and apparently it wasn't cursed.

'The butler will bring it shortly, madam. It's kept in the attic,' said the lad, with the soft smile.

'I'll wait. Would any of you like to earn a modest amount of cash?'

'Is it for the special massage you want, madam?' continued the young lad.

Merrilyn smiled coyly. She felt confident that they'd do anything that she asked.

'I have a proposition for the three of you if you are up to it?'

The lads had to be careful with that interpretation. One woman and three youths would be quite a crowd. Before their thoughts went any further, Merrilyn continued.

'I need you to buy three Halloween costumes and play a trick on an old friend of mine who lives in an old shack next to the Humpletoon quarry. Remove her front fence and throw it into the quarry. It's a very small fence and it's also a very small cottage. It has been a long-time eyesore and needed removal. This will aid in getting a replacement new fence. She likes surprises and so do I. Imagine how she'll feel next morning. You will all be paid handsomely. There are no other benefits available.'

The three lads were almost skint. Other than begging or busking, of which they did neither, street income was non-existent. They didn't do tricks. This offer was in that too-good-to-refuse basket and, besides, they were hungry. The lads all agreed it would be a great lark to theme-dress, receive a cash injection and enjoy a harmless good time. What could possibly go wrong with that trio of experiences?

'We'll do it. There isn't much else happening at night around here. It's goodbye to boredom.'

Merrilyn handed over a wad of cash which had been transferred from its brown holiday bag to her fashionable purse. There was enough to pay for the costumes and a week's party time in town. It was a win- win. After the exchange, three lads ran excitedly into town. Merrilyn's eyes followed closely, thinking why wasn't her Mervyn that active?

Was he cursed?

*   *   *

Aunt Mavis had been unintentionally abandoned at the mug festival. The girls had only thought of themselves as they departed in haste. It wasn't until they had returned to the "dilapidated cottage" that they realised their error. Davidia thought that Aunt Mavis couldn't fend for herself against all those humans; however, she could change facial shapes and that alone might secure her safety.

'We can't go in just yet. We have forgotten her mug. What will we do? The festival will be over, and she may be stolen or end up as junk somewhere. I feel something is missing without her. Do you think it's a family thing? Am I a witch too?' Davidia was crosswording her thoughts to a non-puzzle solver.

'I'm still in mug theme too. How do I retrieve myself?' asked Slirander, tiring of being so small. 'It's so cramped in here. I can't scratch or hug anything.'

There was nothing else to do but wait for what no one knew. It was nearing dusk and as the sun escaped from its daytime routine, three silhouettes suddenly appeared against the skyline. They were heading toward the cottage. Aunt Mavis had said there are never any visitors here, so why now and so many late in the evening? Davidia quickly hid in amongst a group of small shrubs nearby to avoid discovery. She peered through the dense foliage and could only see outlines darting from side to side like nervous bees.

'Are those the legendary black ghosts that appear when

someone has been terribly bad? I hope they haven't come for me.' Davidia shuddered. It wasn't her time. She didn't feel well.

Slirander felt the ground tremors through the base of her mug existence. It tickled her something chronic. After a moment her two, she deducted that they belonged to human feet.

'Davidia, pick me up so I can see.'

'Alright. Be careful they don't see you. I could be turned into something unpleasant.'

The myth of the witch and curses permeated her imaginative mind where she's started to believe all that nonsense about her aunt. Slirander had perfect night vision and realised who they were.

'They are three lads in Halloween costumes.'

'It's not Halloween yet, so what do they want?'

The girls waited secreted behind the dense shrubbery.

'You know the soil here is crap. There is little nutrition living on a clay pan. Replant us somewhere decent where we can make friends with worms and grow taller than being this stunted variety.'

'Who said that?' said Davidia.

'I did,' replied a sound from within a bush. 'You aren't the only species that can speak. Around here, everyone enjoys a gossip. What are you hiding from?'

The world of crazy was just accepted.

'Those moving objects that are over there. They frighten me. They mightn't be real.'

'They are just three lads out for a prank.'

'How would you know that? You don't have any eyes.'

'By feel. That old lady who lives over there has cared for us for so long, whispering strange chants into our foliage; and after a while she taught us to speak. Incredible, eh!'

'You know my Aunt Mavis?'

'Are you a bush too? Those lads are close. I can't be heard whispering, otherwise I could end up on the circus circuit.' The bush shook its foliage, and all went quiet.

The three lads crept like ninjas in the dark crossing the clay pan. Their breath was heavy with anxiety. Fear began to grow like a weed in their minds. Blood flowed at an ever-increasing speed forcing their heart rate up and down in trampoline style. Forget the effect on the kidneys. Sinews and muscles were tightly coiled ready to react faster than a snake bite attack. They signalled to each other to attack the front fence in a tripod formation. The advance was short but sweet. A few zzts and three youth were flat-packed on the ground stargazing. A few groans emanated from their prostrate forms. Their hats had fallen off in the excitement, exposing three sets of lush follicle growth.

'My stomach has burst,' said Agony A.

'My head has been fried,' said Agony B.

'What wow medicinal high was that?' said Agony C.

'That fence certainly has punch. We'll try once more. This time, kick it down instead of pulling it down,' said Agony A. 'That ridiculous little fence is no match for the Toe Destructor Trio. Let's go, lads.'

They stood back about twenty metres for a short-course Olympic event; well, it was in their terminology, to build up speed with devastating kicking ability. Nothing but loose splinters will remain. They were ready to begin their run when a weird shriek was heard overhead. They froze. Had someone called in a drone to scare them? The flapping of wings was heard nearby. Nothing could be seen. Then splosh, splosh and another splosh landed on each of their heads. A runny liquid slid through their hair and onto their faces. There wasn't time to wipe away the offending substance; however, unbeknown to them it was bat guano delivered with the compliments of some of Aunt Mavis' pets. The future Olympic champions didn't hear the starter gun. They just ran and took to the air like a long jumper. Thud, into the electrified fence, which once again delivered a mild safety shock, with further stargazing the result. The fence was made of steel, which in the dark was easy to mistake for palings. Agonies A, B and C rolled around like kneaded pastry dough with all body parts drawn in for pain comfort. The zap of electricity that had exploded on their heads caused fright burn. Their faces were streaked with red welt lines and their hair stood perpendicular with the quality of scouring wire. It would be impossible to cut and it had to grow out naturally. Three grown Smurfs had to admit defeat and crawl away until they could stand. It was a painful lesson to learn that all pranks don't end up as humour. In town, the trio would be easily recognisable with their holiday haircuts.

A bat landed near Davidia.

'You can go home now,' it said.

Before a response could be formulated, it had disappeared.

Was Aunt Mavis home?

*   *   *

Word had filtered back to Merrilyn about the failed attempt. Details of what exactly had happened were rather scant. The electric shock had tampered with a memory file which resulted in blurred recollections.

'A flying bear knocked me over.'

'There was a team of elves with miniature baseball bats on the other side of the fence.'

'The fence was guarded by gigantic ants with the largest pincers I'd ever seen.'

The truth was hidden in there somewhere, but whatever it was, it wasn't being signalled truthfully to Merrilyn. She stood with a thoughtful pose in front of her mirror, smiled and almost scared herself. She was in good form. She thought, *'Perhaps another time then'*. Her mirror smiled.

8 HARASSMENT

The land surrounding the quarry wasn't particularly useful for a range of pursuits such as agriculture, even though it had been rezoned for agricultural use, housing, or even recreation except for a motor-cross activity. Aunt Mavis, upon her early arrival in Humpletoon, had purchased the land surrounding the quarry to a width of fifty metres and depth of fifty metres. She had no idea why those measurements were important; however, in one of those dream sequences she experienced from time to time, a faint voice pressured her subconscious into making such an investment. The voices she heard were apparently from an ancient time. They had selected her, without her knowledge or recognising her future behavioural patterns, to be the guardian of this special plot of land. If there was a special hidden secret, it certainly hadn't been explained to her. Living the life of a mysterious recluse further enhanced the protection of the site. Her rumoured behaviour had kept all at bay except now that a few red rubies had been discovered. It put pressure on its protector. During the construction phase of her underground sanctuary, Aunt Mavis also found a few of the special red rubies and safely stored them never to be revealed to anyone. That ancient scroll, which gave up a few incantations that only Aunt Mavis understood, finally revealed to her the truth of the clay seam and its red rubies' purpose; however, the greed of man, ergo Mervyn and Merrilyn, had interfered with their security and soon the quarry walls would come under threat. Aunt Mavis had undertaken various defensive procedures during her home construction to ward off any sabotage attempts. Only the front fence had been tested to date.

*   *   *

Davidia carried Slirander to the front gate and stood exactly where the lads had been taught a lesson. Was she to receive one too for forgetting Aunt Mavis' mug? She placed a hand on the gate handle and was relieved that the only shock she received was the one she expected but didn't. The gate opened effortlessly, the grass parted like Moses parted the Red Sea, the front door was obligingly well-mannered, and they cautiously entered. It was their first time at a night-time visit. The air felt cool with a hint of movement. Soon they were safely home underground.

'That wasn't so bad,' said Davidia relieved to embrace indoor furnishings again. She placed Slirander on the floor as she took off her disguise. She felt relieved that all of her was still there, whereas all of Slirander wasn't. 'Where's Aunt Mavis? Maybe she's in the bathroom? She wouldn't be out visiting, would she?'

There was no sign of her. The house felt uninhabited. That cool air began to give Davidia a headache. Where's the Panadol? Suddenly, the wall and shelf where the scroll sat seemed to make a movement toward them. Davidia sensed a gloomy feeling and a reduction in floor space. Slirander was still on the floor doing nothing, so it wasn't her. She instinctively picked her up. She had to keep her friend safe. Without warning, Slirander flew out of her grasp and adhered to the scroll on the shelf. Her appearance began to alter. Will she be permanently disfigured? Davidia watched amazed as a beautiful scroll creature stood in front of her shaped exactly like a scroll. There was an opening, a cute pert nose – the type fashion models possess – two beautiful, ruby-red eyes and Slirander's ears, easily recognisable anywhere by their pointedness. A moment passed as she grasped the meaning of the changes – well, she thought she did – but had to ask a question, the depth of meaning wasn't important at this stage. Strangely, she didn't feel threatened. Her persona was invaded by calm.

'Is that you, Slirander?' she asked unsure of any response.

The scroll smiled. It was almost transparent and, if it really was Slirander, there would have been more shape than a flat, straight body design. Perhaps it was probably an eye delusion that she was experiencing? Those piercing red eyes seemed familiar, but for the present that memory file was in the deferred section. There was no one else in the room. She was alone with a tall, shaped page and not a writing utensil within arm's reach.

'Hello, Davidia,' said a husky voice, the type one experiences with a heavy cold. 'Don't be afraid, your friend is safe. She has given me life in your world so that I can communicate with you.'

'I can't see her. What have you done with her?'

'You will see her shortly. My name is Scrool, the keeper of the ancient Scroll of Scrollinger. Our ancient homeland was destroyed long ago by the greedy race known as humans. We were fortunate to survive in this area undisturbed for such a long time and now that we have been rediscovered, we risk permanent destruction. Have you noticed anything about me that attracts your immediate attention?'

Davidia sized up her conversationalist companion and the item that struck her most was those beautiful red eyes. They were magnificent with the reddest glow ever. The rest of the visible anatomy was quite average.

'It's your eyes. They are so impressive. I'm drawn to them.'

'You are observant. I had no way of seeing again until tonight. A precious gift of two red rubies were returned by your Aunt Mavis with the assistance of your friend, Slirander, and her mug mate, Milo Mac. We live in the special clay that surrounds the quarry and a few ferreting worms brought us to the surface recently and the humans discovered us. The red rubies are the eyes of my people, even though we aren't many or exist in an easily understandable or identifiable form. We are greed on one hand and the preservation of a lost race on the other. If rubies are extracted from the clay, extinction awaits us all.'

Davidia thought for a moment.

'What is the purpose of your race? You do have one, don't you?'

Scrool baulked at the impertinence that her purpose for existence was questioned. She could ask Davidia exactly the same question but decided to avoid any unpleasant discourse. Young teenage girls can be formidable linguistic opponents when in disagreeable mode.

'We inject special minerals into the clay giving them magical properties and allowing faces to change and take on the personality of the owner when mugs are made from it. We also form soft clay with special minerals for health benefits that can prevent the skin from ageing too quickly. We are therapeutic saviours. That is why the special clay around the quarry is limited to a specific size, fifty metres wide by fifty meters deep. We exist nowhere else.'

That would explain Aunt Mavis' potter's hands and how her age could be misinterpreted if that was the only part of her that was seen.

'Where is Aunt Mavis? It feels as if she isn't here.'

'Once she gave me the gift of sight, she is being rewarded elsewhere. You don't need to know everything. However, tomorrow she will be with you again and so will your friend, Slirander.

Tonight, you have to cope by yourself. Remember, if you find any of our other missing eyes, please return them to your Aunt Mavis. There are some out there in the wrong hands. Goodbye.'

Scrool slowly rolled up into a scroll again and returned to the shelf. Slirander was gone also. Davidia was physically alone, but not really alone. A pair of red eyes watched over her. She didn't need them. She thought how strange a day it had been. Her visit to meet her aunty was so interesting. That night as she slept, the subconscious section of her brain had visitors all twisting and formulating her thoughts of tomorrow.

*   *   *

'Hello, Eleanor,' said Merrilyn, lilting her soft sounds as if each one was an important statement that everyone should take notice of. 'It was nice of you to bring your mug, the one you won the competition with. Well, where is it?'

It was securely wrapped in her large wicker basket, the type one takes to a picnic, in soft pink crepe paper to protect Milo Mac's delicate surfaces. Well, they weren't delicate, but crepe paper had to have some useful use. After the encounter at the festival with Slirander and learning the discovery of being a relative, Milo Mac was aware that he had more special features than an item to be stared at and be a carrier of a liquid mixed for pleasure. He also had the ability to change his facial shape when stared at long enough. He hadn't practised his new-found skill because he was always stuck on a dusty shelf on his own. Eleanor and grandma never spent enough time with him, not that he was purposely ignored. It was that he didn't get enough "me" time with either of them. His opportunity for conversation was limited only to other special clay mugs. In Merrilyn's home, he was a hearing and understanding mute with the frustration of not being able to respond to anything. When he was out visiting, all he could be was observant.

'I have it in here somewhere,' replied Eleanor, as she fussed like a bossy schoolteacher through her storeroom of essentials. 'Here he is,' she said, proudly holding him up to the light. He shone brilliantly.

'So, this is this year's winner? I wanted to meet the mug that I lost to. Place it over there on that mantelpiece. It will be safe whilst we have a sumptuous high tea to celebrate your victory. I invite all winners to a high tea and, believe me, this is the first time I have had to do it, because I usually win.' Her nice starting smile went a shade nasty. 'Come into the dining room. Sit there.'

She pointed to a high-backed chair, an antique of some sort, whilst she wrestled with her period clothes like a princess. Her dress needed to be spread like peacock feathers for a satisfactory seat placement. Eleanor's seat was riveted with silver studs around the outside to imprison the inner fabric. In the centre of the seat, where the comfortable part of both sides of one's anatomy should reside in comfortable repose, it was littered with unpleasant small barbs embedded deep within the seat in a circular shape to catch a pair of unsuspecting buttocks in a pincer movement. They were invisible to the eye, but body weight triggered their pinprick nastiness. No one complained because they were sitting with Humpletoon royalty. It was Merrilyn's favourite chair as it ensured both an uncomfortable stay and a short visit. Eleanor sat down and emitted a surprise gasp. Merrilyn smiled. Whilst Eleanor squirmed for comfort, Merrilyn signalled to her butler to bring in the high tea goodies. When served to Eleanor, the butler held them outside arm's length so that she had to lean forward for a selection and return to her seat in discomfort. There is nothing like pain to sharpen one's focus.

'Who made your mug? I notice is has been made from striped

clay. That is most unusual. Tell me. Who made it?' Merrilyn leant forward expecting a secret to be revealed.

'My grandma bought it in town at the store. She uses it for her nightly drink of Milo. We thought it would be fun to enter the competition.'

'Did you happen to see my mug with the special red earrings?'

'I'm not sure.'

'You didn't steal them for yourself, did you?'

'Definitely not! I don't wear earrings yet. I haven't had my ears pierced.'

She fondled her ear lobes to emphasise the point.

'Had you noticed anyone else nearby who may have tampered with my entry?'

'No. I wasn't there to snoop on others. I only went to enter my mug in the competition and provide an interest for my grandma.'

Merrilyn sensed a waste of time was occurring and signalled to the butler to clean up, forcing Eleanor to stand and de-crumb herself.

'Thank you for visiting. My butler will see you out.'

'I can't forget my mug.'

'Listen, dear,' she said, whisperingly close, 'it stays here for a week in honour of your victory and then it will be safely returned to you, totally undamaged. It's what I do for every winner.'

'But, but …'

It was no use. Merrilyn got her way. Eleanor was escorted off the premises. Milo Mac saw her leave and wondered why he didn't go too. It was soon evident.

'You intrigue me. I'm interested in your special stripes. What secrets are you hiding?'

Merrilyn picked up Milo Mac rather fondly and caressed his smooth surfaces with her delicate hands. Being an inanimate object, it was a case of receive it and "take it" like a mug.

Something unfriendly disrupted his composition. He stared back at Merrilyn and his shape began to change into her face. He tried desperately to deny it. Plonk! Before a full transition occurred, he was placed back on the mantelpiece. Whew! That was close. As she walked away, he happened to notice a hand ring glinting with a red object. Once again, he had an ill feeling. When he was at home in the quarry, he never had experienced such ill feelings as he had at the show and now in the mayor's home. His world was certainly interesting. However, his life for at least the next week was a waiting and watching affair. He couldn't contribute anything except improve the mantelpiece's ornament range. It was a small plus. At least the room was bright and airy without a stale odour in existence. It may turn out not to be that bad.

*   *   *

'I believe I have the right to mine the quarry,' said Mervyn, sitting in his council chambers picking over his thoughts.

They were strewn haphazardly throughout the room and, without a mind organiser, lay tangled, twisted and confused. There was the one for improving city sanitation, and another for the placement of electricity poles underground, and yet another one concerning public safety which made it a traffic offence for anyone exceeding a five-kilometre walking speed. Council wasn't all about revenue raising. He opened a side drawer of his massive oak desk which had more drawers than a lingerie shop; mind you, some of those soft fabrics were used as liners, but only in one special drawer. It held the secret to what he perceived to be a life of luxury. In it he had a small collection of those magnificent red rubies confiscated from the quarry and the reason he was anxious to continue mining that special clay seam. He thought that it was only appropriate that he had sole access. He didn't hold a heavy machine licence himself. That meant sweaty work and operating mechanical equipment. That was for others, not of his station. Suddenly, he remembered that potter called Chad who said that he was his brother. If that were true, he'd possess a heavy-duty driving licence from his earlier farming days. He wondered whether he would help him. He couldn't risk any local with the truth. It would be eaten for breakfast the next day with the whole town feeding from the same bowl.

Years ago, Chad was as handsome a man ever seen. He had a firm torso with a real six-pack stomach, abs that artists drew for their perfectness, a manner that turned sane girls into emotional jelly and a distinctive gentlemanly demeanour. When he shook a female hand, it was static electricity that coursed through their veins and often he held a limp lady who had fainted and ended their evening early. Mervyn was jealous of his brother's attractiveness and it wasn't totally lost on Merrilyn. The brothers worked together on the land. Beads of sweat often rolled down their arms displaying tightrope tendencies, but only one of them made them jump all the way until gravity dispensed with them. One afternoon, Chad was carting hay bales alone and by hand when Merrilyn surprised him with some sweet lemonade. One sip and an hour later the soft drink had been replaced by an enchanting memory of straw fields. It was never mentioned again. However, Mervyn had finished his field round early and had heard the sound of clucking chickens, only to realise that it was an old hen, and not a pullet, in full voice. He hid behind another a bale of hay and saw his wife emerge plucking straw off her clothes. He never said anything. In that moment, he declared that Chad had to go, so he framed him with the other farmers' wives' dalliances. It wasn't a pleasant time for anyone. He forced Chad to sign his entitlement to the farm in return for not sending him to gaol. Was there any truth to it? Now he pondered whether his brother would forgive him. He had to have an angle. Her name might be Ruby.

He bent over to retrieve very carefully from the open drawer a silk, monogrammed handkerchief. Inside was a set of the most perfect rubies he had ever seen. Their lucidness and brilliant shine were breathtaking. They may as well have been the crown jewels. He delicately unfolded the silk handkerchief which was not for nasal usage. Behold! It was a perfect gem. The red rubies gave out a magnificent and blinding shot of pinkish light. It ran amok around the room seeking every nook and cranny like a detective searching for clues. Then it suddenly withdrew. Strangely, the rubies lost their red lustre and became a duller red. Maybe the light was a signal to others. No one understood or spoke gem talk.

'You are the reason I want that quarry.'

He closed the drawer, locked it tight and went off with a dose of humble pie to meet Chad.

He hoped he was as hungry as he was.

*   *   *

A letter arrived at Aunt Mavis' property. It couldn't be left in the electrified letterbox due to the present danger of receiving fried fingers. The ingenious postal deliverer attached it to the outside of a sock filled with dirt. He swung it like a slingshot and let go. It flew unerringly straight at the front door and fell onto the porch with a dull thud. The vibrations it triggered was like sending an email to a spam address hoping the intended recipient could respond. The postal deliverer took off instantly the delivery had been made. There was no need to wait for a signature, pleasantries or receiving a curse. The pedals of the bike flared red hot with a furious rider in escape mode. Myths persisted with everyone. The vibrations filtered through the steel structure and underground it made a soft "you've got mail" ting. It rarely played, but when it did, was it a signal that somebody cared? There was nobody home except Davidia. Aunt Mavis and Slirander were still absent. Davidia thought that they were probably on some holiday destination or parallel world travels in Scrollinger. The clue cupboard was as bare as an empty breakfast bowl. She made her way upstairs to the front porch. There was no one there except a paper missive resting angled on a step perched so precariously that a slight gust of wind would make it airborne and into the grass and it would never be found. She picked up the piece of paper folded in half in the shape of a rectangle. It wasn't a mathematics problem, but interesting can sometimes be made from uninteresting. You just drop the first two letters from the longer word. It also wasn't a parchment, so Scrool hadn't left it. The paper was stiff and starched to the feel. Davidia sniffed it. Aunt Mavis may have a secret admirer. It smelt official and not scented. Prediction was it was male sent. Davidia toyed with delicious delight in thinking if she should read it. It would be the height of rudeness to read another's mail, but don't girlfriends sneak a peek look at each other's diary?

'It wasn't me. The pages just flew open and I saw a finger drawing me to it. How could I resist? I was hypnotised.' Yeah! Yeah! would have been a normal response.

Davidia returned downstairs. The crowd hadn't increased at all. She was still a single. Suddenly, a laser light so thin that it couldn't be seen with the naked eye emanated from the scroll on the shelf. There was no other movement or the return of the likeable Aunt Mavis. Davidia was warming to her. Where was her odd friend, Slirander, who was equally as clever as she was and missed her? Those emotions were presently kept under wraps to avoid a wet session of solace, by crying. The light wrapped itself around the paper and snatched it from Davidia's hands. It flew like a robot toy that had control. A few dives and it fell onto the floor. It was open. The message read, "Be at council chambers in thirty minutes otherwise your land is forfeited, by order of the council."

'What utter rubbish,' said Davidia, out loud.

She had answered as if she was warning somebody, maybe the mayor. She had to attend. There was nobody else here to speak on Aunt Mavis' behalf.

'They aren't going to steal her land. It belongs to my aunty. I bet this isn't legal.'

Within five minutes, a tempest had left the cottage. The grass made way without argument. The friendly bushes felt an ill wind even though the atmosphere was dead still. A young lady was on a mission. Once she had stepped into her confidence basket, an enormous amount of kicking would ensue.

Would she succeed?

*　　*　　*

The Humpletoon Pottery was in full swing. Mervyn felt threatened by meeting Chad again after their previous encounter had left him confused. His head hurt from an uncharacteristic lack of confidence. He thought, *'My bloody brother, indeed.'*

'What's that parasite doing here in my town? He was a forgotten and wasted part of my memory until now. Am I the one that's cursed? Never mind, I'll see if we can come to a peaceful resolution. It might be therapeutic working together again.' Mervyn was rehearsing his thoughts in case he came unstuck with what he wanted to say.

Mervyn approached the front door and he could have sworn that he had heard someone say, 'What the hell do you want?' His subconscious might be seeping imaginative guilt. He looked around for the perpetrator. There was none. Shadowy thoughts danced on his shoulders. Maybe they were plotting against him? The huge, aged, front door stood in defiance. It had been hewn from two massive trees years ago. That stand of trees no longer existed. Progress had a way of replacing forest with housing. He pushed against the door which opened slowly as if teasing the entrant to go in. He stood there surveying creativity. Potting wheels hummed incessantly like background music in an opera. No one rushed up to greet the town's mayor. He was just seen as another snooping member of the public. He eyed everyone. He was completely ignored and waited. It wasn't council election time. In the far corner sat a lonely figure. All potters sat at lonely stations because it was solitary work.

'Don't just stand there and make the entrance unattractive,' said a new, young potter with attitude to mould. He didn't know who the mayor was and it was his first day.

There was no response. His mood was distracted by the thought of meeting Chad. He wandered to the space where he last had contact. An unattended wheel spun circuitously on an endless journey. A calico drop-sheet hid the small kitchenette where coffee was served in second-hand mugs, the failures of bad pottery sessions. Chad had the tap acting as a mini waterfall into a kettle and was preparing morning tea. This was his down-time. The drop-sheet was suddenly swung open. Chad twirled around, spoon in hand to scoop a tablespoon of coffee, but instead it wrapped itself across a set of protruding knuckles gripping the drop-sheet. The owner wasn't identifiable. A small yelp emanated. Chad pulled back the drop-sheet and thought to himself, *'Drop-kick,'* when he recognised the parcel of lard imitating his brother. Tensions initially arose, but quickly subsided when Mervyn put forward a hand gripper and this time it wasn't refused. The protagonists stared at each other studying each other's face. If there were compliments to ensue, no one heard them.

'Hello, Mervyn. Not lost, are we?' said Chad, who by now had a swirling hot coffee in one hand.

'Hello, Chad,' replied Mervyn. His hands were clammy so the handshake was quite brief. 'I came to see how you are.'

'Life is fine as you can see,' said Chad, waving an arm in an arc pretending it was his palace.

'We may have got off on the wrong foot last time. The shock of meeting someone who said they were related took me by surprise. I couldn't accept it.'

'Imagine my surprise also when I saw you still functioning; and mayor no less. Fate has dealt us a hand that neither of us could envisage. I live here. You live here, so that's it. We both live here. What is it you want? You haven't come to spread niceties or engage in doorstop polling.'

Chad knew his brother never gave out anything for free except unwanted advice. He began to reflect on his farming past. However, he shook his head to clear it of any nonsense before he attracted a shocking migraine. Mervyn stood see-sawing nervously on his legs, whilst formulating that riveting first question about helping him.

'Have you retained your heavy-vehicle licence?'

Chad wondered what that had to do with pottery.

'I still have it. I kept it renewed seeing the countryside was to be my new home somewhere and it could come in handy.'

'I supply the pottery with special clay and I understand that there is a shortage of the good quality clay and it needs replenishment.'

'Why not use the regular operators?'

'I need someone who I can trust and isn't the town gossip. I'd rather keep it private.'

'The quarry is public property, so why the secrecy?'

'There's a special striped clay seam I believe that runs into the quarry walls and an expert operator is needed to extract it. The town operators haven't a clue about real precision and its value, so I need to keep it low-key. If it became general knowledge, the site would become a dog's breakfast with everyone competing for it and there's the chance it will be ruined. This town is well-known for its top-quality pottery and it would be devastating if that reputation went down the sewer using an inferior product. It has to be done at night under the cover of darkness, when no one else is around. There's less chance of being discovered and what's found stays with us. What do you think?'

Chad knew his brother always had an angle and sometimes it was bent.

'What's in it for me if I agree to your proposal?'

Mervyn thought for a moment. He didn't want to give up any of the red rubies or tell Chad that was his real purpose. He intended keeping every red ruby for himself and the lovely Merrilyn. What would interest his brother?

'Fifty per cent of the value of the special clay we find. It's the most valuable in the whole district.'

Chad did a lot of pondering. That old saying about "not being able to lie straight in bed" to Chad meant danger. His head nodded as his thoughts grew in weight. Mervyn thought that movement meant that it was a resounding *'Yes'*. Interpretation often errs.

'Is there any chance that this is an illegal assault on a public quarry? You will need permits to gain access. I don't want to find I'm guilty of trespass by your council if this foray is a failure. Can you guarantee me immunity from any repercussions, legal or otherwise?'

'Yes. If you agree with the plan, all necessary permits will be issued by me personally. I will take full responsibility.'

Mervyn had to do that anyway to keep council workers' prying eyes away from his plan. He would arrange for use of the local state-of-the-art digger which was capable of devouring any clay seam. All risk was supposedly his. Chad wasn't as stupid as the younger man who was fleeced by the older brother years ago. He'd learnt rat cunning and made his own plans if anything foul occurred. In his carrot-coloured khakis, a telephone recorder had been eavesdropping and a digital footprint of the conversation had been made. It was his insurance policy against his older brother. Trust was often as fleeting as a flick-pass. Blood might be thicker than water, but in prison it wears very thin.

'I agree. When do we operate?'

'Tomorrow evening. There will be a dull moon. Conditions will be perfect. Around 9.00 pm. It should only take an hour. I will be driving the truck upon which the digger is transported. Thanks for your assistance.'

Mervyn once again shook hands with his younger brother. That wasn't as painful as he had at first thought. He walked home feeling he was on trampoline legs. There was spring in the air and it wasn't the spring season. Chad watched the departing brother and wondered if what he would be doing held any personal danger for him. A simple job wouldn't, but was this that simple? Be wary, awake and focused.

Sitting quietly in another corner of the pottery were two old women treading the pedal. One possessed a youthful pair of delicate hands whilst the other pair had a delicacy about them, but they didn't appear as soft. They had observed the meeting between the brothers. Nothing was said between them; however, their hearing was acute enough to hear every word. Many potters often wore rags of some description to avoid damaging their good clothes. Sometimes it was a statement about who they were. The two old ladies couldn't be recognised. Their faces were covered with long tresses of curly hair with a bouncy spring to it. Who were they and what were they doing there? A refuge for the aged hadn't been opened recently. Chad looked over at them and waved a generous arm. He knew one potter as "Hands", the producer of exquisite pottery. The other must be new. He returned to his wheel.

He pondered over how much his share of the clay would be worth. Little did he know that the land he was to dig belonged to Aunt Mavis. Mervyn may have set a trap for him. Mmm.

*   *   *

Davidia stood outside the council chambers surveying the monument to questionable good governance. The message she had received for Aunt Mavis was tightly gripped in a strangulation hold. It would be answered with the same good grace it was sent. She started up the stairs and was effortlessly overtaken by a huffing set of lungs inside the body of Mervyn. He had hurried back to meet the appointment threat he had made. Davidia was ignored. He was expecting an older and frailer fry so she wasn't on his radar. The doors were flung wide open with such fury they felt they were unhinged, yet still stayed attached to the walls. Davidia wondered what the rush was. She was well in time for the meeting she wasn't expected to attend. Her watch ticked over at its regular pace. In the corridors, various staff positioned at their posts went through explanations with constituents. Some stood around representing either a wax figure or a fully-clothed mannequin. No one paid any particular attention to her. She was the invisible girl. To test that theory, Davidia ducked into a side office much to her embarrassment. Two staff members were practising the parliamentary method of crossing the floor from one side of the chamber to another. She thought that wasting taxpayers' money and time and should be reported. She wasn't noticed, so she quickly withdrew. A large sign ahead on another two huge doors said, "Council Chambers". Outside the doors, a desk sat forlorn and lonely with an officer staring at her. Had she not washed her hair? Was she wearing odd shoes? That wouldn't be surprising; or had she left remnants of her breakfast on the front of her jacket? She brazenly walked up and thrust the message into the officer's hand with such force he received a paper burn.

'What is this?' he said, surprised.

'Entrance,' was her stern reply.

'You need an appointment to enter.'

'This is it.'

She waited for the door to his mind to open. Blank spaces didn't only appear on paper. The staffer looked carefully at the scrunched-up message. He thought that she didn't look old enough to be someone's aunty, as the note suggested.

'Wait here.'

The staffer disappeared like a wombat down a burrow into the council chambers. Davidia waited. She heard some indistinguishable chatter and as the door opened, noticed Mervyn pacing the floor with a piece of paper in hand. Perhaps he was in training for a heart attack. His next visitor might affect him that badly.

'Please go in,' said the staffer, as he held the door open for her entrance.

Davidia walked in confidently, but her nerves were jangling on an invisible necklace. She walked directly toward Mervyn with her arm held out straight holding her hand with an open palm and thumb standing erect like a gun trigger. Mervyn sheepishly offered his clammy collection and they shook hands. Davidia recognised him from the first day that she had arrived in town. Mervyn remembered who she was too.

'Hello, Mr Mayor,' said Davidia, with the manners of a princess even though inside she was riddled with turgidity and anger. 'It's nice to meet you again.'

'What's your name again? I don't seem to recall it.'

'It's Davidia.'

'Ah, yes, I seem to remember now. You're related to the old lady who lives on the hill.'

'You mean Aunt Mavis.'

'Yes, that's her. What can I do for you? You seem to have picked up someone else's mail. You know it's an offence to open and read it without authority.'

He waved the note as if it were the remnants of a used tissue.

'My aunt is unavailable, so I came to answer your threatening note.'

'I'm afraid this isn't any of your business.'

'You may think that, Mr Mayor, but I don't believe you have any legal standing to confiscate anyone's property unless it is of national significance. If that was the case, the government would issue the relevant order.'

Davidia had relied on her school legal studies where a problem similar to this had arisen. They were in class when Snodgrass, one of the local lads, brought it up. His parents had a block of land near an air force base which wanted to acquire it for a runway safety buffer zone along with many others. The airport had encroached close to the local housing estate and this brought the blocks of land into dispute. They tried to forcibly evict the owners and snatch it without fully compensating them. A court battle evolved with victory on the side of the land owners. She thought that this was a similar case. School was certainly a plus in education and gaining worldly knowledge. She quietly waited for a response. Mervyn was touching his chin where his mind had slipped to and he tried to stop it from dropping to the floor. His eyes rolled like a roulette ball in their sockets, only in this case there was no winning number.

'I think you have it all wrong. It was merely a suggestion to remove that eyesore of a dilapidated cottage. My secretary must have misunderstood what I had said. Wait a moment whilst I fetch my notes from my office.'

Mervyn disappeared. Davidia thought the whole place was full of wombats as she watched him exit. A few minutes later he returned. His appearance hadn't improved.

'It's all a matter of legality. I have checked my notes and conferred with our legal division,' which was himself, 'and it was meant as a warning only. Mistakes do occur, you realise.'

Mervyn knew his note was pure bluff. It was another angle to force Aunt Mavis out. The lads with the holiday haircuts didn't work and this ploy seemed doomed also. He had half-expected Aunt Mavis to comply because he could bully an old lady. He didn't count on the resilience of a long-lost relative to front him.

'Then her house is safe?'

'It is for the moment. When we expand the quarry, her home will be at risk then.'

'I'll warn her. Thank you, Mr Mayor.'

Davidia left. She was so relieved. A quick stop at the ladies on the way out gave her time for her racing heart to calm down.

Mervyn hadn't given up on acquiring that property and his future perceived wealth. He imagined the surprise that would be in store when Chad dug out the quarry walls and the whole area threatened to collapse. His sinister mind had just left his rubbish dump of thoughts where they mostly hid.

Let the contest begin.

9 DISAGREEMENT

Davidia traversed through the streets of Humpletoon after her meeting with the snivelling Mervyn. No one side-walked on the opposite side of the road to avoid her because today she was wearing her normal clothes and wasn't dressed in the Aunt Mavis theme. A lot of nodding occurred as she passed by. A few smiles emerged. She felt good. Her curiosity was tweaked by seeing the sign of the backpackers hostel and she remembered the dancing-queen male receptionist. She wondered what he would be doing. Their last meeting was a little chaotic as he took off in fright blabbering about curses. She knew she was attractive and had the personality of a reality celebrity; but scary, no she didn't believe that. One look at her and a male would realise that she was made of pure honey, so sweet to taste. She wasn't preparing to be licked by anyone; however, she knew she had some interesting attractions. No one can wear an IQ as a segment of clothing. That takes time to discuss.

She stopped in front of the backpackers hostel. She listened. It was dead quiet. There was usually more activity with itinerant travellers in and out on a revolving door visit. She pressed open the door, peered inside and found it empty. There was no attendant. She rang the bell. Its dinging ring echoed off the walls like a playful tune. No one came. She knew there was a small room behind the desk area where staff nipped out for a break. Something smelt in the air. It wasn't dope, a messy dog or body odour. The hair on the nape of her neck stood erect like porcupine needles. She tensed. Suddenly, a loud flush was heard, a door opened and there was the attendant still with ear wires attached. He detached them when he visited the small room and reattached them as he left.

'What are you doing back here? This is private,' he said, surprised at his visitor.

'Sorry. I was passing by and decided to say hello,' replied Davidia, realising that she was outside the male toilets.

They hadn't advanced to unisex ones yet. It sometimes takes longer in the country for development to occur.

'Are you looking for accommodation? Outgrown the shack, eh?' he said.

'No. The last time we met you freaked out about curses and nonsense. I came to set the record straight. There are no curses and I'm not cursed. The mayor might think so, but that's another story.'

'What now?'

'I thought that we could have a date, like together, but not a real date just like that, but an adventure date. There's a risk involved and all you need is a large ...,' he waited for that breathless go-ahead word, 'torch.' His ego deflated rather quickly.

'It sounds weird-like to me. You mean a date that isn't a date, but it might mean trouble? I get it. It's not a puzzle date, is it? I need to know what I'm up for before I agree and not afterwards.'

'I think Mayor Mervyn wants to evict my aunty from her property and probably the town. So, I thought that if the title deeds to her land are stolen – I doubt if they have them computerised in this town just yet – she couldn't be evicted. I'm not sure what she owns, but whatever it is, someone else wants it. I was in the council chambers today and noticed a side door with the words "Tittes Office" written on it. Someone had deliberately scratched out the l and replaced it with a t. No one noticed probably because they couldn't spell in that department. Are you up for it?'

Davidia didn't think of the consequences of being caught and that if she was, she could make up a suitable excuse; maybe some form of adult harassment. It was too early to think negatively. Her idea stood up to good decision-making; however, breaking the law was never a good decision. Contradictions were everywhere. The lad thought carefully.

'My name is Beau.'

'You mean like in bow and arrow?' asked Davidia, with a cheeky smile. Her humour shone. She liked him.

'When do you want this to happen?'

'Tonight would be fine after dark. I don't have a key, but Slirander might know a toolbox of tricks. We'll be here at seven. Wear a beanie and don't forget the torch. See ya.'

Before the dialogue became personal or improved, Davidia had left the building, just like the saying about Elvis leaving the building. She passed the hotel where Mr Hoarse often held his own beverage council. She was in good spirits as she wound her way home. Would Slirander and Aunt Mavis be there?

*   *   *

'This is where we live,' said Scrool, giving Aunt Mavis and Slirander a home appreciation course through the clay world of Scrollinger. Slirander and Aunt Mavis had been transformed into wafer-thin scrolls with an ability to float through clay unimpeded. They felt like seepage winding its way through the earth. They didn't require red rubies for sight as they possessed their own. Strangely enough, they could see through the clay quite clearly, emulating the feats of a well-known comic superhero.

'Why end up in this place?' asked Slirander, who knew of magical beings. 'This is next to a quarry which is a dangerous place for any being. You can be mined at almost any time.'

'It goes back a long time when our world was much larger and we had many more relatives then.' A sad sigh moistened the nearest dollop of clay. It shone brilliantly, having been teased by wetness.

Scrool gave a brief overview of the history of Scrollinger.

'The country in which we lived was inhabited by a group known as the Gemsters who plied the soil in search of anything valuable. They were experts in gemstones and whenever any significant ones were discovered, a ceremony of appraisal was held. The finder was given the privilege of wearing one stone from their find and one stone only. The wearing of this limited precious item was strictly enforced. Most villagers wore it on a necklace of the finest gold. It was the stones that held the value for them. Over the years, almost every villager was successful in obtaining a find from which they could wear their own stone on their necklaces. It was forbidden to give any away to another who wasn't so fortunate to find any. The excess stones were stored in a protected stone cave and used for trade and occasionally a ceremonial ritual. The country was peaceful and all villagers enjoyed the limited lifestyle on offer; however, there was one indi-vidual Gemster miner who had never found anything of value. It held a grudge against all others and felt ignored at being the odd one out. Its perception of acceptability was misplaced. It was included in every event held, but beneath that outer layer stewed the hatred of jealousy. No one knew of that emotion at that time. It must have been imported by some of those impure gems given in trade. Maybe they whispered of other places where they originated from and he lived there. It was an awful posses-sion and invisible to all. It was a sneaky emotion.'

Scrool stopped the explanations for a moment. It saddened him when the past was rehashed, especially with an unhappy element.

'Jealousy also exists everywhere today in my world,' said Slirander. 'At school, Davidia and I are jibed often by others when we near the prey known as boys. Some girls think that they are their specialty, but really, they're not. Emotional greed comes out expressed as stupidity sometimes. We think that they should concentrate a little more on academia than what they see in the mirror each day.'

Scrool nodded. His vocabulary wasn't as expansive as Slirander's, nor his emotional understanding at that level. It was a much simpler life in Scrollinger. Scrool continued.

'As you can appreciate, red rubies were the abundant gemstone that supported the community. To protect them from any unsavoury event, the wise head Gemster, visited the highest hill of the village and unravelled his scroll shape to triple in size as a flat piece of parchment. It lay down in a rectangular formation – the chubbier ones were capable of making a square – and placed three red rubies on one end. No one else was around. It raised an arm and unfolded its hand with the most magnificent ruby of the village. It was folklore made on a hill. The Gemsters believed in the natural universe and a chant emanated repeatedly from the scroll. It was as it was written on one of its curves. All Scrollingers possess a different magical chant. See, mine is there near that curve. Our ancient history is preserved in those chants. Some are more than just written history. Secrets abound that we aren't all aware of. Well, the head Gemster was well into his chant – it was rather a long-winded effort – when the sky opened and out popped a clouded visage. There was no smile or pleasantness in it. It saw the hapless Gemster chanting in the ancient way and spat at it. A large electrical current flashed to the ground and sizzled up its parchment to ashes. All that was untouched were those three red rubies; however, the larger one was nicked by the disgruntled Gemster who had hidden nearby. It headed off to the stored cave to steal what it could. The two red rubies left behind shone brilliantly, charged by that electrical force. That event gave us our eyes. Unbeknown to the thief, the stored cave was now protected from theft. The head Gemster had sacrificed itself to save the cave. When the thief approached the stored cave with the stolen ruby, a great crowd had gathered outside forewarned by a hidden force in the cosmos and were ready to defend their wealth. When it appeared that all hope of thievery was lost, the upset Gemster hurled that brilliant ruby into the cave and an almighty eruption occurred scattering the cave, its contents and the gem population skywards. A wild wind, fresh from its summer nap, was furious to be woken up and it charged the dust cloud with a vengeance. It gathered up all that it could and spat it out in disgust. It consisted of rough particles and solid rocks interspersed with inedible red rubies. We were flung in one giant formation and landed thump where we are today. The quarry was our centre which has now been mined putting the rest of us in the ring at risk. The clay stripes were formed by the force of hitting the ground from the soil mixture that landed here. Our ancient chants have found a saviour in Aunt Mavis and also brought you and your friend here too. We didn't know when we chanted where they would end up or what it would bring.

Goodness is all that we require. Our valuable family members were mixed mainly in the ring that's left. Only a few unfortunate rubies have been found to date. We need them all back as one family unit, otherwise we are lost forever. Now you know the importance of saving the Ring of Clay. If ruined, there could be costly consequences for the town and its inhabitants. We need the return of all red-eyed rubies.'

Slirander suddenly realised the importance of the return of those two red ruby earrings located at the Dimpletoon Mug Festival. Merrilyn had that mug made so perhaps there is more where that came from. Scrool had been given new sight with them. Slirander determined then and there that her friend Davidia and she will find any missing red-eyed ruby. That task may be easier said than done.

'How do you make the clay so soft and give it its magical qualities?'

'It's in the eyes. We transfer elements of light in combination with a chant – it could be one of many – and the clay responds with warmth within itself and the particles party hard to change their composition. It's like a conductor of an orchestra. Wave a baton and the orchestra acts together as one. It's almost magical.'

Aunt Mavis hadn't uttered one word. Was it possible that she couldn't speak underground? Slirander had no problems. The dense clay made the most magnificent pottery. Aunt Mavis was busy determining its use, composition and thickness of seam. She could clearly see underground what no one above ground could see. The rubies were either shy or scarce in number. They encountered only the odd pair. Where were they?

'There doesn't seem to be many rubies here,' said Aunt Mavis. 'Have they been taken or are they in hiding?'

'We don't reveal ourselves to strangers. No red glows are randomly given for discovery. We light up in anger and to massage the clay seams, otherwise we pretend we are invisible. Will you assist in saving us?'

Slirander felt privileged that an ancient race of scrolls had requested her personal help. She put her hand out and touched Aunt Mavis' hand as a gesture of togetherness.

'Don't touch me,' she screamed.

The ground shook with small electrical charges zig-zagging

haphazardly amongst the clay. It certainly invigorated what was a normally quiet place.

Slirander wondered what the commotion was about. She was shocked by the reaction that she received. Aunt Mavis was shaking like a deciduous leaf in a high wind with parts of her scroll dress falling off. It appeared that a series of pinprick holes had aerated her. She immediately made for the surface near her home.

'Aunt Mavis, where are you going?' asked Slirander.

'The tour is over. Someone is at the front door.'

Scrool and Slirander weren't in a disagreeable mood, so they followed along the tracks made by the ferreting worms to the surface where it was nearing dusk. They emerged as thin pieces of parchment any breeze would easily blow into the quarry.

'We must get inside quickly or our fate will be sealed,' said Scrool, who knew only too well what devastation would be inflicted by exposure to fresh air and daylight on an ancient parchment. It would disintegrate into a pile of paper compost, a no longer readable or existing item.

The three scrolls returned via the shelf in Aunt Mavis' house. Slirander and Aunt Mavis re-emerged as themselves and Scrool wound itself up to rest on the shelf once again.

'It's great to be back to normal,' said an excited Slirander. She had been too small for too long.

Aunt Mavis returned to her chair of buttons as an exhausted, older-aged adult.

'That physical change certainly takes it out of you. It seems that I have been chosen to protect the Ring of Clay. Maybe that's my curse, to live here alone hidden away from the world to manage a clay seam that others want to destroy. There has to be a way to save the seam and for me to lead a better existence.' Aunt Mavis was expressing far deeper thoughts than she'd allowed herself before.

Slirander felt an emotional change in the reclusive behaviour of Aunt Mavis. Perhaps with her and Davidia visiting, it may have enlarged her perspective on a solitary existence that it didn't have to be this way. Often, it's said, "That's food for thought"; however, for Aunt Mavis it was the beginning of a real life snack.

*   *   *

'Anyone home?' Davidia called out.

She wasn't keen on entering a house from the dark by herself. In one's mental shadows lurks unknown and damaging forces that may scare you. Fast heart palpitations are acceptable when trying to meet an attractive young male at school whose attention you require, but a house not even on the radar? No one replied. She quietly made her way underground into the main part of the house to be met by two people sitting quietly.

'And where have you been?' asked Slirander, like a scolding mother of her daughter who had crept out at night after being grounded and then hoped to sneak back undetected.

'Me?' she said, exasperatedly. 'I was left alone to defend my thoughts, which no thanks to you, I mastered. Where did you go? It wasn't out by the front door otherwise I would have seen you.'

Slirander explained to her friend where they had been, the importance of the Ring of Clay and that they were entrusted to save it, after which Davidia agreed that it was slightly left of centre but believable. Aunt Mavis sat impassively, then silently pressed a button. There were many to select from in her technological home. She turned toward a wall. The girls were wide-eyed as it disappeared from view. It was at about two-thirds of the height of the quarry, safe enough not to be affected by mining at the base. A one-way mirror emerged with the most magnificent views of the opposite quarry wall. It was a sight to behold, perhaps to a miner. There wasn't the expected picturesque landscape inclusive of magnificent tall trees, burping frogs, chirping birds and art-designed lily-pads patterning the surface of a wide lagoon. It was a vista, nevertheless.

'What's it for?' asked Davidia, and continued, 'It's definitely not for the views.'

'Safety,' replied Aunt Mavis. 'It allows me to monitor any activity within the quarry. It can't be seen from the outside as it is camouflaged as the quarry wall. During the day scavengers rummage through the refuse and I note what they take, not what they do with it. Sometimes people turn up with a pick and shovel digging everywhere, maybe hoping to find a treasure, or better still, a gem. I sometimes feel like the quarry warden. When all that mining went on recently, I sat here and watched the eagerness of the mayor sifting through the debris and exalting in the find of a few red rubies. I knew from that day trouble would follow. Gemstones have a natural attraction for greed.'

Davidia wondered whether she should tell Aunt Mavis about her plan and the title deeds she hoped to steal. She knew it would be disapproved of and she would be breaking the law and that she could possibly receive a prison sentence of some sort. She knew it was wrong and she would endanger two of her friends and she could disappear from town like those earlier tourists did and could be sent home with a reprimanding note from the police. She could even sustain an injury in the dark and could be up for trespass. She could also be convicted of a criminal offence which would damage future employment prospects and she knew it was unacceptable behaviour from a young lady. She wondered if she should make it worse by telling someone. The die was cast.

'Aunt Mavis, Slirander and I have to go out tonight and meet that young lad, Beau, at the backpackers. He told us that he's lonely here and could he meet up and have a coffee together with someone his own age. So, we said we would. We won't be late.'

What did Aunt Mavis remember about the behaviour of youth? She thought it seemed healthy and normal to go out and meet friends. At least they had some to meet. It might be a lonely, thoughtful night for her. She saw two young girls experiencing the joys of life and what an inspiration they were. No one could see any emotion under all that hair. Maybe it was time to remove it? It was just a ridiculous thought, but was it? Change was upstaging her solitariness.

'Be careful. Take this.'

She handed them an object each which felt like a gooey gel toy one throws flat on the ground to spread and then reassemble as the object first thrown. Tourists often bought them. Whatever importance it held, they accepted and placed it in their pockets.

'Slirander, dress in black.'

The girls left the house. 'Black is black, I want my titles back' they hummed, as they walked in the dark. Only their shadows followed, but they couldn't be seen. High above flew a few bats that followed them as aerial bodyguards. Bat guano is a formidable deterrent for enjoying oneself.

*　　*　　*

'Do you trust that brother of yours?' said Merrilyn to Mervyn. 'He has been a bit shady in the past.'

It was a remark that Mervyn wasn't prepared to comment on because he knew who else had been shady in the past.

'We have to give him the benefit of the doubt. He's family. Who else in this town would you trust? Besides, he has the proper licence to operate the digger. I certainly can't do it with my manager's hands and blister-free palms. I'll be there to supervise. I can at least drive the truck to the quarry. No one will be there after dark. It's too far out of town and if anyone sees a light from a distance out there, they will immediately think of that old lady performing witchcraft.'

'You haven't told him the real reason you are mining the walls, have you?'

'He might be related, but my trust doesn't extend to the truth. We'll be wealthy after we discover where those red rubies are.'

'What about the waste you dig out? Won't he be suspicious that it's not being dumped in a truck for transport to the pottery? If he sees you discover the red rubies, he'll want some of them too, won't he?'

'Let's find them first and I'll handle that hurdle when and if it arises.'

'How will you identify them in the dark?'

'I have a special light that reflects on anything red. It will only be a flicker. He won't notice that whilst he's in the digger. I'll pretend to drop something and pick them up. The waste can be left overnight because it's too difficult to select the correct seam to transport in the dark. He'll buy that. I'm his older brother.'

Older brother or not, he was still a gigantic rat not to be trusted, but Chad already knew that.

'Have you safely locked up that set we have?'

'They are secure in the old, oak desk drawer under lock and key. No one knows of their existence except you and me.'

Merrilyn smiled. Treachery was never obvious. True, she was married to Mervyn and had been for many years, but these days her planet was aligned with Uranus. There was definitely a change in her cosmos as she dreamily fondled in her mind *her* magnificent rubies. They would be a most suitable necklace to show others and gloat about their wealth and beauty. Had she plans to dump Mervyn and reset her eyes on Chad? It was a catastrophe in the making. Reason didn't enter the space of greed and want.

'Can I see them again? I feel something in my aura that tells me that I must see them.'

Aura, my foot! It was the need to see and feel, not dream and imagine their beauty. Mervyn thought it a simple request and why not show her why he was risk-taking for their future retirement. He withdrew the keys from his pocket, went to the desk and opened the drawer. The red rubies were all present. Not one of them shone. It was as if life had been drained from them. They were unhappy and their dull-red colour emphasised dissatisfaction with their current predicament, separated from their own families. Would they ever be reunited? It was an unhappy drawer of occupants.

Milo Mac sat still. He couldn't move anyway. The mantelpiece gave great vision around the room. His emotional state was aroused. It wasn't an attractive female mug that triggered the feeling, but rather the innocuous action of opening a simple, modest drawer with lingerie lining and a few red stones. It was about relationships, but a symbiotic one. Mervyn took them out and displayed them on the desktop. They were perfect. Merrilyn ran her fingers over them. Static electricity tingled through her body at their exquisite feel. She shut her eyes and whatever occurred in her mind at that moment wasn't explained, but she screamed out a loud, 'Yes.' Mervyn had no idea. Had she a panic attack? Had she imagined that she wore them as a necklace or was she lost in another hay shed? She wasn't repeating the emotional response into verbal discourse. It was just left with her and that exhausted smile.

'Are you okay, darling?' said Mervyn, 'I thought I might have to arrange an ambulance for you.'

'Nothing could be finer. All you have to do now is find me

some more, lots more. I feel that those rubies need me. Someone has to protect those itty-biddy gems.'

Merrilyn had succumbed to the emotional aura that the stones had generated. Sane people often had their personalities altered by their red greed. Merrilyn had the early stages of WAP (wealth and power). It was an insidious, money-based wealth creator that didn't show up on the Stock Exchange Index, but it was sought the world over. Humpletoon had now been officially incorporated into corporate greed via the mayoral office.

'Have patience, my love. Tomorrow night, all your desires will be met. Chad and I will find them and I will bring home, not the bacon, but the rubies.'

Merrilyn smiled again, wondering what those desires were. She suddenly twirled on her light feet like a whirling dervish with her petticoats flying at right angles to the floor. Her fluffy, frilly pantaloons that covered her legs resembled fairy-floss and she went so fast, she fell over. The excitement was catching. She stopped and stared at Milo Mac with the hardness of a chisel. He shut his eyes tight as he didn't want to morph into her face.

'Throw that stupid mug out,' she said. 'I don't know how it won the competition with that facial combination.'

Merrilyn picked herself up off the floor. She didn't want clammy hands on her old-style outfit placed under her armpits as a hoist. She left the room, which suddenly felt empty. Mervyn was still present but one never felt that he could "fill" a room on his own.

The red rubies were still lying prostrate on the desktop on their lingerie rug. One of them shone a laser light at Milo Mac. He responded by glowing the stripes on his surface. An under-standing passed. Where was that nice mug he had met at the Dimpletoon Mug Festival? He was now aware of a dastardly plan to decimate his home and friends. He needed to tell some-one. He felt hopeless. His anger with what he had heard had upset many of the particles he was made of so they began to fight with each other. It felt as if a wind tunnel was within his mug walls with nowhere to go. It was more exhilarating than having his inner surfaces filled with hot water and Milo granules. The rumbling was short-lived as he was only a modest size mug; however, during the skirmish, signals had been released into the atmosphere. Where they landed or what had received them was an unknown. Things resettled and once again, he sat quietly and forlorn. All he could do was wait and hope that his warning had been received. Mervyn replaced the red rubies, the cause of all the greed and disagreeable language, into the drawer and securely locked them away. At least they were familiar with the dark and weren't stressed in that confined space. They too, had to wait.

*   *   *

Things were deathly quiet at the backpackers hostel. One could be forgiven for mistaking it for a morgue. In town, shadows lurked from every mass, moving or stationary. They weaved interesting night patterns for the animals and the girls to walk through or evade. One minute they were cloaked by a black, smothering coat and next, by soothing lights from the street lamps which operated as a "seen" friend. There weren't any villagers scurrying around as if a curfew existed. They approached quietly. There was no benefit in making any noise and being discovered with a, 'What are you doing?' question. Tonight needed to be a no-noise activity. Town gossip would ruin their plans and the thrill of discovery. They neared the front door. It wasn't locked, but gave the impression it was. A ring bell waited patiently to be pushed, but it wasn't.

'Use your shoulder to push,' suggested Davidia.

Someone had to stand guard. Slirander complied. It creaked,

warning entrance. Once it was opened wide enough, they peered inside. The lighting was on a cost-cutting exercise with a solitary lamp pumping out minimum amps. There was no one there. They slipped inside like Ninjas ready to pounce on any prey. The floorboards were worn with years of foot traffic and lack of repair. It was an early-warning intruder alarm as their weight, albeit from two slim and modestly-built girls, was still too heavy to avoid the loud and awkward creaking. Suddenly, a young man appeared at the top of the stairs, baseball bat in hand.

'Identify yourselves,' he said, 'otherwise you'll be hit for a home run.'

'Beau, it's us, Davidia and Slirander. We're supposed to be here, remember, seven o'clock.'

'I knew it was you.'

'What's with the third arm?' Davidia said, referring to the baseball bat.

'I thought it might be a good friend to have in a crisis. You two could have been real thieves and here's me, ready to protect my space.' He smiled broadly. The stairwell shadows prevented that from being seen.

'There is to be strict quietness tonight. We don't want to be found foraging through council records. A criminal record on our school resume would haunt our futures. All understood. Did you bring a torch?' Davidia wanted to ensure all bases were loaded with the correct information.

'Wait a minute. I almost forgot.'

Beau fumbled under the front desk for the crusading light to become the leader of the three-world youth into battle against a formidable foe, the darkness. They needed to penetrate its heart. Only a torch had that capability or infra-red night goggles, which they didn't have. Davidia had no idea and neither did the other two about how the evening would transpire.

'Let's go and kick a…' said Beau wound up with his maleness and being the leader; well, assumed leader.

They walked quite briskly to the council chambers, keeping to doorways and shadowy spaces remaining undetected. They were undiscovered on their short journey. What an achievement! Those few stray bats that followed them from Aunt Mavis' hovered overhead as protectors without them knowing. No one had ever heard of bat bodyguards. They were so small it would be perceived that they would be ineffective. Just ask the boys with the holiday haircuts about that. The front entrance to the council chambers was quite dark. A poorly-lit street lamp did its best to cheer it up, but it flickered incessantly with a case of electronic nerves from an infrequent power source. A group of mosquitos coloured its glass as they had their last gasp of light causing a filtering effect as well. It was a gloomy place at night. During the day when council was in full voice and happy discourse was raised throughout, disagreements about governance confirmed the gloomy concept. The three stood dwarfed by the building.

'Where's the alarm system?' said Beau. 'I'll disable it with the baseball bat.'

He swung it menacingly, almost swatting the girls. Length and the concept of dark are often difficult to determine accurately.

'They don't have an electronic alarm. You need a key about the size of a fist to open that door. Check to see if it has been left unlocked,' said Davidia.

'They wouldn't be that stupid, would they?'

No one thought that they would be, but doubt can be an ugly relative. All three pushed to make sure. It was locked solid.

'Now what?' said an irate Davidia. 'How are we going to get in? Who wants to climb on the roof?'

That was a ridiculous suggestion everyone ignored. No one had any climbing gear.

'Stand back behind me,' said Slirander, in an authoritative tone which didn't need a responder. 'I will attempt to open it.'

'But, you're ten feet away. It's impossible,' said a disbelieving Davidia.

She knew that Slirander was very clever, like she was, but even this task was too far out for her. All she could think of was doom, doom and one more doom. Could they be defeated before they started? The darkness played into their hands. It felt like a safety blanket as they stood in the open. Even the homeless didn't overnight near the council chambers. It was also too gloomy for them. Slirander sat on the cold, stone steps, cross-legged in a lotus yoga position, placed her hands together under her chin to give her head a rest and closed her eyes to dream of where else she'd rather be. Her body tensed and a statue was born. Davidia gave her a gentle nudge. She was immobile and solid to the touch.

'Ugh! She's gone cold.'

'Shall I hug her?' Beau offered, in a moment of chivalry. She was pretty enough to hug.

A small cloud began to form around Slirander. The air became icy. The cold emphasised her breath as she inhaled and exhaled. Each breath seemed to consume more oxygen. This lasted a minute or so. Her mouth began to open slowly like a drawbridge.

'I hope she flossed this morning,' said Davidia. 'You can have awful bad breath in the morning if you don't clean your teeth.' No one was listening. They were watching Tower Bridge opening.

Slirander's agape mouth was as large as a small dessert bowl. Suddenly, an awful gurgling sound like a belching bellows began from her stomach which was pulsating on its own to internal disco music. Davidia thought something said, 'Hello, there,' as it brushed around her. A strong exhalation sent a stream of cold air into the huge door lock and it disappeared. A few moments later, that same stream of air returned to Slirander as she inhaled.

It was her next breath. Her mouth slowly closed. When shut, she still didn't speak. Davidia and Beau didn't know what to do.

Then, the strangest thing happened. It was a first for all three – one participant and the two startled onlookers. Slirander's head began to bobble and burble like a hot mud-pool. It changed shape from the pretty person she was known as, to a mass of brown, popping sounds that emanate from unsavoury jokes men often perpetrate. The transformation was remarkable. In the dark it was difficult to see the full impact, but what was seen had them mesmerised. Her head had turned into the shape of a key. Before there was time for real shock at what they had seen, Slirander spat – usually a most dirty and unattractive habit; however, this time it was for a good cause – a white stream of hot air in the shape of a key. It flew into the lock and amazingly, as if a miracle had been performed, it opened the door. The moulded key disappeared as quickly as ice on a hotplate. Davidia turned around to her friend who by now had regained the shape of her normal head.

'That was a nice nap. Let's go,' said Slirander.

She was totally unaffected by her ordeal. There wasn't an explanation lurking nearby. Had she learnt something from Aunt Mavis who might really be a witch?

'How did you do that? I mean it was incredible.'

'A girl never gives away her secrets, especially on a first date.'

Davidia wondered what that meant. Does she think she's on a date with Beau? If she thinks that, her mind needs to be rewired. It also wasn't a date for her, but because the night escapade was her idea, she felt that she had the front running if an embrace occurred. Girls, we are on a break-and-enter. Let's focus.

They slipped inside and the door automatically shut behind them. They were now officially felons.

It was pitch-black. Vision was short-sighted. Not even one of those beautiful mirrors that Davidia and Slirander often stood in front of could improve the situation.

'Beau, the torch,' insisted Davidia. They needed their guiding light.

Beau fidgeted about in the dark trying to locate the switch. He had to do it by feel. A clumsy thumb pushed down on a protruding object and lo-and-behold, there was light. It began beautifully. The solid light rays danced lightly like a ballet troupe all over the walls searching for corridor access. They carefully headed toward the misspelt name on the Titles office door. On the way it became harder to see. The torch was malfunctioning with uncooperative batteries. Where was the light escaping to? It certainly didn't want to be arrested like they might be. Zap! It was pitch-black as they struggled and stood outside the Titles office door.

'What's happening to the light?' asked Davidia.

'The batteries have gone flat. I could have sworn they were new,' replied Beau, holding a useless inanimate object whose assistance had expired. 'Now, what do we do? None of us are nocturnal and can see in the dark. What a damn waste of time. We mightn't be able to find our way out. I could be late home for supper. Will I get arrested?' The fun personality he thought he had wasn't on show at this very moment.

'Stop the wimping,' said Slirander. 'Follow me.'

The trio lined up as obedient schoolchildren in a single file behind Slirander, who, instead of changing shape, pushed the door open as it had been left unlocked. Internal security arrangements had been quite lax. The staff must have been in a hurry for a council freebee somewhere. A musty smell greeted them. It was clean-sinus territory. The air was full of leather-bound book smells, old style title deed parchment aromas and dust particles that always welcomed a visitor because if disturbed they had the opportunity to settle elsewhere. Life, at time, had its exciting element. The room was fully enclosed so the risk of turning on the light was minimised. There were no windows leading to the outside world. Beau, being the keeper of the light, had the honour of locating the light switch inside the door. It wasn't a difficult task, but he had the knack of lengthening any given simple task. His hands went up and down the architraves almost splintering them with the damaged woodwork. The girls waited patiently. Finally, a switch was found. He flicked it. Nothing happened. He repeated the process a few more times and gave up. It might have been another council initiative to reduce costs by not connecting the electricity supply.

'It's probably not connected,' he said. 'It's so dark in here.'

'We've no torch and no lighting. How do we locate any files in this mess?' said Davidia, thinking that the night was the disaster that could have happened. Hardly a shadow could be sighted. It was an impasse at the door. They waited a minute or so to allow their eyes to adjust to the conditions.

'Davidia, take out that gooey gel ball gift that Aunt Mavis gave you before you left the house. Hold it at eye level in your right hand only and lightly squeeze.'

'This isn't time for silly games. I want to see to search for the files.'

'Please do as I say and you will be surprised.' Slirander often had a firmness in her voice. It was a non-tampered with sound. 'Don't waste our time. Just do it.'

'Alright, keep your shirt on. I'll do it.' Davidia thought she could be so bossy at times.

She extracted the gooey gel ball from her pocket. It had an unpleasant, sticky feel to it. She held it aloft and gently squeezed. It slipped through her fingers like runny jelly, then retraced its shaped displacement. All eyes were riveted to the exercise in the dark that no one could see. It was a feeling exercise.

'My hand is vibrating. I'm not getting an old age person's disease, am I?' she said, nervously.

The answer was a moment away. Her hand began to glow. There was light. The pulsating gooey gel ball was a squeezy light known only to a few in the witchcraft world. So how did Slirander know? There wasn't time for debate. It lit the room sufficiently bright enough to see what they were doing.

'It also has another quality,' said Slirander. 'It has a voice-absorptive control system that can be directed as a discovery tool without wasting unnecessary time looking for an item, in this case, old title deeds. It has been used before to discover hidden secrets.'

'And I have three heads,' said an unconvinced Davidia.

Slirander gave the instruction, 'Search for the title deeds to Humpletoon quarry.'

They all waited. Davidia noticed a tiny movement within the gel ball. She peered closer. There was a series of tiny minute particles oscillating in random circles like dandelion seeds in a wind storm. Cohesion had been left at the gate post. She watched entranced. Finally, they settled. It was a speckled interior. Her hand suddenly felt lighter. The gel ball took flight, albeit at a modestly slow pace. They followed in line as if a pied piper had hypnotised them. At first, it operated as a confused robotic toy.

'What's it doing?' said Davidia, as the light ball rotated and disappeared behind shelf space, over old files covered with dust, and finally bumped upright and kerplunk, it fell to the floor. 'It's damn dark in here. Where did it go? It's not a kid's game toy, is it?' Davidia was becoming frustrated as she crawled along the floor in search of that disappearing ball. She banged her head, skinned her knees and finally found the object of her annoyance. 'Gotcha, you rat.' She picked it up and in doing so squeezed it gently and it took flight once again. 'Slirander, how do you manage this thing?'

'It will find its own space. We have to wait.'

Beau kept silent and followed carefully. He didn't want to trip over and sue the council for untidiness because if he did, he would have to admit to trespass. Any injuries sustained during any fall would have to be personally carried home in pain, if it applied. He marvelled at the lack of filing discipline. When he was younger, he'd been a scavenger in garbage tips combing the heaps for spare bicycle parts. It had better organised refuse than this so-called Titles office mess. Maybe the misspelling Tittes Office was correct. Can't spell, can't file, can't clean, can't find. No wonder fees were high if a council staffer had to do a "search" in the office rubble. He doubted if the titles they were after could be located even if they did actually exist. He played along. He was part of the trio now.

The slow-moving flight pattern of the gel ball allowed them to keep pace. It lit the walls that were filled with bound ledgers, the occasional empty space and rounded scrolls similar to a solicitor's brief bound with red ribbons. It hovered, moved, hovered, moved and hovered again. The light it generated, once again, quickly faded. The darkness was in charge again.

'You stupid b…. ball,' yelled Davidia. She grabbed for it and squeezed it hard. It lit up once again, but this time it didn't move. 'Lost a gear, have you?'

'Davidia, it's showing you the location of the deeds to Aunt Mavis' property,' said Slirander.

'You know I don't dine on teasing,' she replied.

Suddenly, a thin, fine shard of light flickered from the gel ball onto a file covered in dust. It was at head height. There was no point in proving if it was alphabetically filed. Davidia moved closer. She put out a delicate hand and touched the dust-encrusted file. It was in a scroll format, not unlike the one that sat on the shelf at Aunt Mavis' home and had turned into some weird behaving thing. She thought that was curious. Her hand firmly picked up the file. There were no identifying marks on the outside. She huffed and puffed and blew the dust away to reveal an old, parchment-type scroll, tied neatly with a red ribbon. A small table nearby beckoned a visit. Amazingly, it was empty – at last, a useful item of furniture unencumbered with disorganised mess. Davidia carefully untied the scroll which had nibbled edges of decay. Parchment is a delicate paper that can easily be damaged. She placed it on the table and opened it as carefully as a doctor performing a surgical operation would, ensuring any creases didn't part. The writing was in a beautiful cursive script as if a professional printer had performed its best artistic work. The presentation alone was worth heritage listing. The gel ball hovered above for ease of reading. All three sets of eyes were glued to the fine print. It was the true title deed to the quarry. Who did it reveal as the true owner?

A folio reference and file reference together with a draftsman's drawing of the land plans that are subject to the title deed, reeked authenticity. The signatures were written with a flourish, but there wasn't an available comparison to a current existing signature. It was naturally assumed that Aunt Mavis had signed the original title deed. True, the title deed read that Aunt Mavis as the real owner; however, the date of the sale and transfer to her name preceded her arrival in Humpletoon. She was an unknown and had never been, seen or heard of Humpletoon before she found herself outside the railway station at the start of her new life.

Slirander suddenly felt a jolt in her aura. No explanation was given. It was time to go. Davidia rolled up the scroll and as she did so, she saw two red lights flicker within it and then fade. She felt a weirdness developing the more she thought of the scroll. Was it related to the "home" one?

The gel ball received a final squeeze and just as Davidia held it tightly before release, she turned to Slirander and asked her to instruct it to find the title deeds to the mayor's property portfolio empire. It was only on instinct that it came to her; however, those two red lights may have instructed her subconscious mind.

'If we stay any later, someone will arrest us,' said Beau. He'd tired of being their protector. 'I've enjoyed the date. I'd prefer a nice, warm dormitory-style mattress rather than those lumpy, saggy and overused mattresses at the police precinct.'

'We got what we came for,' said Slirander.

'Not quite,' said Davidia. 'I want to see the mayor's deeds first. Something is nagging me and this time it's not either of you two. Now instruct the gel ball to get moving and this time, make it go faster. It is getting late and we need our beauty sleep and non-arrest.'

Slirander stopped dead in her tracks. She wasn't imitating a tombstone. Her eyes turned a bright red and a burble of unintelligible syllables lightly dressed and camouflaged as words, fled in fear from her mouth. The room filled with swishing noises. The gel ball had escaped Davidia's grip and acted erratically, flying around the room in precision manoeuvres. Slirander's head had turned into a huge sound-bowl on her shoulders. Davidia didn't have time to be terrified. Slirander was her friend and harm would never be allowed to visit. Beau froze like his favourite icypole, what flavour it couldn't remember. Once again, the empty table was full of deeds, dumped by the gel ball and the ancient incantations of Scrollinger. Suddenly, all sound and activity stopped. Peace and quiet had replaced the din. Slirander was her normal self again without giving an explanation to her behaviour. Weird was a given state to be in.

Davidia was interested in the deeds. She opened them with less respect than the scroll and hurriedly read what was owned by the mayoral family. Slirander trailed a finger over them using its end like a third eye. Actually, whatever it touched was absorbed via a magical vein within her system to her brain where it remained until it was brought back to memory. She didn't know she was doing it. Her time of disappearance into Scrollinger armed her with a formidable array of unknown talents. Her outbursts weren't all under her control.

'The mayor and his wife own almost all the town. I wonder how come they don't own the quarry. Maybe Aunt Mavis can tell us. Quickly, replace the deeds. We don't want to warn anyone that something in here has been stolen or tampered with.'

No sooner said than done, the deeds were miraculously replaced with another series of incantations and a busy gel ball. They headed toward the entrance doors of the Titles office, pleased at their discovery. No one would know. The gel ball returned to Davidia's pocket. It had lost its glow and settled. Slirander was leading and as she was about to open the door, she heard voices. It wasn't magic this time. It was a policeman and the mayor standing to the side of the front door.

'Hello, sergeant. How are the rounds going tonight? Is there anything suspicious to report?' said the mayor in a convivial chit-chat mood.

'There's nothing of importance that I've noticed. I thought a disturbance might have been here at the council chambers, what with all the backpackers in town seeking a sleepover spot. Some could end up here. We can't have the council chambers used as a public bed and breakfast and amenity block. Besides, Mervyn, what brings you here at night?'

'I forgot to lock the Titles office door. You never know, riff-raff might try to break in. Could you wait whilst I lock it?'

The sergeant shone his powerful police-issue torch which lit up the interior. Nothing could slink past undiscovered. Mervyn clunked the heavily-keyed door shut. There was no other exit. Those doors were far heavier and secure once locked because of the valuable documents they protected. Were the girls and Beau doomed to discovery?

'Goodnight, sergeant.'

'Goodnight, Mervyn.'

The Titles office door and main door were now securely locked. Escape seemed impossible.

'Now what?' said Beau. 'There's no way out.'

He began to regret his bravado foray with dates he hoped to have in the future. His baseball bat had no use nor did his withering repartee. It was a night of outs.

'No one ever leaves home without an exit strategy,' said Slirander.

She happened to be the only one with one. Davidia wasn't on the table with a good idea. It was a night off for her too. Slirander reached into her pocket and withdrew the other gel ball that Aunt Mavis had given to her.

'Stand back.'

Beau fell over in the darkness and on the way down to the floor, his hand caught hold of a light fabric which was attached to Davidia. It slipped off her shoulder and in the dull, faded light, a moonbeam ray of light glinted from her shoulder. Beau glimpsed some of the female human form in that reveal. His distraction made the pain of hitting the floor non-existent.

'Let go, you fool,' said an annoyed Davidia. 'I'm not falling on the floor for you. I want to get out of here. Besides, if we are incarcerated all night, what are we doing about a toilet break? I haven't seen any buckets in here.' The pained expression on her face remained unseen in the dark.

'Shut your eyes,' commanded Slirander.

She waved her arm around with the second gel ball and once

again, a ridiculous-sounding burble emanated from her mouth almost identical to her last effort. What one wouldn't do for a good book right now? She threw the gel ball as hard as possible against the back wall. A mysterious swishing sound arrived. It was fresh air from outside. The wall had parted.

'Quickly, we don't have much time.'

Like three frightened chooks, they scrambled through the exit into the night cold. The wall closed behind and the three friends were safe outside having stayed up past their curfew hour. What teenager has a curfew hour?

'We had better hurry home,' said Davidia. 'Aunt Mavis will be worried we're so late. We are supposed to be on a team date for coffee with you; well, that's what we told her.'

'I enjoyed the date too,' said Slirander. 'There may be a next time before we leave Humpletoon.'

'Thanks for the date, girls. Perhaps next time I can hold hands with one of you and hug the other. You did say a team date?' Beau had a broad smile as he said it. He liked them both.

The girls headed home after leaving Beau at the backpackers. They faded into the night as two silhouettes. It had been a magical evening. The bat bodyguards relaxed and they flew home, job done.

What would Aunt Mavis think of the truth of the title deeds?

10 THE CHALLENGES

The girls arrived home safely. They were now familiar with the tricky entrance techniques to the house. Once safely downstairs, they were confronted with Aunt Mavis still sitting in her chair of buttons waiting like a doting parent for the safe return of her two guests. She eyed them with caution. Someone had used the gel balls this evening, which was unexpected. They were given only as a safeguard and not an all-out attack object. Their use had triggered a signal to Aunt Mavis that they were rather active. An explanation was required. The normally placid and polite Aunt Mavis definitely had a burr jabbing her emotional plate.

'Was the coffee pleasant?' she asked.

Her hands flittered over her button range wondering which one to push. Once she felt a special tingle, bang, down went the finger. She had ten fingers jingling at the moment.

Both girls had the word "guilty" emblazoned across their foreheads with the peevish looks they gave out. Who was to step forward with the truth? It was better coming from a relative. Davidia swallowed hard. When a lie has to be refuted and a truth has to replace it, the dryness in the throat creates the "lump" which is difficult to swallow. Is it a guilty saliva wash?

'We did meet Beau, but the coffee wasn't on the menu,' started Davidia. Whew! That's the first sentence out. 'We visited the council chambers uninvited so we let ourselves in. No one saw us. The words on the Title Office doors were misspelt, so we entered wondering why a grammatical error would be allowed to exist in a public space. Perhaps there were more words inside that needed correction such as proper labelling?' Davidia was meshing the truth with a dose of non-reality. Aunt Mavis waited. 'Whilst in there, the gel balls lit the way. Curiosity got our interest and we located the title deeds to this property. We have them here.'

Davidia withdrew the scroll with the red ribbon and placed it on the table. It rolled slightly. Was it alive? What secret movement was it going to make? It settled, but no one took any notice of Scrool who sat quietly on the shelf. Slirander returned the two gel balls as an interruption technique to allow Davidia a breather. Guilt is not easy to manage.

'These are the title deeds to this property, your property, Aunt Mavis,' said Slirander, taking the lead. 'The mayor is suspicious of you and this land. He has an interest in acquiring it possibly for the red rubies that you have seen that exist in the special clay seams. I believe that the clay seam is a pretext to mine for the rubies. It was Davidia's idea to find the truth about this property.'

'Thanks for the responsibility comment, girlfriend.'

'The title deeds show you as the rightful owner. If they fell into the hands of the mayor then they could be manipulated with a forgery and, hey presto, no more ownership. There is one peculiarity though. The deeds were signed over to you years before you arrived in Humpletoon. How is that possible?' Slirander was using her clear-thinking techniques because it created a puzzle to solve.

'We only did it to save your home and learn more about this area,' piped up Davidia, who could fight her own linguistic battles.

She was almost spoiling for an argument. At home her parents offered advice many times which didn't agree with her opinion of whatever it was they were offering. Tension grew like a tempest until reason arrived somewhat surprising the opponents. Was Aunt Mavis going to offer "parental advice" or accept the best intentions of the two girls? Her hands were still flitting, but at a reduced pace. Finally, she removed her fingers from above the buttons to rest on her lap. Confrontation avoided. The three females sat quietly staring at the title deed scroll. Before any further bright ideas emerged, the scroll had unravelled itself flat. No one had touched it. It covered the small table completely. Suddenly, a large cursive letter arose from the scroll and stood tall. It was immediately followed by a series of other letters as support. It was a community gathering of members of the alphabet spelling out the name of Aunt Mavis.

'This isn't a pantomime, is it?' said Davidia, thinking that Christmas had come early given the show by the alphabet performers.

'It's a message,' said Slirander.

She'd heard of dim, dark stories of past places that remain hidden inside documents for safety and their true selves only revealed in a trusted environment.

'What sort of message?'

Before any further guesses were made, Scrool came to life on the shelf. It shone those beautiful, red eyes at the other scroll and Davidia could have sworn it said the word, 'Aunty.' Scrool then unravelled into its scroll shape and was as flat as the other, albeit in an upright position. It delicately floated toward the table, careful not to damage its fragile shape. The words on the deed scroll lit up like a series of Christmas lights, the bright LED type. A short, sharp repartee of incantations filled the room as both scrolls emitted their ancient greeting ritual. The girls didn't understand them, but Aunt Mavis did. Then, an amazing thing happened. Both scrolls floated in the air and turned to Aunt Mavis and bowed.

'What's this all about?' asked Davidia. She had to know the ins and outs of all the weird events. 'I didn't know Aunt Mavis had any servants.'

'Thank you, Scrool, now I understand,' said Aunt Mavis, sounding appreciative.

'Understand what?' Davidia had to know.

Aunt Mavis ignored the question, stood up and approached both scrolls. She placed one hand on each scroll and rolled them into a fist. She lit up like a Christmas tree too. The girls were mortified. Was aunty a witch burning at the stake? Fear arrived uninvited and gave the girls a few tough moments. As quickly as it had begun, it finished. Aunt Mavis was still with us and hadn't changed in any way. Both scrolls returned to their previous locations and performed as expected, rolled up and immobile as records of an ancient history. It was quiet once again. The girls waited breathlessly for an explanation. It was exciting being in the company of Aunt Mavis. Davidia thought her mum would be impressed when she returned home with stories to tell of the recluse everyone had an ignorant opinion of. Aunt Mavis gathered the girls close by. They all sat cosily on soft cushions, legs crossed and ears open. There was a short history to be told; however, once said it couldn't be repeated. It was to be an informative but forgetful experience. Live in the moment to enjoy the details which fade almost as quickly as given. It goes like this. Aunt Mavis began.

'A long time ago, when Scrool's family was dumped on the area of the Humpletoon quarry, one relative had to be sacrificed as a title deed to ensure the safety of the group. They were separated from their family to live a lonely existence as a scroll of truth. The Scrollingers knew of the importance of ownership, having been evicted from their own country. They didn't want any repeats, so one member became the title deed scroll to protect them all. The name of the member was called Aunty and that name was entered on the deed. It was filed in the council titles office archives. No one knew or cared for its existence until the discovery of the red rubies, the eyes of the Scrollingers. The title deed needed a real person in human form to legally protect the quarry land. It was unfortunate that there was no real deed in evidence to avoid the land being turned into a quarry. It was assumed that the council owned it. So, a search began for a protector. I received a vision when young. It was unexplainable, but there it was, "Come save me." As a young child, I was receptive to suggestions and the Scrollingers took that as a sign and changed the title deed into my name, Mavis. They had no trust in anyone who wasn't receptive to their message. It turned out I was the only receptor. Later on in life, when things took a turn for the worse, I heard the message again and for some inexplicable reason, I chose Humpletoon to settle in without knowing why. I needed to escape my past. This land was all that was on offer at the time and when I turned up at the council offices to purchase the land, imagine my surprise when found out I was already the owner. The title deed has been seen by the mayor and the councillors. They tried for years to remove me. Now you know why I live here as I do.'

'But you live alone,' said Davidia. 'Don't you have any friends?'

She felt sad under all that hair. Her pain couldn't be seen. Aunt Mavis replied, 'Only two.'

The girls were pleased that they knew the truth about the scrolls and Aunt Mavis.

'How is it that you are a distant relative of mine? I'd never even known you existed before this trip,' said Davidia. The connection hadn't been quite made yet. 'My mum said that you were a distant relative and it wasn't meant to be that you live far away.'

'It's a technical term really. As a child, I was great friends with your grandfather and spent many years sharing school times, stories, visits and attending family social functions. I became sort of an adopted family member. When families moved away as time passed, the association diminished; however, I occasionally sent a postcard wondering how things had turned out for your family. Your mum was too young to really remember me. Stories, myths and misunderstandings have perpetrated history about me. So, I'm not really a blood relative, but a distant one. It's been a heavy night. I thank you for what you did tonight. I originally thought that you had been up to real mischief and problems would come my way. I was wrong. The title deeds are now safe and I have just the place for them.'

Aunt Mavis placed the title deed scroll on the shelf next to its other family member. Davidia could have sworn that a red light greeting passed between them, but couldn't be sure as she rubbed her tired eyes with both fists which blurred her vision. It was a nice thought anyway.

Aunt Mavis now made real sense to Davidia.

Slirander was restless that night. She had received a distress signal from Milo Mac. Tomorrow she would follow it up. Where was he?

*   *   *

It was dark. Mervyn had requisitioned the council digger for a few days on the pretence that his farming property needed a new dam to be repaired. The council staff prepared the correct paperwork so he had a legal permit to operate that machine.

'I wasn't aware that you had a heavy vehicle licence to operate the digger,' said an observant staffer.

It must have been mentioned after their coffee break that

each working day was short. That's when the brighter questions arise.

'My staff possess that capacity,' said Mervyn.

'Any damage to the equipment is payable by you,' the staffer continued.

'I'm well aware of that. Is there anything else you want?'

'That about does it. Sign here and we are all sweet.'

Mervyn signed and didn't read the small print. It was assumed that he understood it. He mumbled that he could understand the public frustration at times with council workers.

He went in search of Chad to pass on his good news; a permit.

*   *   *

'I need to see Milo Mac. Something is bothering him. He signalled me last night,' said Slirander, who had actually frowned her perfectly wrinkle-free forehead with worry lines.

'Where is he?' asked Davidia.

'I think he went home with Eleanor, but I'm unsure if he's still there. It's just a feeling I have.'

'He hasn't been stolen or smashed, has he?' queried Davidia.

'I think he's in a bad place. It's the vibe he sent me. It shook my comfort zone of trust. It's difficult to explain.'

'Ring Eleanor and we can visit him to check on his safety status.'

Slirander rang Eleanor who was busily fussing over grandma and explaining that her new mug had been misplaced for a short period of time and it would turn up unscathed.

'But where is my mug? I loved its handles and funny face,' said grandma, who saw by feel. Suddenly, the telephone rang. It was Slirander. She had taken the lead over Milo Mac's safety and whereabouts.

'Hello, Eleanor speaking,' she answered, wondering whether it was a pest or one of those waste-of-time calls from an Asian country wanting to check her electricity plan, suggest fluorescent light replacements or a dating site for an emotional rip-off. Fortunately, it was none of those.

'Hello, it's Slirander speaking. I met your mug at the Humpletoon Mug Festival and wanted to catch up with him.'

Eleanor wondered if it was a crank. Who meets up with whose mug? It sounds plain stupid. She carefully posed her follow-up line to fathom a truth.

'What is it you want to discuss with the mug?' She didn't really believe she was having a discussion about a mug as it if was "alive".

'He sent me a message and I wondered if he was in any trouble.' Eleanor was about to hang up when Slirander continued. 'His name is Milo Mac and I was on the same table right next to him. We got along very well.' Eleanor went to reach for the insanity pills if there were any nearby.

'We are discussing my grandma's mug, aren't we? You haven't taken a voice substance or pill to derail any common sense, have you?'

'Certainly not!' replied an indignant Slirander.

Then the penny dropped. The realisation that they were chatting about the same thing, but from different pages dawned on Slirander and she agreed that it would sound weird to Eleanor. To her, it was an inanimate object, not a fellow conversationalist. A quick correction of misunderstanding was needed.

'My apologies, I'm off in forgetful land. It was my Aunt Mavis mug that was next to yours on the table and sitting there together, they seemed to be a perfect set of matching mugs. I still have mine and thought that a photograph together with the festival winner would be a lovely gift for my Aunt Mavis, who doesn't get out much these days.'

That sounded far more plausible. A U-curve in explanation had landed Slirander with the positive result she was after.

'That sounds a great idea, but my mug isn't here at the moment. I took it to the mayor's house where Merrilyn, the lady mayoress, is looking after it for a week. Apparently, all mug festival winners get to visit and stay at the house for a week. It's a tradition of some sort. I don't know what she does with them. She could use them to drink from or just admire them as an ornament.'

'Perhaps I should visit, take my Aunt Mavis mug and have the photograph taken there? Would you like a copy? We may even get Merrilyn to hold them both for us. It would be great for a local charity fundraiser.'

'That sounds like an excellent idea. I look forward to a signed photographed copy by Merrilyn and thanks for calling. It did sound a little weird at first, when you rang speaking personally about a mug as if it was a real person. I'm glad you cleared that up. Bye.'

Eleanor hung up. Slirander hung up. That was the end of the conversation. Silence followed. It was occasionally known as the shadow of the mind that let thought seepage occur during that quiet lull. Slirander's brain operated as a permanently empty thought bowl constantly filled by replacement thoughts. It was a high-intensity space. Davidia had the manners not to interrupt during the conversation, but once completed, her high-intensity area had to have a refill also.

'What did she say?'

'Milo Mac is at the home of the mayor being looked after by his wife. I feel our help is needed.'

'What shall we do?'

'I need to go as an Aunt Mavis mug. You will have to take me there. We also need a camera. Aunt Mavis may have one.'

'Do I have to carry you all that way?'

'I will go with you dressed as Aunt Mavis. The villagers will stare at us, but who cares. No one will bother us as they think we're cursed anyway.'

Slirander selected an Aunt Mavis' costume, because that's what they really were, a clothing shell in which to hide. When fully-rigged, she bent over in theme and was a perfect replica of Aunt Mavis. God, she was a good actress. Davidia went as herself. No one was going to curse her. Will the real Aunt Mavis please stand-up?

'Take this with you,' said the real Aunt Mavis. 'This town has taken an intense dislike to rumours, myths and an old lady near the quarry. If trouble erupts, there may be an intelligent thought hanging around town and this might be handy.' She gave Davidia a child's toy which looked exactly like Aunt Mavis.

'Do you want me to drop this in at the opportunity shop for resale?' said Davidia. 'It's not a sale sample, is it?'

She thought that she was too old for kids' toys and didn't want to start playing with them again. She was a growing teenager and the past sometimes had to be left behind.

'Be careful. The lady mayoress is a formidable opponent and someone not to trust. Her knives of retort and her eyes of daggers have destroyed the happiness of a few townspeople especially where male counterparts have been involved. You two will be impossible to intimidate. I know I've tried and you rise above it. Your friend Milo Mac does have a problem, but it can only be solved by you two. I'm inert to assist outside my home. That is part of my caretaker role. I can protect what I own, but not what I don't own. Stay alert. If Mervyn is home, pass him off as a parasitic insect.'

There was an edge of venom in that comment. Only Aunt Mavis had it.

Davidia took the toy. Slirander was dressed to annoy and

enhance the myth. Two bright-eyed girls left Aunt Mavis sitting in her chair of buttons and headed off on their mug mission. She tracked them as they left, thinking she'd like to join them, but that was impossible.

Bats normally don't fly during the day, being nocturnal, however a small invisible bat-force flew after them. They had been retrained for daytime activity by Aunt Mavis and were a safety strategy she employed each time she left the sanctuary of her home. Not everything that flew in the sky was a seagull. Plop!

Who were the mugs?

*   *   *

The walk through the main street of Humpletoon to visit the lady mayoress was a statement of defiance in support of Aunt Mavis. Slirander imitated her perfectly. A group of ladies had gathered outside a clothing retail store, the only one in town. The girls stopped nearby and Slirander deliberately coughed with a dreadful hacking sound. The women scattered in all directions.

'That young girl must be cursed to be in her company,' one worried woman was heard to say.

'Did you see that control stick she had steering her. It was placed directly in her back,' said another.

'She's infectious.'

'Her breath is green.'

'Did anyone see her legs? I didn't. She must have some, mustn't she?' That lady wasn't too sure.

'Those clothes are the worst anybody could dress in this town. The sooner she is got rid of, the better.'

Common sense often had a holiday when myths and misunderstandings arose. It was a field day for the uncommon sense today. The girls stood amused. Slirander had only coughed.

What's the big deal? Davidia realised that maybe a small town wasn't for her in the future. Had they overstepped the mark in testing the town sanity? They were alone. The street was deserted. Even a stray cat eyed them suspiciously. They passed the backpackers hostel and wondered what Beau was doing. He was watching them from an upstairs window dreading a visit once he had seen the ladies' reactions. The window pane acted as a window into the real world and not to be a space for nosey busybodies to peer through and assess others. Curiosity can never be eliminated. They passed by, much to his relief. He liked both girls, but had only seen Davidia with the old hag. Was she now cursed too by being in her company and if he had a date, what ills would befall him? His relationship was on a tenuous footing; well, if he had one in the first place.

The mayor's house with an opulent appearance greeted them with the large front doors supposedly built to reflect the intelligence of its owners. It was early morning. The sun struggled to warmly greet the population. Merrilyn was fully dressed in her period clothing as was her want every day. No one could fathom the need for such an unusual dress code in modern-day Humpletoon. She wasn't auditioning for an English soap opera or an early Australian documentary. The heat would be unbearable in summer. No one knew if she wore it as a protective shield to keep Mervyn away. Idiosyncrasies are difficult to deal with until an understanding is given. Perhaps she would unburden herself to the girls? Yeah, fat chance!

The doorbell waited patiently. A firm push would be today's first function for it. Davidia pushed the button marked Press Here. A music played the familiar tune from "Who wants to be a millionaire?". The ambience was destroyed when a sour-faced Merrilyn opened the door. She hadn't invited anyone for morning tea nor did she appreciate hawkers, especially in the mornings when she was at her most fragile. Her ensemble of good looks hadn't quite been completed. A few wispy strands of hair gave her the appearance of the look of a lady who had enjoyed a night on the tiles. Mervyn wasn't a tiler. She brushed them away. Now a clear visage was available. Appearance improvements aren't always automatic. The shock of seeing Davidia in the company of her Aunt Mavis frightened her. The old lady had never been to her home before and now she was ruining the doorstep. It hadn't cracked. Aunt Mavis was slightly built. The look of horror said it all.

'Stay out of my house. You aren't welcome,' she said, in a high-pitched voice. 'Go. I don't want a curse to be left on my doorstep.'

Suddenly, a few bats imitating a flock of seagulls dropped their welcoming cards on all three, plop! plop! plop! The three of them screamed so loudly the bats considered wearing ear plugs on their next foray. Two performed as actresses and the other as a reality contestant. In the mayhem, Slirander's cloak hit the ground without her inside it. Where did she escape too? Davidia was left alone to clear up her mess and aunty's coat.

'May I come in? This accident needs to be cleaned immediately or the clothing will be ruined and that includes your beautiful dress. These droppings are very acidic,' said Davidia, in the hope that entrance could be gained.

'Five minutes and you are out of here,' yelled Merrilyn, in a state of high panic. She didn't want her dress to be ruined. She dashed inside to the bathroom. 'Sit in the lounge room until I have finished.'

It was all quiet. Mervyn was lurking upstairs and had heard the commotion. He came downstairs to notice a young lady seated in his lounge room. His face turned an ashen colour when he realised who it was. It's that girl again. That Aunt Mavis girl. She reappears like a repetitive, unwanted, boring television commercial. Davidia eyed Mervyn and gave him a courteous smile. She had lots more to share if needed. He acknowledged her presence with a fake smile, the one with the automatic facial reaction to widening one's lips sending a message of pleasure to the receiver, but in reality, it was the non-reaction in the eyes that held the real message. His shot out danger in small, stabbing rhythms at the same rate of his increased heartbeat. Mervyn knew how to squeeze a hand. He put his out for a response.

'Nice to meet you again,' he said, with charming, good manners.

He knew he needed to play the nice card with the relative of the aunty he was trying to evict.

'Good to meet you, Mr Mayor,' replied Davidia.

A first name basis of introduction had not yet happened.

'Call me Mervyn, not many do.' It was obvious he was aware of the town's public opinion. 'Your name seems to escape me each time we meet.'

'It's Davidia. It's a boy's name with an extension.'

'Davidia. It has a nice ring to it. What brings you here to our humble abode?'

What untruth did she have to conjure up? Whatever it was, it had to be laced with bluff. She had only five minutes within which to achieve it. She thought hard. Her reservoir of witty ideas and deep thoughts were on a picnic. How does she explain the disappearance of Slirander; but wait, he doesn't know that she was with him and she was in the lounge room first? A glimmer of brilliance was about to explode. She glanced around the room. On the mantelpiece there were two mugs, Milo Mac and now Aunt Mavis, pretending to be oblivious to the conversation. There was her Aunt Mavis' jacket, worse for wear with a few stained spots and her damaged outfit waiting its turn on a wash. She felt in her pocket for the camera. If Merrilyn doesn't surprise them, then she may get away with it.

'I had heard that the winner of the Dimpletoon Mug Festival

was here and the winning entry had been made from an extraordinary clay. I also had an Aunt Mavis mug made from the same clay and wanted a photograph of them together as a memory for my mother back home. It's odd isn't it that both mugs were made from the same clay.'

'And how do you know this?' Mervyn queried.

His sense of intrigue was aroused. No one knew about that special seam of clay or, more to the point, what it held. Was he to be tripped up?

'My Aunt Mavis told me. She lives next to the quarry.'

'Not for long,' he whispered quietly behind his hand. He almost spat out the words with distaste.

'That's my mug on your mantelpiece next to the festival winner. Don't they make a lovely pair of book ends? I put mine there to take a photo. I hoped Merrilyn could hold one in each hand for me. It could also be placed in the local newspaper; however, if it was you, Mervyn, who held them aloft, it would be a great publicity campaign shot for you.'

Mervyn thought that he'd make a better mug holder than Merrilyn; besides, he was the Mayor. In his anxiousness to impress Davidia, he fumbled in his pocket for the keys to his oak desk drawer. An impressionable young girl might be influenced by what he was about to produce next. Bragging rights can often lead to downright stupidity. Older-age men can have a fat cheque book, wealth and trinkets to shower a young girl and forget that they have a long past, the young girl a long future and the means to achieving both is not necessarily as a duo. Fools don't have to be born at birth; they emerge all throughout life. There is no guarantee that it won't happen to anyone. It felt as if one of those moments was about to emerge. He opened the desk drawer and took out from among the lingerie the red rubies that he coveted. Milo Mac suddenly felt a surge in his aura. Slirander, felt the same as the red rubies were freed momentarily from their incarceration in a desk drawer, albeit made of the finest quality wood.

'This, young lady,' said Mervyn, in a boastful manner, 'is a pair of the finest red rubies ever discovered.' He carefully opened the covering and showed Davidia.

'They look like fake glass to me,' she replied. 'How do I know they're real? I'm not a jeweller. Have you got a certificate of authenticity?'

Questions, questions, what else did he expect? She was a teenager and not yet educated in the wiles of understanding real wealth. Mervyn's jaw sagged with shock at the rebuff. How dare she question his word? He's the mayor. He placed them on the desktop and stood back like a proud parent. Davidia moved closer and as she did so, Mervyn put out an arm to stop a closer inspection.

'That's close enough. Nobody touches them except me.'

'Where did you find them?'

'Nearby,' was all he was prepared to say.

'Can I have that photograph now? You can hold both mugs up like this.'

Davidia acted like a stage director. Mervyn momentarily forgot himself. He was in the company of a beautiful female, yes, she was a young teenager and not unpleasant to the eye; however, recognition of both elements together got lost in the vision and a long memory. He smiled this time with warmth that was previously missing. He stood next to the mantelpiece, picked up both mugs carefully and stood like royalty with two prized polo trophies. Davidia withdrew the camera. Click! The photoshoot was done. She replaced the camera in her pocket and Mervyn replaced the two mugs back on the mantelpiece, one with a minor controversy.

'You look familiar,' he said, staring at the Aunt Mavis mug.

Who did it remind him of? It twigged that was his nemesis. The blockage to his wealth plan. He slammed it down hard enough to send a painful feeling through her base. She wasn't going to morph into his rotten facial features no matter how hard he stared even though it was a condition of her construction. The distraction was sufficient for the red rubies to send an unseen alert signal to Milo Mac. He responded with his striped glint glow. Slirander recognised the distress signal. It was now up to Davidia to keep Mervyn's attention whilst she changed her appearance. Davidia got the message.

'Mervyn,' said Davidia, 'have you ever been married before?' Her eyes shone like blue sapphires.

What interest is it of hers about my past? It was odd to say the least. Questions weren't usually of such a high standard. He thought that she may be far older than sixteen. She acted like it.

'No. One life sentence is enough,' he muttered. He surprised himself with the directness of his answer.

'Have you any siblings? I have a brother who drives me crazy at times, but I love him.'

'I have a brother and used to have a sister. Have you met Chad at the pottery? That's him. I had forgotten him and he suddenly turns up at the pottery. Some people are cursed with bad luck. Apparently, he's been there for years probably in hiding, who knows? I never visited that place with all that filth and the smell of clay. Now it has the smell of money.'

'What about your sister?'

'What about her?'

'Haven't you kept in touch?'

'Not for decades. I have no idea of her whereabouts and what's more, I don't care. She was nothing but trouble. She had weird and unusual habits. I can't stand her.'

Davidia sensed a pensive Mervyn and couldn't understand

why? His head was staring at the carpet, a forlorn and lonely object even though it was still attached to all his other parts. He wasn't trying to detect any dust mites, determine the depth of pile or trace a footprint he'd made; it was as if the lump on his shoulder, his head, was becoming too heavy with its in-tray of information, responsibility and how he'd cheat that old lady out of her land. It was a thought mixture that was toxic. Whilst an element of feeling sorry for himself existed, Davidia, for an inexplicable reason, put her hand in her pocket and withdrew that Aunt Mavis toy that peeved her off so much for having to carry it. The child had left home. It felt squishy in her hand rather like those squishy gel balls. Was the substance similar and would it react in the same way? Mervyn was in sorry land. Davidia squeezed the toy. It shrunk then expanded. It didn't do much, so she left it on the table. She glanced over at Milo Mac and Slirander who sat there silently and immobile. The red rubies sat on the desktop, ripe for stealing or recovering. All this seemed to have taken far longer than five minutes and Davidia wondered whether Merrilyn would arrive at any moment and kick her out. Time seemed suspended.

'We need to retrieve those red rubies,' said Slirander. 'This is our chance.'

'Well, I can't do anything from here,' replied Milo Mac.

'Stay alert and keep guard. There is a way.'

The Aunt Mavis toy on the tabletop began to spin. Small flecks of dust flew directly at Slirander and settled on her surface. She glinted in acknowledgement of the visit. Her mug shape began to flatten — quite similar to what occurred at the mug festival — and before long she was a misshapen mug masquerading as distorted rubbish tip molten glass that had been melted in a fire. It was a most undignifying shape. She began to move along the mantelpiece toward the red rubies, leaving dirty scrape marks requiring a repaint. She thought, '*The deeper, the better.*' A flashing red light emanated from the red rubies and suddenly they were sucked up by Slirander in a vacuuming extraction, leaving behind a lingerie home that could double as another useful item. She regained her shape and once again represented a perfect identikit of Aunt Mavis.

'How do you do that?' asked Milo Mac.

He had talent, sure, but felt inadequate with that powerful female display.

'It's a family secret,' replied Slirander.

'Won't the mayor notice the disappearance of the red rubies? It will be rather obvious that they aren't there.'

'Watch closely.'

Both mugs waited a few seconds. The Aunt Mavis toy floated across to the desktop and settled into the previous lingerie home of the red rubies. They noticed a few moments of bumpiness and then it settled. It was done. A duplication and replication had taken place by the Aunt Mavis toy. It carried within it a duplicate set of red rubies of inferior quality that weren't the eyes of the Scrollinger rubies. They were the fakes that Davidia mentioned earlier pretending they were fakes, but those ones weren't.

'You still here,' said Merrilyn, in a high state of alert. She wasn't meeting Chad, was she? 'What's this? He hasn't shown you those red rubies, has he? I'll have your guts for garters if any have gone missing. You stupid man.'

Mervyn innocently mumbled that he'd shown them because they were so beautiful and matched the sapphire coloured eyes of their guest. He wasn't quite colour-blind, but blinded nevertheless. Youth had a way of deflecting the truth. Merrilyn wasn't convinced.

'How do you know that little tart wasn't purposefully sent here to spy on us?'

'My Aunt Mavis wouldn't do that. She has proper manners and is honest. I'm not a food item either,' replied Davidia.

Merrilyn was getting up her nose and if she had the magical powers, she would stuff her in there and have the most gigantic sneeze to dispense her into a waste tissue. What happened to the nice – was she ever nice – Merrilyn that some others knew? She wasn't currently at home. Perhaps she was visiting elsewhere.

'Where are those rubies?' Merrilyn made a beeline for them.

She flipped open the cover and saw that her precious items were accounted for. She quickly folded them up.

'It's time you left and took your stupid mug with you. Whilst you are at it, take that other ugly mug that won the festival competition too. I don't need to be reminded that I didn't win the title.'

Merrilyn was a boiling kettle almost ready to spill its contents. She had a duo of hot air and hot water swirling around her.

'What about washing my clothes and my coat?'

'Let them rot. Where's that old lady you came with? Lost in the toilet, is she? You ruined my dress too. Those spots have rotted the fabric. It will cost a fortune to repair. I'm sending you the bill. Why haven't you left already? You do know the meaning of exit and get out, don't you? Act upon it. Go!'

The nasty ambience was getting worse. Davidia picked up both mugs, her Aunt Mavis coat and walked toward the door.

'I suppose a photograph is out of the question,' said Davidia, cheekily.

'The only thing I'm giving you is your marching orders. Don't ever set foot in this house again.'

'It mightn't be yours for much longer,' replied Davidia, with her own nasty twang. She had no idea where that came from, but it was now said and one must live with the spoken word. 'I have a photograph of Mervyn instead of you. The three mugs will be the highlight.' She smiled one of the many she possessed.

'You cheeky little b…. I'll have words with your mother.'

It was a silly, veiled threat. She didn't even know who her mother was or where she lived.

Once outside the front door, Davidia dropped the Aunt Mavis coat on the ground and it instantly inflated. Her friend Slirander was back and she had one less mug to carry. Milo Mac was grateful for being removed from the mayor's house. As they walked away, a loud female voice overrode the stereo system and it sounded like someone was in the doghouse. There was no barking response, just a low-level whimper.

'Aunt Mavis was right. You don't cross swords with that maniac. Are we unscathed? I wonder what she is up to. Those red rubies have gone and now all the eyes of Scrollinger have been returned. What next?'

The two friends and their new mug friend happily walked back through Humpletoon. They ignored the window snoopers. Slirander had a stroke of genius and instead of stooping to perpetrate the bent over, old- lady myth, she stood tall and straight as a steel pole. There were gasps of disbelief from inside many a home. What had they witnessed? It was a miracle of sainthood proportions. A few members of the public were in the street walking pets and chatting with friends when they saw Aunt Mavis walk toward them. Their mouths stayed open in shock. After so many years feeling sorry for the old lady, had she magically been cured of her stoop? It would take some convincing.

One lady they passed shut her eyes to avoid being cursed with a direct stare – not that her face could be seen – and yelled out, 'I've been infected.' With what she had no idea. Inside her eyelid a vein had quivered with nervousness and she mistook this as the cause of her new affliction, which was only a case of nerves.

'Where did you get that cure? It's not possible to straighten a deformed spine so well. There must be a trick to it,' said another.

The recovery spread like wildfire around town, even though it was still awash with persistent rumours about the curse. Ask anyone in town what was Aunt Mavis' curse that had secretly been put there and they would only shake their heads. No one could definitively explain its existence, but everyone knew it existed.

'My son fell over on the way to school today. There was no hump where he fell, but I'm sure he was deliberately tripped. He said he saw someone lurking in the bushes nearby wearing a long coat. That could only be that witch on the hill. Nobody else dressed like that.'

A few days later, a suspicious character who had been spending more time in the bushes than necessary had been apprehended. It was these movements that had distracted the boy and caused his minor accident. Aunt Mavis was nowhere near. So, the myths abounded about blaming an innocent, old lady for the ills of Humpletoon inhabitants. From little things, big things grow. That was certainly true about witchcraft, real or imagined.

Another lady was seen running frantically down the main street with a face full of pain. She dashed into the hotel where Mr Hoarse witnessed the commotion. She ran through his establishment, slammed open a door which barely withstood the impact and later, a quiet rush of running water followed by a huge 'Ah!' She returned with a ruddy complexion, wet hair with water from the wash basin and panting heavily.

'Who was chasing you?' asked Mr Hoarse.

'I had wind from that end of town to here,' the lady replied. 'I was desperate to locate a respite centre such as this establishment.'

'That's where that old lady lives. Did she scare you? I bet she sent a wind demon after you.'

'It was constipation.'

'So, that's what the wind was called. She even gave it a name. No wonder you were frightened.'

The story of a dangerous wind myth chasing innocent folk had arrived. The local press gave it a kick-start too.

'She really does have legs,' observed a male across the street. 'They don't look too bad from this distance for a senior person.'

The ripple effect of walking tall had everybody abuzz with curiosity. The coat no longer dragged along the ground as a street sweeper. Her legs acted in a coordinated fashion as they should. She was taller than many and her whole demeanour had changed her appearance. Slirander felt as if she had unlocked a part of Aunt Mavis that was afraid to embrace the general public.

What will she say now?

11 CONFLICT

Aunt Mavis was waiting for the girls' return to confirm that the red ruby eyes had been returned safely to Scrool and passed on to the country of Scrollinger. All missing eyes had now been found. There were no further outstanding stolen rubies to search for. Harmony could once again exist within the clay seam. It felt whole again. A peaceful life should be a future improvement for the Scrollingers.

What about Aunt Mavis' future?

She felt that the visit by the two girls had been therapeutic for her and gave her a glimpse into enjoying life if others were let into her emotional family. For too many years she had deliberately remained hidden. Perhaps it was time for a personality and social rebirth. The art of stooping and not acquiring any friends had left her emotional sack rather light-on; in fact, near empty. Within the confines of her home she was able to be herself which nobody else had seen. To the outside world she was a witch to be feared and not the nice person she really was. Her past created the problem, perhaps now it was time for a correction. Her delicate pottery hands also hid the secret occupation she had practised in full view of the townspeople. Nobody had ever recognised her "other" personality. Can you think of who that might be? Before melancholy visited, that wasn't the name of another unhappy relative, she heard the twitter of two girls probably discussing their latest beaus, or was that Beau? She decided not to sit in her chair of buttons. Instead she would stand to face some of her own fears and not use a mechanical object to do her bidding. Her comfort blanket, her chair — even though it was for the lower part of her anatomy, sat alone and ignored. It didn't misbehave with the sleight it had just received. Happy homecoming was about to erupt. The tension was electric, filling the room with emotional uncertainty. Beads of sweat gathered together to gang-tackle her body with a wet outcome.

The girls arrived in good spirits. Davidia felt immediately, that something was different. Slirander, still in theme, standing tall, felt it too. Milo Mac was only visiting and his involvement wasn't warranted.

'Aunt Mavis, you aren't in your chair,' said a very surprised Davidia. 'Is something wrong?'

She couldn't see that there was. This was the first time she had seen her out of the chair in her home. She really could walk and those rumours about floating without legs were quite untrue.

Slirander was almost as tall as Aunt Mavis. The two of them stood eyeing each other with what they could see from underneath all that hair. They could be identical twins. The shock of the stand-up had three women frozen in time. It took a moment or two before the brave Aunt Mavis walked forward and firstly hugged Davidia then Slirander. The tears of relief and joy that cascaded down her face unseen matted some of her long tresses and made an embarrassing puddle on the floor.

'You haven't, have you, Aunt Mavis?' said an astonished Davidia, observing the growing water trickle on the floor.

'No. I'm sorry. I haven't hugged anyone in years and I was afraid to do it. Now, it is such a relief. I had forgotten how warm another person could be and the good feelings that emanate from it. Thanks. Do I really look like that?' she directed at Slirander, who nodded with a big smile also unseen.

'I think it's time to take off the façade and reveal your true self. For me, it's a game of theatrical proportions for a short-term purpose, but maybe for you it's rather more serious,' said a sixteen-year-old girl, wise beyond her years.

Often Slirander and Davidia would jokingly add up their ages to make thirty-two and then act as that older-age adult. It was a girl thing. You had to be there in the moment.

'I'm afraid,' said Aunt Mavis, trembling.

Davidia walked over and gave her a huge Davidia hug. Any young nubile male would be impressed with that feeling and wish that they were all Aunt Mavis mugs when those were being given out. The embrace was eagerly received and they stood there like conjoined twins, shedding tears of happiness.

'Don't be afraid,' said Davidia, 'we are your friends.'

That word "friends" sounded like a symphony orchestra playing its heart out.

'I'd give her a hug too, if I could,' yelled out Milo Mac.

He didn't want to left out of the goodwill games.

Slirander suddenly gained everyone's attention by clapping loudly. Look at me, look at me, she seemed to say.

'Aunt Mavis, I am going to remove my costume because that's all it is and I encourage you to do the same,' said Slirander. 'Do you think you can do it? It's time.'

'I've never undressed in front of anyone before. I've never been married or had that other experience of male associations. I assume that happens sometimes.'

Both girls nodded knowingly. They were avid readers.

'Kindly concentrate on the now. Copy me.'

Aunt Mavis had realised that to improve her life maybe, just maybe, she had to dramatically change her existence and that may include leaving the Ring of Clay as its custodian and the curse that she lived under as its protector. It wasn't a witch curse, but one nevertheless. She was tired of hiding and from what? Her past was about to be faced with a kick fair-and-square up its backside. Even with the routine of disrobing, although there were plenty of underneath subsidiary layers of clothing to avoid any modesty embarrassment, it was the outer layer that hid the truth. There was no sensuous pole music played or stage on which to perform. It was only the hat, hair and coat performance, a quick three-act play. In there amongst Aunt Mavis' three items was a recent lifetime of emotional baggage. It clung like Gladwrap inside her mind. Slirander made the first move as leading lady. At school she often had that role in the plays. It was a position she enjoyed most, being first.

The audience of Davidia and Milo Mac waited patiently for a new beginning for Aunt Mavis. Off came Slirander's hat. She flicked it with the flourish of an expert frisbee competitor. It landed perfectly on the table as if it was a thrown quoit.

'You next, Aunt Mavis,' encouraged Slirander.

'I've got a migraine. I need water. I need rest. Where's my chair?'

Aunt Mavis had raised her hand to remove her hat when an emotional paralysis gripped her arm. It was a muscle cramp; however, that could be easily soothed and overcome. Davidia stood in her space to prevent her seeking refuge elsewhere. Seeing her escape passage blocked, the girls were surprised to hear an unpleasant expletive. It had unintentionally escaped during her emotional panic. A minute passed. No one was going anywhere. Aunt Mavis raised her arm again and there was no barrier this time to grasping her hat and elevating it from her head. The scene depicted an old, silent movie in black and white with characters making all sorts of gestures without sound. She held it for a few moments delivering, in her mind, its last rites before it was permanently discarded as an essential perceived witch's accessory. She placed it on the table carefully as if bidding goodbye to a long-term friend. It was goodbye and hopefully good-riddance. She no longer needed it. When it rains an umbrella would adequately suffice. A small applause erupted from the girls.

'Well done. How do you feel?' asked Slirander.

'It was rather heavy. I feel light-headed. My head moves much easier.'

A few more head rolls and calm pervaded her. The first chink in her emotional armour had been chipped, well, placed, away. Next item was the cloak. It was her emotional armour. It had to date deflected many an inquisitive look and conversation. It had been her prime defence of defiance against anyone wanting to know her. Today, it was just an old, worn piece of clothing that needed replacing with a modern look. The girls could provide an exciting shopping excursion to purchase clothes for the "new me".

Slirander removed her coat first. It was simple and easy. She threw it over a chair. Underneath she had her normal clothing. To her it was a game of charades.

'It's your turn, Aunt Mavis.'

Without her hat, her long tresses cascaded around her body like a hairy waterfall. It hadn't been cut in decades. No telling what the ends were like. However, the coat! It was all about the coat. The particular one she wore was duplicated by many others so the removal of the one would be symbolic that all of them are removed together. Her body began to sway. It was turmoil in there. How vulnerable would she feel afterwards? She had a feeling of nakedness, but wasn't. It was a waiting game.

'Can I assist you, aunty?' offered Davidia, hoping to ease the trauma.

'Stay away,' she snapped. 'Can't you see I'm busy? I can't find the buttons. Did you take them?'

A slender pointed finger headed her way with menace dangling from the fingernail. Davidia wondered if she was going to be stabbed. Fortunately, she stood at a safe distance and aunty's arm wasn't long enough to reach, otherwise a painful jab would have occurred.

'Take your time. It's not a game of strip-jack-naked.'

That was a popular card game when alcoholic bravado overrode good sense. There wasn't any alcohol in the house. The girls waited again. Firstly, a few jittery fingers searched for the release buttons with some success. Her hands shook quickly as if cooling them under a hot air-drying machine in a public convenience. A second button released its defensive hold. The coat loosened. Then a third button agreed with the first two. Harmony pervaded. Aunt Mavis was frightened to finally reveal what she was under her coat. She was really a tall, striking woman and not the insipid, old witch she had played to a treat to the townspeople of Humpletoon. A vast emotional rearrangement was occurring as the coat loosened even further. Finally, she felt progress had been made and she was excited by the prospect of removing the coat permanently. There was more to life than old clothes and loneliness. If only she had recognised her predicament years earlier. The fanfare chorus was about to erupt. Aunt Mavis had all buttons separated from their hugging epaulets and it was ready for discarding.

'Girls, would you each take a corner?'

The girls did so. They spread the coat like a flying saucer and without a hint of nerves Aunt Mavis took three giant steps, one for each of them, and walked out from under her coat. The girls gasped in surprise. She was wearing their favourite coloured pantaloons, which were now a fashion icon.

'Aunt Mavis!' Davidia squealed, excitedly. 'You're colour coordinated. Wow! That's a surprise.'

'I don't feel naked,' said Aunt Mavis, still shaking like a recoiled spring. She walked around the room free of her burden. 'It feels good to move so quickly once again. Perhaps tomorrow I'll jog.'

'Don't get too excited. Your hair has to be reduced as the final emotional makeover. Then we can see the real you. You might even look like me,' said Davidia.

'She definitely won't look like me,' yelled out Milo Mac, reminding the girls of his presence.

'How do you really feel?' questioned Slirander.

She'd seen a friend of hers at school tell fibs about how well she was. After a trip to hospital with a ruptured appendix requiring removal, she wasn't that well after all. Psychiatric counselling followed.

'Better than I thought. I need a mirror.'

She walked to a wall and her reflection bounced back beautifully. It revealed a tall woman with strong thighs and finely shaped legs. Her body had retained its shape quite well. It wasn't just at that model standard level, but for older-age men, it still appeared to possess appeal. She admired herself. Her confidence of de-shackling her life with two simple removals of a hat and coat made her nod with approval to take the next step. She was also intrigued at what she looked like. It had been many years since the last sighting. Her femininity was returning. Should she have a perm, a blow wave, a gel basin special or a crew- cut wave with hair channels? It hadn't taken Aunt Mavis too long to embrace future possibilities. There was probably a new set to experience, seeing it was years ago since she last embraced her femininity.

'Aunt Mavis, please sit here,' said Davidia, directing foot traffic like a traffic warden to a large chair nearby. 'I'll cut your hair.'

'No, you won't. I'll do it,' said Slirander, as she pulled off her wig and tossed it randomly into the air. Where it landed didn't matter. Her performance was over.

'She's my aunty, so I'll do it,' reinforced Davidia.

'You don't know how to cut hair, but I, on the other hand, can,' replied Slirander.

'I don't recall shearing your pet dog and that mangy cat of yours. A proper certificate in hairdressing doesn't qualify either, whereas I cut my mother's hair and she complimented me about how nice it looked.'

'Does she also tell you that on the same day she visits the proper hairdresser for a redo and repair job?'

The childish spat was getting out of hand.

'Girls, I will do it myself. It is my problem.'

Aunt Mavis was very firm. She went to her chair of buttons, pressed an impressive array of them and soon a small robotic butler entered carrying a set of very sharp garden shears. It was followed by a short walking ladder followed by a bucket with legs sloshing fresh water, followed by a set of the finest manicured scissors set every hairdresser would die for, followed by a team of individual shampoos, conditioners, skin creams, make-up remover, blush, rouge and a pile of hot towels.

'Where did all this come from?' asked a stunned Davidia.

The girls had paused in their disagreement.

'I once was a real hairdresser myself in the town I lived in. When I left, I thought that my skills stayed too; however, with you two arguing over who should cut my hair, it was only fair that I did it. I didn't want any fallout between two friends who have helped me enormously. Besides, it will give me an opportunity to test myself. I have to try.'

The girls sheepishly looked at each other and laughed. The tension was kicked to the curb.

'Is that a remote in your hand?' asked Davidia.

'Yes. Watch closely.'

Aunt Mavis whispered into it. It was voice controlled. The robotic butler placed the ladder at the rear of Aunt Mavis. It picked up the garden shears, climbed the ladder and began snipping. Her hair was clean from an early morning wash. It sliced cleanly and fell onto the floor in a huge pile. There was enough to fill a queen-size doona. The robot had cut to the base of the skull. It was a simple basin cut as if a pot had been placed on her head and cut around the edges. The 1920s were looking good. Her face hadn't still been revealed. She needed a moment to feel the freedom of the weight being removed.

'That's an amazing feeling,' she said. 'A burden has been lifted from my shoulders. I feel so light-headed.'

The "new" aunt was slowly adjusting to the weight loss. She pressed another button. Wild screams could be heard. They saw about ten bats flying toward them. They hoped they weren't a target for guano.

'We are being attacked,' said Davidia, as she ducked behind Slirander for protection.

'Meet the hairdressing team,' said Aunt Mavis. 'This is Simpson, that's Precipity, over there is Hyacinth with Metamorphis, Lemondal, Mygrain, Blutentail, Jugalong, Jogalong and Singalong. They know what to do next.'

Like a set of precision team instruments, they selected the various products on the floor and did a complete make-over. Aunt Mavis' face was now revealed. She took a moment before she turned around. The girls were anxious to see if she was as pretty as them. A surprise was in store. What was it? Had she three eyes, one ear and no nose? Was she Uncle Mavis? It couldn't be that much of a surprise, surely? She only had a hairdressing appointment.

'I was a little firmer there. Had fewer wrinkles there and was

much fresher. It's nice to meet you again after all these years.'
Did she expect a reply?

Aunt Mavis smiled at herself. She had actually worn rather
well. There were still a few years left in her tank. The reveal, it's
all about the reveal. Aunt Mavis slowly turned around and faced
the two girls. Their eyes glowed brightly. She was beautiful for an
older-age woman. A visit to town would certainly create interest.
No one would know what or who she was. Her new title would
be "stranger".

'What do you think, girls?'

'It certainly is a surprise. You have the most brilliant red eyes
and your forehead has the implications of a scroll shape that's
barely visible. Are you really my Aunt Mavis?'

'In every way; however, the Scrollingers have made me part
of their family also. It's a sort of complimentary compromise.'

'It's your eyes. Are they red ruby eyes?' asked Slirander. She
had a feeling about them.

'Yes. That last pair you obtained from the mayor's house
belonged to me. They had been misplaced. Mine are a dull red
usually, but brighten up when danger appears. The return of that
last pair has given me the vision to see past my pert little nose
and realise, with your help, that I shouldn't hide any longer. We
have a job to do and that is to protect the Ring of Clay.'

'It isn't under threat, is it? There's nothing happening in the
quarry,' said Davidia.

'How do you feel about your reappearance?' said Slirander.

Aunt Mavis thought for a moment.

'Comfortable. To prove it to myself, we should walk into town
and see if anyone recognises me.'

'No one has seen your face, so how will anyone know who you
are?' commented Davidia.

Davidia wondered who she expected to see and know her after

all these years. Maybe Humpletoon should be called Simpletoon if she believed that to be the case. She may be drawing on emotional straws as a desperate effort to be known. It was a mystery. Why is it so?

'There may be a surprise. Grab our hats and coats, oops, I mean let's go. I don't need that emotional camouflage anymore. What a relief.'

She grabbed one hand from each girl and the three little kids left the building for town.

Was any shopping on the agenda?

A new Aunt Mavis had arrived.

*   *   *

That afternoon, three skittish girls descended into Humpletoon for an afternoon of girly treats visiting the one main clothing shop with outdated apparel, the local pub for a sip of probably recycled fluids and, of course, the town's pride and glory, the pottery. That was about it, except for the mayor's residence. Aunt Mavis wore sunglasses to protect her eyes from the glare. The streets were littered with scurrying residents all going somewhere in a complex pattern of movement. The backpacker residents still used the side streets as their piece of paradise, a cement pavement to sleep on and a doorway arch as a roof. What else did they need? It was a busy day. Three good-looking women don't go unnoticed very easily.

'Who is your friend?' said the shopkeeper of garments hidden under plastic. She hadn't seen this lady in town before and naturally her curiosity arose.

'This is my Aunt Mavis' younger sister,' said Davidia, being a bit mistruthful. 'She arrived earlier today to visit my Aunt Mavis. She's ever so much fun.'

'You mean she's related to the old witch out at the quarry. Do you carry the family curse?' It was direct and straight to the point. She didn't want to risk an infection.

'What curse would that be?' asked Aunt Mavis. 'You aren't selling any, are you?'

'I don't sell them. I'm affected by them.'

'Can you kindly show me what one is like? I'm curious to know. It's all new to me.'

'Personally, I'm fresh out of curse stock, but someone brought one in the other day. It was terrible. I'm not sure where she found it. It was nearing dark when she heard a wild scream coming from behind a paling fence. It scared the living daylights out of her. She carefully crept up to the fence and a knot that had its centre missing was the ideal peephole. She squinted to get a closer view when a gush of water squirted her. She was convinced it wasn't a fountain, but there it was. A small fountain wet her. Suddenly, a ferocious roar arose and a fight ensued. It was awful. She managed to peer over the fence and saw a long coat disappear into the bushes. No one around here wears a coat like that so it had to be the witch. I'm not going near that fence. It's cursed.'

The truth of the matter was that an owner had taken his two pet dogs for a walk at night and as sniffing animals do to mark their territory, it had light relief on the snoopy peephole at eye level and the lady was the unintentional victim. C'est le vie!

Aunt Mavis knew better not to reason why, just nod and accept it as a colourful interlude in someone's life.

'It's nice to meet you face to face.'

'Have we met before? You seem familiar but you're not. It's these tablets I'm on. You should take some. Frisky is the word. Enjoy your walk.'

'There's nothing here worth buying,' said Davidia. 'We've been here before and, believe me, the city is the spot; however, if we all wanted to dress like the previous Aunt Mavis, then this would be that spot.' All three smiled. It was great for Aunt Mavis to relax.

'I'd like to visit the pottery. There is someone I want to reacquaint myself with,' said Aunt Mavis, wistfully.

Her mind wandered along an untrodden path that had been hidden under an emotional cloak for years and now she was daring to reveal that darkened past or at least put it to the test.

'Who would you know there? You have always lived out of town,' said Davidia, wondering if she had forgotten to take her sanity pills. How could she know anyone? She was a recluse.

'Life is full of surprises and disappointments. This might be a sharing of both.'

Davidia was thinking about the what, why, when and how of the visit. She shook her head in concern. Was a disaster waiting? More to the point, was anything waiting? Ah, well, go with the flow and see what arises or erupts. Slirander had been there once before with Aunt Mavis when in theme so it was just simply a return visit for her. She had no concerns about Aunt Mavis handling herself. She had a deeper insight than Davidia. They passed other townspeople on their way.

'She's new in town,' one commented.

'I haven't seen her before.'

'She's obviously a city lady,' said another.

'I wonder where she is staying.'

There were lots of sideway glances and conversations hidden by hands. A new topic of conversation had arrived in town. Little did they know that they had discussed her for years.

'Isn't that Merrilyn walking over there?' Aunt Mavis pointed out.

'Yes. She's not wearing her period dress. It was ruined by some bats crapping on it,' laughed Davidia.

'She had your red ruby eyes,' said Slirander, 'and she wasn't giving them up to anyone, not even Mervyn. You were right about her being a nasty bitch.'

'Introduce me.'

'She's too dangerous.'

'Good. I'll be careful then.' Aunt Mavis smiled and this time many others could see it.

The trio diagonally crossed the road. Jay-walking was not a criminal offence, but if brought up at council, it probably would be. They confronted Merrilyn by blocking the footpath. Her passage of forward motion had just been halted. Her face said it all. Anger spits everywhere. A snippy lip was preparing for a blast. Kaboom! Out it came, not as a parcel of saliva, but as a brutal rude grouping of the Queen's best English. Nobody dared block her especially those two girls she had recently ordered out of her home. Who was their guardian? She looked too old to be their mum. If it was, words would be crossed.

'How dare you impede my progress? Public nuisances should be gaoled. Remove your sorry selves or you'll regret this encounter. This is my footpath and my town. Get out of my way. I've important business to attend to.'

Her nostrils flared like an over-exercised horse. Did she stamp her legs preparing to kick someone too? The four women glared at each other; the trio and the tripod. Aunt Mavis' heart skipped a beat. She didn't miss it. She realised that the rude, arrogant character that Merrilyn portrayed still existed, but had hoped the years would change that behaviour. Aunt Mavis had personal insight, but not that of a psychic regardless of how much they got paid.

A very sensible Davidia sensed hostility. It didn't matter who the opponent was. The expectation of wielding power and abusing others rested often in the weirdest of characters. Merrilyn represented herself true to form.

'Mrs Mayor,' began Davidia, repeating the fib, 'this is the younger sister of my Aunt Mavis. She is visiting like we are during school holidays.'

'What do I care who visits that old witch near the quarry? It's time she left town. She gives it a bad name.'

Aunt Mavis stood impassively.

'Has she caused you any harm?' asked Aunt Mavis, careful not to remove her sunglasses. She disguised her voice also.

'What business is that of yours?'

'I would have thought that a harmless, old lady wouldn't be a threat to anyone. My sister might be slightly eccentric but she is rather shy.'

'Tell your sister from me that it's time to move. Progress can't be ignored just because she lives at the quarry. There are expansion plans and she isn't included in them. Now move, otherwise you'll be arrested as a public nuisance.'

David and Slirander were about to unleash their tightly-held tongues when Aunt Mavis gestured that they hold their outbursts. She immediately took off her sunglasses and for a brief moment, stared directly into Merrilyn's eyes. A dull, red light flashed momentarily between them. She then replaced them feigning sun glare. Merrilyn felt empathy, for what she didn't know. Her nastiness abated.

'Have we met before?' she said.

'It's possible; however, I usually stay away from people who are rude and arrogant and think that the sun on their behinds shines brighter. It's not always true. Thank you for your time as precious as it is to you. Come, girls, we have another important errand on behalf of my reclusive sister. Oh, and by the way, Merrilyn, would you like to meet my sister?' Aunt Mavis was sort of asking a schmaltzy question to which she already knew the answer.

'Never. Why ruin my dignity?'

The girls stood aside as a petulant and self-important egotist collated her thoughts that were spread erratically like a nasty flu virus, but the only illness it caused was to the thinker of those thoughts. Merrilyn brushed past. Davidia felt a good rugby tackle would level her horizontally, but she wasn't into violence. Young girls stay away from that characteristic element, don't they?

'She didn't recognise me,' said Aunt Mavis.

'How could she? She's never met you before so she wouldn't know you. You seem rather keen that somebody should recognise you even when they've never met you.' Davidia was slightly confused.

Her aunt seemed to possess a need for someone to know her. Perhaps she should do a genealogy course to trace her family history. That might help to satisfy her emotional hunger.

'She hasn't changed.' Aunt Mavis flipped out the comment as a throw-away-line. Only she knew its real meaning. 'We'll visit the pottery next.'

The three girls walked in silence. It wasn't far.

*   *   *

The pottery was familiar territory to Aunt Mavis as she had worked there for years undiscovered and was known colloquially as "Hands". No one had ever asked her real name. She was reclusive and rarely spoke to any other potter except to pass the occasional word, sometimes a grunt and a nod. Her name given was due to the delicate nature of her real hands that had been kept young by the special clay used at the pottery. It was a pseudo anti-ageing cream, the quality of which hadn't been scientifically discovered or proven that's what it did, yet it had kept them in a pristine and healthy condition.

'Here we are,' said an up-beat Aunt Mavis. Whatever tune she was hearing, it must have had good lyrics.

Davidia quite liked visiting the pottery. Somehow, in there, things seemed real. Items were created from clods of clay mostly into a meaningful object as an expression of the potter's imagination. She looked at her hands and thought she'd rather have her nails decorated with nail polish and the latest skin cream smoothed all over. There wasn't enough time to get them dirty by potting.

Chad heard the door open. Three women entered. He looked carefully. Who were they? It wasn't visiting hours and besides, all tours were run in the mornings.

'Excuse me, can I help you ladies?' he said.

Aunt Mavis walked forward and extended a hand in greeting.

'Hello, Chad,' she said.

Chad had no idea who she was and it showed by the surprised look on his face. He didn't publicise his name, so how was he known to her?

'Hello, madam,' he replied.

'I hear you make the most amazing pottery.'

Compliments were like food to the mind. It grew larger with each positive utterance.

'I have been known to produce the odd masterpiece. Have you seen my work?'

'Every item you have produced over many years. They are almost as good as mine.' Aunt Mavis chuckled.

Chad thrust out his roughage hands to embrace the delicateness that Aunt Mavis offered. He felt their smoothness, softness and strength altogether. He'd never before touched anything so electric to the feel. His hand did the involuntary jerk. It wanted to go home. It sought refuge in his pocket.

'How is that possible? I haven't seen any of your work and I only work from here.'

'Don't you recognise anything about me at all?'

Chad took a long, hard look. He saw a set of nice, shapely legs, an upper torso still full of interest, a face with a pleasant view, a pair of small feet rather femininely petite and height about a good match. That was his current observation. The puzzled look on his face said, *'Not really.'*

'What about these?'

Aunt Mavis raised both hands in front of her as if she was presenting them to a manicurist. She wiggled her fingers. She alternately smoothed the back of them by crossover movements and then held both palms upright. Chad was confused. A woman doesn't display naked hands as a mating ritual if that was her intent. He couldn't see any purpose in the display. Where are her rings? That's probably it. She's missing her rings and signalling that she's single.

'I'm not sure that I understand your approach. You don't have anything of mine that I recognise.'

Aunt Mavis removed her sunglasses. Her reveal didn't add any clues to the knowledge list that Chad didn't have. He saw a feminine, well-preserved lady. That was a non-recognisable move. There should have been more. Time had dimmed his memory. Aunt Mavis replaced the sunglasses realising that her cover wasn't blown. It was that he had no clue as to who she really was. As she placed her hands by her side with the backs facing outwards, it suddenly dawned on him. He was besieged by a pottery thought. It swirled busily in his brain causing a slight pain. It must have some meaning if it hurt.

'Hands! It's your hands. I've seen a similar set of those before. They belonged to an old lady who sat at that wheel over there. She made the most incredible pottery. She hasn't been in this week. Could be ill, who knows? People come and go.'

'What if I told you that was me?'

Chad's Adam's apple developed into a huge, chunky pie as he tried to swallow the surprise.

'I don't believe it. It couldn't possibly be. You aren't using hypnosis on me, are you?'

'I almost had you fooled, didn't I? That was my older sister who sat there and she is ill at the moment, but that will soon pass. Do you have any siblings?' asked an innocently expressive Aunt Mavis.

The question didn't exactly floor Chad, but his ribcage took a kick by the mention of siblings.

'I have a brother,' interrupted Davidia. 'Only one, though. It's enough.'

'I have a sister,' said Slirander. 'Only one, though. It's enough.'

'We are visiting family during school holidays,' continued Davidia. 'This is my Aunt Mavis' younger sister; you know the lady that lives at the quarry. So, she has only one sister too. Do you have any brothers and sisters?'

Chad wondered what damn business it was of theirs to question him about his family. He wasn't sure of his response when he gave it.

'I'm aware that I have a brother who I haven't seen in many years. Time drifted us apart. That's it. Small families ran in the area I once lived in.'

'Was that a farming community?' asked Aunt Mavis.

Once again, Chad's Adam's apple turned into a curry pie this time, still unable to swallow the comment.

'Why, yes.'

'Me, too. Years ago.' It was a dismissive comment. 'Girls, thank Mr Chad for his time. It's been a real pleasure to meet the supreme town potter that I'd heard so much about. I'll tell my sister that you were concerned for her non-attendance today.'

'Are you staying in town for long?' asked Chad.

Mavis had no intention of leading Chad on for a fling of any sort. She knew the truth about Chad. She could sling a court subpoena in his direction once further information was obtained.

'It's only for a few more days. I'm sure we'll meet again. I can guarantee that.'

The girls thanked Chad for his hospitality and left.

'He didn't know who you were,' said Davidia. 'What about Hands? Does she exist?'

'Yes, she does. It's me. For years I've worked at the pottery under a disguise. Slirander came with me the other day to observe my skills. I haven't always been "hidden". It was my one perfect escape into the real world without revealing my true self.'

'I suppose we are going to meet someone else who doesn't know you either,' said Davidia, convinced that Aunt Mavis' journey of recognisability was dead-duck territory.

'What we need is a refresher.'

Only one place in town had the credentials to comply with what Aunt Mavis had in mind – the local hotel.

It was a brisk walk.

* * *

'We aren't of legal age to go in there,' said Davidia. 'It wouldn't go down well with mum if we were caught in an illegal situation where grown men frequent, swill and use debatable language. I still want to finish school without a criminal conviction.'

'Lighten-up,' said Slirander. 'We could pretend that we are actually over twenty, but have been cursed also without realising it. We don't want to look so young, but there it is. Do you think that will work?'

'As long as we don't have to produce proper identification. Besides, Aunt Mavis will know what to say. She's the adult.'

The hotel seemed to be a popular place for myths and curses. One more will add to its notoriety.

'I have never been in this establishment,' said Aunt Mavis. 'Mr Hoarse is well-known in gossip circles around town. I'm aware his information is not always reliable. Apparently, he is a "secret" newspaper source for many myths and rumours. His "source" is apparently found inside small bottles of chatty water he serves at the hotel. No one except him knows what is written on the inside of the bottles. He only discovers these secrets after dark. He must have great vision from behind the bar. Let's introduce ourselves, curses included.'

Aunt Mavis was relishing the expression of humour once again. It had been a while. They entered like three western cowgirls with their six-guns above the waist. Two were nervous and fidgety as all eyes rained down on them. At the bar were a few locals addressing their hand-held companion, a drink, as the oracle of all knowledge. Mr Hoarse was behind the bar walking up and down pouring liquid into any empty glass. He was surprisingly accurate. He spied the three "Texans" and gulped a breath of air. It wasn't really fresh, but it was imbued with a malty taste. His eyes stood out on stalks as he followed their every step. He came out from behind the bar, greeting them in a gentlemanly manner. He wiped his mouth first with the back of his hand. Dribbling was only permitted after 10.00 pm.

'Are you ladies lost?' he said. 'This is a hotel, not a public convenience.'

'Hello, Mr Hoarse, is it?' said Aunt Mavis, hand extended in a salutary pose.

'Why, yes.'

'These are my two bodyguards. They cannot speak "local". They only speak "city".'

Mr Hoarse nodded as if he actually knew what was said.

'Those two seem to be young. Are they of legal age? I don't want to lose my licence for under-age drinking or offering respite to youth in a public premise.'

Aunt Mavis took off her sunglasses and stared into Mr Hoarse's eyes. A red glow was released. It must have done something. He smiled and agreed that they could stay. Before any refreshments were ordered, a solitary figure was noticed occupying the end seat at the bar. His head was bowed disclosing the signs of baldness. A lot of worry wrestled inside that shape. He raised his head to peer at the newcomers. There was no recognition; however, Aunt Mavis knew immediately who it was. The body had changed shape, but there was no mistaking the life marks on the face. It was Mervyn, the mayor, sitting with all his friends. He twirled his glass as an activity to thwart finger stiffness. Aunt Mavis now took that deep breath with the malty taste. She wondered whether he would recognise her.

'Can I order a stiff drink without the starch?' said Aunt Mavis. 'I need it after a long day.'

Mr Hoarse poured a neat drop of whisky. It was drunk in a second.

'May I have another, please?'

That went south too.

'You aren't getting intoxicated are you, Aunt Mavis? It isn't a good look sculling and you aren't in a boat on the water.'

'I'm fine now. I just had a minor shock. I'm approaching the mayor. He might share a drink with me.'

Aunt Mavis and her entourage approached Mervyn. He seemed disinterested. It wasn't election time to meet constituents. He didn't move.

'Hello, Mervyn,' said a confident Aunt Mavis.

'Don't bother me. I have business to attend to,' he replied.

'Is it a think-tank that you are engaged in all by yourself? No one else around here seems to be contributing.'

Aunt Mavis waved her arm like a windmill. The hotel wasn't full of councillors just yet.

'How did you know my real name? Very few people do,' he said suspiciously.

Was she a spy for a fellow councillor who wants to oust him at the next election? Had she spoken to Chad? Was there a something else?

'I heard it earlier today. I visited the pottery and it could have been mentioned there. It was said in positive tones.' That seemed to satisfy him. 'I wanted to congratulate you on all the good work that you have done for the town. The quarry is an important industry. I'm glad it's preserved for the future.'

Mervyn blinked. Preserved? He hadn't preserved anything. He sat bolt upright and recognised Davidia, the annoying young girl who had been to his house and was booted out. What's she doing here in a pub? She hasn't been hoodwinked into breaking the law, has she? Whose her other young friend? She could be booked for good looks. Before any threat emanated from the town's knowledge font, Aunt Mavis took off those wretched sunglasses again and stared at him. He wasn't going to morph into a mug. He already was one. A red glow flashed. Mervyn didn't see or feel it. Who is this strange lady staring at him? The moment passed.

'Have we met before at some convention? I don't believe I've seen you in town.'

'You probably have, but not that you would notice.'

'This is my Aunt Mavis' younger sister. She's visiting, like us,' proffered Davidia.

Mervyn winced in pain at the mention of that old lady's name. He spun around on his seat and eyeballed the trio.

'Is that so? I'm pleased for you. No one else has ever visited her. Can I do anything for you? Free advice or a ticket out of town.'

'Don't become one of them tourists,' interrupted Mr Hoarse, 'they disappear from town all the time. It's a mystery. I'm sure that old lady is responsible. Once people stayed here and now they don't. That didn't happen until she arrived.'

Mr Hoarse hadn't quite twigged that there is a difference between residents and tourists. He must be reading the insides of too many bottles. Mervyn stood up and retreated out the door. His encounter was over. His sparkling repartee went with him.

'He didn't recognise me at all?' said Aunt Mavis.

'I don't get it. You want people to know you that you have never met as you now appear. It's crazy to think that they would. Your disguise has been almost perfect so no one would ever know who you are until it was your funeral. The death certificate would have to state who the real you is.' Davidia shook her head. Why doesn't Aunt Mavis get it? No one knows her. She should accept that fact.

'I suppose so, but I thought that he might know. It was a long shot. It's time to go.'

Aunt Mavis was visibly upset and the cause wasn't the two drinks consumed. Her emotional in-tray was bulging with information overload. In one day, she had encountered three people from her past and not one, not one lousy one of them, recognised her. Age and selective memory had deleted her from existence in their minds, for whatever reason. That would soon change.

'Mr Hoarse, my two bodyguards are actually of age. That old witch near the quarry cursed them with eternal youth. It's not known how it happened, but it was a few days ago and they don't yet realise that they are both approaching forty. Imagine their surprise if they return to their true selves. What will their husbands say? Three scotches please?'

'Aunt Mavis, he won't believe that nonsense, will he?' said Davidia, hearing her aunt take the mickey out of herself.

'We'll see.'

The three scotches were served. None were drunk. Aunt Mavis winked at Mr Hoarse. Rarely had a female enticed his eyes to function with a winked response. He complied. Slirander and Davidia were puzzled by the ordering of undrinkable drinks. None of their friends would leave an unfinished glass on a bar, not that they drank.

'Why did you leave those three drinks? It's a waste of money,' said Davidia.

'Au contraire, it's a good mythical investment. Whisky is one of Mr Hoarse's favourite story-telling beverages. I have now ensured that you two have eternal youth. The town will be buzzing tomorrow. Your popularity will soar and everyone will want some of it too. My, how easy is it to manipulate the minds of others. Over the years I have been credited with the absurd. This time, I credited myself with the myth of the day.'

Davidia and Slirander looked at each other with exclamation mark expressions.

What have they let off the leash by freeing Aunt Mavis from her lifetime of isolation?

It was a free spirit full of humour.

Where's that bloody curse now? Which one?

12 CONTEST

 'll be late home tonight,' said Mervyn. 'I have some unsettled and unfinished business at the quarry.'

'It's dark. What are you going there for?' said Merrilyn.

'To mine for our future and create an issue about safety as an excuse to rid ourselves of that old witch at the quarry. We need her land.'

'What can you do on your own? Take a pick and shovel? That'll take years to do.'

'I have reliable help who can operate a digger. It's Chad. He can operate the heavy machinery whilst I advise.'

The mention of Chad had Merrilyn's lips moistening.

'Be careful. Remember witchcraft is a powerful magic.'

She wondered whether Chad was still magical.

'I feel tonight is the time for the settlement of our future and that of the old lady.'

Mervyn left home with a positive goal. It didn't matter who was harmed in his pursuit of selfishness. Money had an evil element to it. It made a good slave, but a bad master. He envisaged that by excavating the side walls of the quarry, the surrounding walls would collapse and ruin any residence alongside of it. There was only one residence and only one to suffer. Guess who? He felt it was going to be a win, win for him.

It was early evening as he made his way to the council depot to pick up his pre-arranged hire of the council truck and digger. The moonlight was in a full flourish, often hiding behind darkened clouds. The digger sat atop a tray truck looking like an angry insect, pincers ready to inflict pain. It was easy to imagine its terrifying capability. Mervyn stood next to it admiring its ferociousness. He thought that it was a perfect match for him.

'It will do the job perfectly,' he said.

He opened the door of the truck and out flew a blowfly that had been imprisoned for a few days. Its loud buzz made him jump instantly. It was the fear and guilt trip that startled him. He checked for any other bugs, but the coast was clear. His hands felt sweaty. A good grip of the steering wheel was impossible. He wiped his hands on his pants to dry them. It reduced their clamminess, but they weren't completely dry. The palms of his hands felt like soft leather. He was, after all, a pen pusher and not a he-man tradie with the chaffed palms. The front seat had cracked with age, weight, lack of maintenance and drying. A split was strategically growing where a posterior was placed. Parts of the under foam were exposed. The constant wear and tear indented the seat in two uneven dips. As Mervyn sat down on the cushion for comfort, the crack didn't match his own and made sitting rather uncomfortable. He wriggled for a better fit. The ignition key was at the right side of the steering wheel. He turned it on and a huge roar erupted. The truck burst into life. He felt like a parent giving birth to an inanimate object. He didn't have any children of his own so any substitute was acceptable. A quick flick into first gear and the road to fame, fortune or ruin had begun. A mobile monster had left the council depot. It was supposed to be returned in one piece. The written agreement said so, otherwise penalties would apply. There's no reward without taking a few risks.

The moon followed its journey.

*   *   *

'What a day,' said Aunt Mavis, who now had no further need to sit in her chair of buttons. Instead, a more comfortable settee was available.

The three females sat exhausted after a day of real change and discovery. Davidia and Slirander found Aunt Mavis to be a nice lady who needed a boost to change elements of her existence, hopefully for the better. Aunt Mavis found elements of her past which were disappointing, but were they really? Does pain and suffering have an end date prior to death? Does it have to be rectified during life? Questions. Questions. There were answers to them all, but at what cost?

Scrool suddenly unfolded from the shelf with the title deeds in tow. They lay pancake-flat on the floor, not to be used as a rug, but as further explanations, especially for Aunt Mavis. The girls wondered what the approach meant. Was trouble afoot? Had they blown off the shelf although there was no wind inside the house? Was there a message to be delivered? Slirander bent over and balanced on all fours – she was the closest – and waved her head over them as a surveyor does when mapping territory. A hand was placed on the surface and it disappeared into the floor. It was a concrete slab. She quickly withdrew it. Her head was next. It entered Scrool and the title deeds right into the concrete floor.

'She's wearing a cement necklace,' wailed Davidia. 'I hope she's not dumped at sea.'

That was a reference to what crime gangs did in the past. Her friend was no criminal.

'She will be fine,' assured Aunt Mavis. 'Wait until she returns.'

Inside the scrolls, Slirander mentally walked around in a version of a three-dimensional video game; however, this was serious and not a game. She noted that the clay seams were in turmoil. Red rubies were scurrying around within the confines of the seam walls. They were deep in the ground, but something had upset them. Her mind travelled all the way around the underground realm. She used the ruby eyes to discover the source of the panic. There, in the middle of the quarry, was a ground hunter and gatherer that ate dirt, dust and soil in huge gulps then spat them out as they didn't ever taste nice. How did something so huge fall into the quarry? It was a terrifying intruder. Slirander's head popped out of the scrolls in one piece. The look on her face registered deep concern. She had a message to deliver. Inside the house with its windows closed was impossible to see or know what was happening in the quarry unless particular attention was paid to it. The Scrollingers felt and knew peril was at their doorstep – or should that be wall.

'What is it you saw?' said Davidia. 'It wasn't Justin Bieber, was it? No wonder you look worried.'

'Trouble with a capital T. There is a machine of some description in the quarry. It's hungry and probably hasn't been fed for a while. Danger lurks out there. It's huge.'

Aunt Mavis opened the walled glass window and down below she saw the mechanical pest. It had only just been unloaded off the tray truck.

'There are two people down there. No one visits the quarry at night time except the bats. It's a dark and dangerous place. People have been known to disappear down sinkholes, uncovered mine shafts and get crushed by loose rocks. I wonder what nuisance value they are up to.'

It was impossible to recognise the two intruders from the

distance they were at. The scrolls returned to the shelf having warned them of the impending danger. Defence! It is all about defence. Aunt Mavis thanked Slirander for her input. It was now time for the girls to earn their visitor's card to meet the real Aunt Mavis. Which element of real was it this time?

'It's never too late for adults to learn a lesson,' she said. A feisty adversary was born.

Aunt Mavis sat in her chair of buttons. A few were depressed – by fingers not by mind – and it slowly moved towards the glass window.

'What shall we do?' asked Davidia, not quite yet the action girl.

'You and Slirander have to be the infantry whilst I do General from here. My position here means I cannot go outside to deliver whatever is necessary, but you two can be my messengers, eyes and enforcers. I can easily observe from the window. My powers are strong within the walls but not outside them. That's a legacy of the Scrollingers.'

'What? You want us to bash and belt whoever that is down there with pugilistic intent. The only black belt I have matches a fetching number purchased for last year's school prom. I must admit, I was a candy stick treat in my outfit.' A smile of remembrance embraced her facial muscles.

'Concentrate,' said a firm, voice-controlled Slirander. 'I'll have to improvise my methods of attack. My father taught me some moves that would save my life and not to use them on the boys. No male enjoys being beaten in an arm wrestle.' Slirander ran a slender figure over her "guns".

'You will each need a cloak of deceit and invisibility. Take this hammer and a pointed wand for a surprise. That should be sufficient equipment to teach the invaders a lesson. They have been upgraded from intruders. Be careful not to be seen. We also don't want those grown men being hurt.'

The small, female posse, minus their steeds, were ready for battle.

'This is all well and good,' said Davidia, 'but how do we get into the quarry unseen. Do we fly?'

'You can't imitate a bat; however, there is an elevator I had installed for such an occasion.'

Aunt Mavis pressed another button and a hole in the wall emerged on the other side of the room.

'Me first,' said Davidia, thinking it was a running contest, and dashed for it.

Slirander covered herself with her deceitful cloak and when Davidia had made it across the room she was already standing there with not a heaving bosom or hair out of place.

'What the …?'

She knew she had a strange friend and now an equally strange aunty. Oh well, accept it and move on. The small elevator was cramped. It was fortunate they were such good friends. Small spaces can be claustrophobic and a breeding ground for unpleasant germs. Down into the bowels of the earth they went. It was so dark their fingers were invisible. No one could see what one could do with them. Rude gestures would go completely unnoticed if any were signalled. In her haste to get out of the elevator, Davidia accidentally jabbed herself with the pointed wand. It didn't yelp in pain, speak sweet whisperings, or turn her into a frog. It gave her night vision instead. She wasn't supposed to jab herself, just wave it over her body.

'Slirander, I can see,' she said. 'Stab your arm gently and you'll be able to see as well.'

A soft jab and night-time sight was bestowed upon her too.

'We won't trip over now. Let's see who is visiting the quarry under the cover of darkness. Remember to wear your cloak so you remain invisible.'

Sometimes at school, invisible meant you were seen but often ignored. The "flavour of the month" girls who popularised themselves as the wanted ones, often walked past giving sideway glances but no real attention to you. The boys were supposedly puppy dogs following every woof. Here, it was a dastardly strategy of undercover operations, the type a sleuth employs.

Invisible was the "in" word.

*   *   *

'There's no one else here,' said Mervyn, as he unhooked the digger excavator. 'Chad, drive it off the truck.'

The engine purred. In the circular shape of the quarry, the sound echoed loudly. It sent shivers down their spines. The dark with its strange shadows gave the quarry an eerie feeling, like wanting to be elsewhere. The night beasts lived in their minds, so if they got scared, they were only afraid of themselves and their imagination. Fear was a personal acquisition which couldn't be given away as a gift to another, not even at Christmas.

Chad placed the gear in reverse. It grated and crunched the synchromesh without damage. The digger rolled backwards down the steel planks and onto the ground. As an actor, it was ready to perform. The stage was the quarry walls. If it could think for itself, it would probably baulk at what was expected of it. It was madness to dig direct into the base of a wall, but that was Mervyn's plan to collapse the walls on his way to red ruby wealth. Not every idea is a good idea regardless of how intelligent the thinker is. The night was graveyard-silent except for the purring engine. Fumes spewed into the air choking good quality breathing. Mervyn had a mud map of where he believed the clay seam ran. His fingers tingled with excitement as he mentally tuned in to destruction and discovery.

'There, that's it. That is where we'll start. Chad, firstly gouge-dig over there to see if the special clay seam can be identified. I've got water to pour over the dig to see it glint in the night light.'

Chad wasn't chatty Chad tonight. He was there to work and be rewarded for it. That special clay seam for him held the makings of further, future masterpieces. Mervyn couldn't care less about Chad's pottery aspirations. He was on a different level. A test dig near the base of the wall was performed. The ground refused to give in. The digger's cold, steel teeth gnashed in anger as its bucket filled with a huge quantity of clay clods. Eureka! The first bucket load was dumped successfully into a pile. Mervyn sprayed water from a watering can and the moonlight shine did the rest. This was that special clay seam. The deep gouge became the assumed pathway to those red rubies.

'Keep digging,' urged Mervyn.

Back at Aunt Mavis' house, a special Milo mug was hurting. Milo Mac was experiencing sympathy pains as his friends were brutalised by the digger. There was nothing he could do, except bear the angst with them.

Bucketload after bucketload were piled like a mini-mountain range on the quarry floor. The trail neared the walls where danger was greatest. Mervyn poured over the debris searching for the red rubies. None were found to date. He kept searching. He said that there surely must be some here somewhere. He kicked the ground in disgust. Sure, failure was an "f" word. He thought of another word commencing with the same letter "f" which was used repetitively when failure occurred, but it couldn't be put into print. In the dark he didn't see the two sleuths nearby. They had observed proceedings and they also wanted to use the "f" word, but theirs was "fool".

'Mervyn, that wall is rather high. It might collapse if we dig right into it.'

'The ground here is rock solid. Tunnelling is possible. Keep going. I've had the quarry surveyed. It's safe.'

Chad wasn't totally convinced so he did an exploratory dig. Ding! Ping! Sing! Ding! Ping! Sing! These sounds bounced off the digger's metal surfaces. The digger stopped dead. It disliked its treatment. What had stopped it? Mervyn ran over ready to blast his brother's ineptitude as an operator when he noticed his strange behaviour. He sat giggling like a silly girl or stupid boy in his seat. Chad had been struck with a mild electrical, hallucinogenic jolt from a force field that protected the quarry walls. His equipment went limp like a soft jelly and his loud laughter was accompanied by visualising imaginary cats crawl across his face pricking his skin with sharp cat claws. This rendered him momentarily useless. The scenario lasted for a few seconds but created enough nervousness for him to almost reconsider continuing. Whilst the delay was in progress, Slirander and Davidia seized their opportunity. They crept close enough to the other side of the digger and raised their hammers, not in a salute, but in a menacing manner. They had both seen the movie Thor. Before they could slam them down, they slipped from their grasp and flew into the bucket at the front of the digger. The clang attracted Mervyn's attention. He ran around to the front of the bucket and noticed two hammer claws withdrawing all the rivets without a human hand in sight. He couldn't tell if they were remote-controlled or not. He tried to stop them, but his fingers were flattened almost into a web. There was no pain as the hammers had an inbuilt anaesthetic. It was an Aunt Mavis innovation. His hands replicated a sub-standard frisbee. Chad had recovered from his mild shock and was so incensed that he threw the digger into gear and hit the accelerator with such force it almost stood on its hind tracks like a bucking bronco. Bang! It hit the ground spluttering and swearing in machine language.

Stuff the synchromesh. No "f" words were heard through the noise; however, they had probably been stated expressively and often. The girls hid. Mervyn ran with his own version of constipation. The digger was uncontrollable. Chad was certainly on the loopy train.

The force field within the wall was fully charged and spoiling for a fight.

'Particles,' said the leader, a fully-charged electrical atom. 'Prepare to repel an intruder. It's ugly, has bad breath, lacks manners and has a mouth it never shuts. How rude is that? It approaches.'

The zapped atoms within the wall awoke to their leader's request. They were a formidable team of electrons and other charged particles.

Aunt Mavis had the force field installed for the protection of the Ring of Clay and all elements within, especially the red ruby eyes. She was a genius, guided by the Scrollingers on how to achieve the outcome. Their ancient chants and scrolls hid many meanings, not the least of history, from other ancient places. Her lifestyle suited the arrangement with the Scrollingers and if she kept her end of the collaborative agreement, then in time, a release from the "curse" was possible. It had to be an earnt release. If the quarry and the Ring of Clay are saved, then Aunt Mavis might be too. There were no guarantees.

'I'm coming wall,' yelled Chad.

He had that digger at maximum capacity and charged straight at the quarry wall. The impact would reverberate throughout the quarry, the night sky and his shaken body. Sound reasoning was drowned out with noise. Clunk, grate, clunk, then whoosh. The bucket, which had been loosened by the hammers, had a tenuous hold and was first to fold. The walls were solid clay and the bucket was hopelessly out of its depth. It fell off at first impact. The digger stuck fast. Its rear end elevated at a forty-five-degree angle pointing to the solar system. It appeared it had bitten off more than it could chew. No favourites on the menu tonight. Chad was riddled with a dose of "buzz loader", an insidious condition called stupidity caused by mechanical ineptitude. It was a new name for an old, well-known failing human trait. Mervyn ran forward, worried that he hadn't discovered any red rubies. He was frantic.

'You idiot! You've smashed up my digger. The insurance company will be livid. Did you find any rubies? I mean that special clay seam?'

Idiot or not, there was nothing wrong with Chad's hearing.

'You said rubies. Is that what this is all about? You selfish bastard! I risked my life for you and the truth is that it was for a different reason. That's the last time you con me, brother.'

'Did you hear that?' said Davidia. 'He called him brother. I would have called him something else.'

'I heard it too. There's something not quite right in Humpletoon. Aunt Mavis met both of them earlier today and wondered if they recognised her. If they are brothers, then what's the connection?' replied Slirander.

'They can't see us, can they? Creep up behind them and give them a jab with the wand. It's the only magical thing we have left.' Davidia practised a swipe as if immunising for the flu.

Suddenly, an electrically charged mist with spitting sparks enveloped the digger, Chad, Mervyn and the girls. It swirled around them like rounding up sheep. A vision of a monstrous toy appeared in a teddy-bear suit. It floated, enlarged, then deflated. It came near, then moved away. Chad and Mervyn felt a chill. It had a child's face with a sad smile etched across it. Clarity was missing. A grainy, stippled visage teased their visual senses. The boys thought it looked familiar as it faded away into a stretched, grey, speckled mist.

'What do you make of that?' said Chad, who had regained what sense he had left.

'Rather weird if you ask me,' said Mervyn.

'It may be the work of that old witch. We are in her territory. Your machine is neutered. It's only good for recycling for spare parts. You are covered in red dust. Where did that come from?'

'So are you. Maybe it's from that mist. I've had enough tonight. It's been an unmitigated disaster. Merrilyn will be disappointed.'

'With what? You turning up empty-handed or turning up at all.'

A hint of sarcasm was dealt with that comment.

'I have to rethink what to do.'

'That machine is stuck fast and cannot be removed. You will need a crane. I'll leave you to it then,' said Chad as he walked away from the scene. 'Don't bother offering me a lift. I'll walk.'

'Will we wave a wand at him and see what it will do? We were given night-vision, so what else can it do?' suggested Davidia. 'It's been given to us for a purpose. I don't believe it's a sole-purpose wand. I'm curious. It might turn him into a pleasant personality.'

'Me first,' said Slirander, wanting to take the lead role. After all, she had more magical qualities than Davidia. It was a magician and witchcraft thing, yet she wasn't actually in the witch category. Her schoolmates would be mortified, or would they, to learn the secrets about her oddities? 'I'll tackle Chad as he slinks past. He needs a friend at the moment. Mervyn certainly messed with him tonight. Here he comes. Not happy, Chad.'

Slirander stepped out from behind her camouflage and waved the wand in a big Z formation. There was no chant or hocus-pocus spell to accompany the wave.

'That's it?' said Davidia. 'No drama, flourish or theatre with that? It was so simple. Mervyn needs some attention. He's mine. Should I show as much enthusiasm?'

Slirander waited for the effect of her interesting wave. There was no reaction. Chad walked past oblivious that he'd been wanded. He faded into the dark with his own thoughts because no one else can carry them for him. His brother had once again taken advantage. Tomorrow might be clarity day, an addition to a normal week day. Shall it be in conjunction with an existing day and not a weekly extension to the calendar to be expected? Confusion might visit also.

'How will I live down this embarrassment?' wailed Mervyn, surveying his failed attempt to destroy Aunt Mavis and locate anything red. His face reflected his disappointment. 'Where did this bloody red dust come from? No one knows I've been here. I'll spin a story about the stolen digger and truck. The council will believe me. I went to pick up the pre-arranged hire, but it was gone. Who left the gate open? It was a mystery.'

He was frustrated with the evening and spoke out loud as a stress reliever. He had inadvertently informed the girls of his plans to relinquish any responsibility for the evening's mess. That wasn't going to happen according to two young ladies. He had no idea anyone else was there spying on his antics. The moon infected a sombre mood on the quarry. The reflected light exposed a future rust bucket if not removed, the pate of a balding older man, and shadows where the girls hid in their invisibility cloaks. Mervyn carried a head full of regret as he walked past Davidia towards the exit. Suddenly, she jumped out of the shadows pretending to possess ninja qualities with one arm raised at a right angle to her face. She wasn't sure whether it was in attack formation or to hide her face. Drama followed Davidia like a shadow, hand in glove, etcetera. One gets the impression of a mobile theatrette. She waved her wand in a parabola shape like a huge U and stood back admiring her handiwork. Waves aren't solid objects to be retained. Once again, there was no reaction.

'This damn wand doesn't work. Who's interfered with it? Did Aunt Mavis issue us a dud pair?' said an annoyed Davidia. She had expected an instant result.

Aunt Mavis smiled from within her home. The girls had done well. Tomorrow would reveal the effect of the wand waves. They weren't duds. They had been impregnated with a truth spell of the Scrollingers which would determine a future for them and avoid all future unnecessary interest in the quarry. It had been a successful evening for one party.

Mervyn trudged out of the quarry with a huge invisible weight on his back. It was poorly packaged.

'I suppose we'll go home. There's nothing else to achieve around here,' said Davidia, wistfully hoping the evening had more substance.

'Not yet,' said Slirander. 'I feel a signal from the ground.'

She popped down on all fours, which was becoming something of a popular position for her. Her hands ran over the rough ground like a metal detector. There were no loud blips discovering gold or mistaken gold metal objects. It was deathly silent. Shades of a cemetery filtered through. Hopefully, a new, dead mummy wouldn't be discovered. Inexplicably and painlessly, her fingers turned upwards and bent backwards, acting like keys on a piano keyboard. They went up and down in see-saw fashion for a few seconds. Then they stopped. Both girls were amazed. It was a trick that couldn't be done normally. Her bones weren't that flexible. She could make a fist, but not do it backwards.

An underground burp from deep within the bowels of the quarry emitted, bringing to the surface in a protected bubble a set of the most magnificent red rubies ever seen. They popped out with a slight plop. There was no dialogue. Slirander knew exactly what to do. Make a set of earrings from them. No, they needed to meet Aunt Mavis and Scrool. Once again, the ancient Rubes of Scrollinger had emerged in a time of crisis. It was a rare event. Had Mervyn discovered these beauties, he would be wealthy beyond belief. Slirander stood up with the pulsating bubble in her hand. No offensive odour had accompanied its arrival.

'What's that?' said Davidia. 'They look fantastic. Let me touch.'

'No. That isn't allowed. I must personally deliver these. It's a requirement and a selfish task. It's time to go. Aunt Mavis and Scrool are waiting.'

'Are you sure that I can't touch them?'

'Yes. No, is a two-lettered word. Which letter do you not understand?'

'You don't have to get picky.'

The girls made their way to the hidden elevator and the sanctity of inside the quarry wall. Aunt Mavis and Scrool formed the welcoming committee, anxious to greet the ancient Rube. The bubble arose from Slirander's hand and oscillated in mid-air. It had no legs, so it didn't need to stand up.

'Hello, Mac. It's been a long time. No feel. We have been parted for a while.'

'It's great to see you again. The fun times underground have gone now that I'm a different shape. I was discovered by an intrusive digger, like many fellow clods. Now I have a new life to live and enjoy,' said Milo Mac.

As a mug, he was limited in his abilities, but communication was a special feature that very few mugs possessed, yet it was endowed upon him. His special clay held secrets only a few special mugs were allowed. They were impregnated with these talents to ensure that as a mug they could enjoy a quality of life not understood by humans before they were chipped, broken, smashed and finally ended up as a discarded object or land-fill. His journey had a final ending. Long life was wished upon all clods; however, they existed for various lengths of time. 'Such is Life,' is a comment once made by a famous Australian bushranger.

'Aunt Mavis, we thank you for your continued protection of our special country. There are still some matters to be cleared up for tomorrow's meeting at council. Be there and clarity will follow. Take the title deeds with you. Scrool has been our voice above ground and keeping our world informed of any dangers. Now you understand why Scrool is on your shelf. Who are these two clones of you, Aunt Mavis?'

'My new, young friends.'

'We understand that you have enjoyed your school holidays.'

'How would you know? You aren't following us or having our movements tapped, are you?' said Davidia.

'There isn't anything around here that we don't know of. The real purpose of our visit, at our peril, is that after the defeat of those intruders who wished us harm in the name of greed, is to advise you that the Ring of Clay is safe forever. In the ancient scrolls, which Slirander had contact with, it is written, "When the beast is defeated, the land can never be cheated." Those humans have failed to destroy all we stand for and at council tomorrow, our representatives, you three, will ensure that it never happens again. We can't stay much longer. We will perish in the impure air if we are exposed to it too long.'

Suddenly, the oscillating bubble spun faster and faster. A red light completely filled the room for but a second, then it was gone like a mirage in the desert. The girls were stunned. In fact, all present were stunned. Their memories had been sucked dry when they concerned the red rubies. It was selective brain drain.

The group of three sat down to recover from what it was that they had just experienced, whatever that was. Milo Mac knew that all their futures would be fine. He had received, in amongst all that whizzing, a personal comment from the Rubes to the effect that his features were fantastic and no other mug had them. They revealed to him that he was a statement mug, with the face of a male angel. There would be no prouder ornament. His side protrusions were ears and all his other indentations and bulges were segments of a face. He now sat proud and contented on the shelf.

Where was Eleanor, his owner?

The night enveloped the warriors. Rest was nigh.

*　　*　　*

'That bloody digger. That bloody brother. Those bloody rubies. That bloody Aunt Mavis. That bloody quarry. That bloody curse. The whole bloody thing is a bloody mess.'

Mervyn, the wailer, had arrived home in a not too happy state. The front door was the first to suffer. Vertical became horizontal with a thunderous kick. A kitchen chair where many a grateful meal had been shared lost a leg and the other three bent like twisted thoughts. His favourite chair was brave enough to resist a fist punch. It was well-sprung and the recoiled fist hit Mervyn on the sensible part of his chin, which was receding with each minute. He sat down exhausted, poured a shot of liquid and it sank into his stomach like a lead weight. His Santa Clause paunch had no Ho Ho Ho left. A dropped page leaf fell to the floor. It was the hire agreement he was to deny. The small print, and it was in very small print, read, "Any damage to the machine is at the user's cost." He was stuffed financially for its use.

'Is something wrong, Mervyn?' asked Merrilyn, with probably the dumbest line for a greeting.

She could see that he was stressed and upset over something.

'That Chad fellow, why do we keep calling him Chad. That isn't his real name. It's Barnaby. I remember the little turd well. The quarry was a disaster. No rubies, no digger, no truck and no brother. I told him to piss off.' In anger, no matter what is said, it has more impact if a nasty range of language is used whether it's right or wrong. Mervyn was having his moment. 'Thank God we still have those red rubies safely locked in the desk drawer. We'll get them valued tomorrow. I have a council meeting at 11.00 am. You'll have to forego your high tea with your society frumps and be in council for support. I'm going to bed. What a waste of an evening.'

'What's that red dust on you?'

'An accident.'

'How was Chad, I mean Barnaby? He wasn't hurt, was he?'

'I don't care. The last time I saw him was when he walked out on me at the quarry.'

Merrilyn thought that she could do the same, but money was a type of glue that some people loved to stick to their hands. It smelt gluey and Merrilyn loved to sniff.

Chad made it safely home after his miserable date with his brother, Mervyn. There was no love lost between them. He vowed never to assist him again. Pain was brought about by a sense of loyalty. It was time the pain stopped. It apparently ran down a single alley of lifeline in the one direction. That night Chad thought that tomorrow he would have it out with his brother, mayor or no mayor.

The council meeting at 11.00 am was an appropriate meeting place where each week, members of the public could air their views but most didn't get the opportunity. They were either bullied into submission via a lengthy verbal diatribe or question time was curtailed if anything difficult or unpleasant arose.

Who slept well?

13 REALITY

It was the start of a beautiful day in Humpletoon. Normally, a Council meeting had no real interest for the locals, but given the opportunity to air an opinion, today was a not-to-be missed occasion. Locals had drawn up lengthy questionnaires in the hope that they could offer one to the council. It was to be a purely verbal event without animated hand gestures like a Punch and Judy show.

The sun beat down on the council chambers windows with warmth. The town was abuzz and not from a swarm of bees. There was a hint of cloud. No one bothered to contact the local weather station. Whatever was forecast it usually had too many elements of doubt.

Mervyn was at home pacing the floor with worry, a mentally adept companion, whilst Merrilyn decked herself out in regal refinery as a showpiece to the community.

'This blasted council meeting should be postponed. I'm not well. That red dust I was sprayed with last night has tinged my complexion.'

Mervyn had a poor night's sleep. His mental jousting had tired him. He had no brilliant solutions to his problem, except to pander to the gullible and make them believe that everything he said sounded truthful. His oratorical skills were exceptional. A lie could be presented as the God-honest truth and, hooray, support was given; however, there was feeling today that the gull-ible and stupid would not be there. The town had grown an IQ.

'I'm off to have the red rubies valued,' said Merrilyn, in high spirits. 'I'll catch up with you at council.'

Her footwork was nifty and light. The valuation of those red rubies was to be her Humpletoon highlight. She danced out of the house with her head in a cloud of some number. Was it a nine that could end in a zero? There was plenty of time to enjoy the day, or not. Mervyn heard her go, but wasn't interested in where she was going. He had himself to consider. His mirror said so.

*   *   *

'Good morning, aunt Mavis,' said a chirpy Davidia.

'Good morning, aunt Mavis,' said a chirpy Slirander.

'Good morning, to you both,' replied aunt Mavis.

'Good morning to all,' chimed in Milo Mac.

With the morning pleasantries dispensed with, it was prepara-tion time for attendance at the council meeting. Everyone was well dressed and modestly made up and displayed an attitude of confidence, not one that came from inebriation. The feeling was one of interest for the girls. At school, they had attended various excursions in the name of education and often the outing didn't bring the education element with it. Once they attended a day swimming camp and learnt about the obnoxious behaviour of boys ogling young women in swimming attire. It wasn't what was anticipated. They wanted mind improvement, not better eyesight. That day wasn't a complete waste of time. Later in the week, some male attention was directed their way. The girls just smiled. They knew they were attractive in anything they wore. Confidence is a great asset when you have the assets to be confident about. Today was all about the mind. Perhaps they should do a yoga session before they go?

'Are you taking me today?' asked Milo Mac.

He had an interest in council proceedings, notably about his homeland and its future.

Davidia agreed to carry him. He might even be reunited with his real owner, Eleanor's grandma.

*   *   *

Chad fumbled about the pottery with his musings and mutterings not adding much to a beautiful day. Clay pots aren't renowned for their conversational ability. He had nothing to offer except attend as a character witness, probably for himself and not Mervyn. He wanted his name cleared from any wrong-doing his brother had lumbered him with and wanted to ensure that there weren't a series of mistruths told about him to the council. His complexion had also been tinged by the red dust he was sprayed with last night.

*   *   *

'Could you value these red rubies for me?' said Merrilyn to the town jeweller, who wondered where would one come across this type of gem in this town.

As far as he knew, only pottery was produced in town. He eyed her suspiciously before he took them in hand and attached his special jewellery eye-piece for a proper view. He had one eye covered and could be excused for frightening young children with his pirate patch. He stared at them from every conceivable angle, grumbling comments as each side reflected different colour configurations from dull red, transparent red to high-quality dark red. His inspection movements took a few minutes. Merrilyn became anxious to know what her prized possessions were worth.

'May I ask where you obtained these?' asked the jeweller.

His interest was certainly high. It was so obvious he'd unsettle anyone who entered his shop at that time. Were they from a jewellery heist and Merrilyn was trying to fence them? Jewellers knew of contraband gems via their associations' reporting to police and maybe he wasn't sure of what he had. Should Merrilyn be arrested? Tension began to fill empty-bucket thoughts of both parties.

'They are a family heirloom passed down through family generations,' Merrilyn said, proudly.

She ruffled her dress with pleasure at her clever answer. There was no one present to dispute it.

'I have no doubt they were,' replied the jeweller, a trite more settled.

His next comment exploded like an incendiary device strategically placed between her ears.

'You do know that these are fakes? It's costume jewellery at best. Rather worthless, I'm afraid,' he said politely.

It is preferable to deliver this bad news politely when you know the response could be quite shocking and offensive. He returned the red rubies to Merrilyn who looked as if she had been hit with a stun gun or worse still, tasered. Fortunately, there were no other customers in the shop.

'What do you mean, fake?' she yelled, hysterically. 'You substituted them whilst I wasn't looking.' She had to sit down to recover from the shock.

'Merrilyn, I assure you that this is the exact pair you brought into the shop.'

'That's not possible. They came from ...'

Her mouth almost bit her foot when she realised that she had nearly given away a town secret; red rubies at the quarry. That would cause an intolerable stampede of greedy miners.

'Are you sure?' she wailed.

Her face had disappointment, complaint and disbelief written all over it in patchy red spots. Her veins were trying to escape their facial prison. She turned a crimson colour that almost matched the original red rubies before they were replaced. At least she had colour in common with them. They would have made the perfect set of red earrings unable to be seen clearly because of her red face. The wind had certainly escaped from her tyres. Now what?

'I am certain of it. They are an excellent imitation. The family must have been cheated, not knowing all those years. The true value is that you make others believe that they are real.'

'That's a great lot of good that does me. I wanted to sell them for other retirement purposes.'

Merrilyn angrily snatched them back and exited the shop quickly. Her disappointment needed to be shared with someone, Mervyn. She wondered whether he had cheated her by replacement. A dry storm was heading up the main street building up strength as it went. The ground experienced a minor tremor.

*   *   *

Aunt Mavis and the girls walked through town to the council chambers.

'Where are their children? I heard she has twins.'

'Where are their husbands? They shouldn't be travelling without them.'

'I don't fancy looking that young forever. It's a disgrace. How dare older women pretend that they are teenagers?'

'I want some of that. I'm not quite ready for a trade-in.'

The rumour had hit town from an unreliable source that the girls had been cursed with eternal youth. A few villagers wished that they were cursed too. Suddenly, a whirlwind brushed past with a splayed, swirling skirt clearing a dusty runway in the direction of the council chambers. It moved like an irate willy-willy preparing to blow over something. This time it was Mervyn.

'She's in a hurry and no one is chasing her. It must be important. She ignored us and didn't trade any unpleasantness,' said Davidia.

'We'll catch up shortly,' said Aunt Mavis. 'Nothing is going to bother my day today.'

It was in the girls' auras.

*   *   *

Merrilyn charged headlong into Mervyn's office where the duelling mouths were filled with angry words. She slammed the red rubies hard onto the table and they shattered like single-strength window glass. Shards of glass flew wherever they chose. It was a release for them.

'You cheating bastard. What did you do with the rubies? These are fakes?'

'What nonsense. Those rubies are as real as you and me.'

'That might be coming to a close. You have stolen them from me.'

'That's impossible. No one ever touched those gems except me. The only other person in the house near them, albeit sitting on a settee, is that old hag's young relative, what's her name. It sounded like part boy. Dav? David? No, there was more to it than that. Davidia! Yes, that's it. Davidia! She could have stolen and replaced them. Her aunt might be a true witch and did it by magic. I can assure you no one else had access.'

'We are ruined. That fortune train has left the station without us aboard. How do we get them back if she stole them?'

'The Council meeting is at 11.00 am so if we usher them in here prior to the meeting we might learn the truth before I front the peasants.'

Politics is a difficult occupation especially if you believe you are in control. Mervyn was mayor. How could anyone be more important? The expectation that council is full of brainless, ill-trained sheep, even if true, still meant that someone had to be head shepherd. There wasn't any wool to be pulled over his eyes today. He fussed over the shape of his tie. A small amount of spittle nestled in his hands to double as a hair-flattening agent and an invisible eyebrow pencil. There, almost perfect.

'Mervyn, I feel helpless,' whined Merrilyn, feeding Mervyn's sense of control.

'Let me sort it out. Get yourself a nice cup of tea at the staff canteen and don't forget to put in your dollar.'

Even council didn't get everything for nothing.

Mervyn sat in his large, soft, leather chair and constantly fidgeted. It felt like his whole being wanted scratching. The sound of the ticking digital clock, which was a technological impossibility, because they were usually made soundless, played on his mind. There was no mouse to run up and down it.

What nursery rhyme would play for him today?

*   *   *

Before anyone was allowed into the council public forum, everyone gathered in the hallway like milling cattle ready for milking. It was a prime opportunity for small-time chit-chat to catch up on local gossip or to discuss important issues before entering, like lawyers do on behalf of clients.

'That fetching Chateau Grigio was the most exquisite wine of the century.'

'We must do lunch again.'

'Oh! The murder charge. Give him ten years; but that wine, what a winner. I'll organise a few extras next time. You can bring your new secretary along too. I'm sure she would like a fine wine with a dash of law.'

Aunt Mavis, Davidia and Slirander were the subject of much gossip being the most recent visitors in town. When acknowledged, the head nodded and sometimes, a brief smile with an innocent hand wave was made. Chad was hanging around like loose change when Aunt Mavis spotted him. He saw her coming and tried to avoid a meeting. Aunt Mavis was too quick. She still had pace.

'Hello, Chad,' she said, charmingly. She still wore her sunglasses. Behind that screen she could visualise reaction to her visit and sort out what it really meant. Chad was evasive. 'It's me, Hands,' she said, holding them out for a shake or caress, either was acceptable. 'What business brings you to council today? Have you got a heavy parking fine to attend to?' Small chat was the order of the day. Chad stared blankly. He had his screen working too.

'The mayor is speaking so I thought as a community-minded citizen I might hear what he has to say. It's a first for me.'

Aunt Mavis knew that to be true remembering he had the truth wand waved at him.

'Is Chad your real name?' she whispered, boring a stare at him that he couldn't see.

'Of course, it is. Why do you ask?'

'I believe it to be Barnaby. Is that correct? I'm doing genealogy research for the Bury family and somewhere in its history, you show up.'

Chad almost filled his orange-coloured khaki pants with more than wind. His stomach hurt. There was no escaping pain. It was withheld in-house. He stroked his beard and it almost turned into a real stroke. He felt winded. No one except that shit of a brother knew his real name. Now, someone he had never met knew it too. Had he been cursed as well? Sort of, as it was Aunt Mavis "the witch" he was speaking to. Before he could answer, Mervyn approached through the crowd. People made way for His Excellence or whatever he liked to be called. He made a beeline for Aunt Mavis. Chad took full advantage of the bag of wind approaching and slipped away feeling ill about his name discovery. He had tried to hide his past, but now it had visited him again. Doesn't it ever give up?

'Aunt Mavis' sister and girls, it's nice to meet you all. It's a pleasure that we can develop. If you will come to my office, there is a private matter to discuss.'

Mervyn was full of proper expression in public. Inoffensive conversation was a vote winner.

'Thank you, Mervyn. Is Mervyn your real name?' asked an inquisitive Aunt Mavis. She knew damn well it was; however, a cleverly phrased question can exhibit doubt.

'Of course, it is,' he replied as a matter of fact. 'Please come this way.'

He led them down a corridor past the Titles office to his palatial suite of a worn leather couch, faded paintings and a mahogany desk that dwarfed any occupant seated behind it. The room had a furniture smell. He courteously showed them to the settee. He took his position at the desk and clasped his hands to avoid losing them. His face was tinged with redness from their previous meeting that he didn't know he had.

'Why are we here?' asked Davidia.

'To determine if you stole anything from my house when you visited the other day.'

'I haven't taken anything. What is missing?'

'Something special from my desk drawer. It's a family heirloom from my wife's family. They have been handed down through generations and the latest visitor to our home has been you. She's so upset at its loss.'

Mervyn played the emotional card and waited for the dealt reply.

'What was stolen?'

'Some precious red gems rarely seen. Just tell me where they are and we can forget this nonsense.'

His nice smile was morphing into a nasty smirk, which didn't have far to go for an anger burst.

'I repeat, sir. I didn't steal anything from you. My parents always taught me honesty. You'll have to find another culprit.' Davidia stood her ground. 'Who's this old bloke threatening me when I'm innocent,' she whispered under her breath.

Before an explosion of bad manners emerged, Aunt Mavis interrupted.

'Is your family name Bury and you have a brother called Barnaby, whom you know as Chad?'

Mervyn had an emotional transfusion. His face looked like a ghostly apparition with the shock of hearing the family name and his brother's real name which he already knew, but no one else did. How is it possible that this woman knows it? He stammered a response. Where was his Adam's apple going? Was it into a stomach pie? He didn't want to choke himself.

'Yes, that's correct. Where did you find out this detail?'

His words were barely audible. He began to sweat.

'I'm doing a genealogy study on behalf of your sister, Tabatha. You do remember her, don't you?'

He hadn't heard that name for years believing that she was

dead. Guilt lives within your mind as long as a memory retains it. Mervyn recalled it from this section and nodded.

'Yes, sadly she was lost to us years ago in an unfortunate house fire. I miss her. There's not a day that goes by that I don't think of that tragic event. She was a special person to me.'

Suddenly it twigged.

'You said on behalf of my sister. Explain what that means.'

Sweat tickled down his inside legs and he was unable to address the irritation in front of three women who could quite easily be offended.

'It means that she isn't dead. She is well and truly alive and now thriving.'

'Do you know where she is?'

'I can put you in touch with her. Family negotiations are very delicate. As Davidia is innocent of stealing, we'll make our way to the council rooms for your meeting. I hope it's a success.'

Mervyn was unsettled. His sister can't be alive. He and Barnaby made sure of that in that fire. Unfortunately for him, a full keg of consumed alcohol had blurred all their visions on that night and no one saw the fleet-of-foot, light female escape in the chaos. The past was now the present. He dashed to the canteen to find Merrilyn and explain the extraordinary meeting with Aunt Mavis' younger sister and the two girls. It was the second shock of the day for her.

Were there any more to materialise?

They both hoped there wasn't.

*   *   *

The council meeting room was full of locals. There wasn't a spare seat available. The meeting was brought to order. The council discussed road rules, staff canteen improvements, quarry development and a host of local issues. No one interrupted as the language flowed with energy, disbelief and triumph. A show of hands in the majority won the day on that particular issue. The forum for public questions was fraught with uncertainty. The mayor was the council spokesperson. He never enjoyed answering a question without notice. It was the danger component of the meeting.

'Does anyone have a question?'

A sea of hands went up. One person was selected.

'Is any action being taken to get rid of that eyesore next to the quarry and its inhabitant?'

Wouldn't you know it? The first question was the worst one to ask. Yikes, it will require a clever response. Mervyn adjusted his tie and took control.

'The council is in the planning stages of compulsory acquisition of the site. It's already been rezoned for farming and we have more research to determine that possibility.'

'What about that old witch?'

'We hope to rehouse that inhabitant, who is a bad influence on our society, to another region far from here.'

'Does that mean all those curses will be lifted?'

'I can guarantee it.'

A round of applause erupted.

'You can't do that,' yelled Davidia, as loudly as she could. 'She is my Aunt Mavis and lives in the most incredible house.'

'She's a wombat, is she?' someone yelled out.

'She owns the quarry and the land around it.'

'Davidia, sit down,' said Slirander. 'You are making a fool of yourself. They don't believe anything you say. They are scared and too superstitious.'

Davidia ignored Slirander's request.

'It's commendable that you want to support your Aunt Mavis,

who by all accounts is a real witch; however, your emotional support has no weight with council. Are there any further questions?'

A sea of hands went up again, but for an unexplained reason, the next question came from the tall, striking woman in the sunglasses who stood up to command presence. It was Aunt Mavis.

'She's that witch's younger sister. Sit down,' someone yelled.

There were a lot of anonymous interjections. Chaos could have reigned supreme, but Aunt Mavis held sway.

'I have in my hand the original title deed to the land that surrounds and includes the quarry.'

The rolled-up parchment scrolls were tossed into the air like confetti. The crowd were mesmerized as it unfolded into a flat page and flew without a magician's trick. It floated directly to the council table and laid itself flat on its surface.

'Where did you get this?' asked Mervyn, rather dumbfounded.

'From your council archives where they had been deliberately hidden for years.'

'I don't believe this to be true. They have to be a masterly forgery.'

'How would you know if it is a forgery unless it has been copied or seen before?'

Davidia was stunned with her Aunt Mavis' performance. She was really a woman of substance and not the old hag everyone made fun of. Mervyn had the councillors assess the deed. It looked in perfect condition. There were no errors or names scrawled across it. The owner was clearly stated as Aunt Mavis. The parchment was definitely original. The signature on the deed suddenly sat upright for a clearer view.

'There's a signature that can't be verified,' said Mervyn, thinking he had prevailed and his council could do otherwise by passing a compulsory land grab.

'The signature can be verified. I have the evidence with me.'

The crowd were stunned. The mayor was stunned. The council was stunned. Davidia and Slirander were stunning. Aunt Mavis moved forward. She stood directly opposite Mervyn.

'Where is this compelling evidence?' he said, as if presenting a challenge to her.

Aunt Mavis rummaged in her bag for a moment and withdrew a pen. It wasn't monogrammed or skilled in the art of black magic, it was just an ordinary everyday, commonly-used pen. In a theatrical play, she turned to the audience and waved it above her head. There were no magic flashes, witchery spells or flashes of light to dramatise the moment.

'This is the compelling evidence that you requested. Will you please pass me a piece of blank paper?'

'Your evidence is a cheap pen anyone can purchase from any newsagency or supermarket in bulk.'

'Go on. Show us your evidence,' yelled out a local.

Silently, Aunt Mavis signed her signature on the plain piece of paper. It wasn't a magical A4 page. Once again it was as normal as paper could be.

'Compare that signature with the signature on the title deed. They will match perfectly,' she said.

Mervyn and the council compared the signatures. They were a perfect match. Amongst the council, one councillor was a writing expert. He added his own worth of knowledge. He confirmed their identical form.

'That means you are Aunt Mavis, the old witch who lives next to the quarry. How is that possible? You look nothing like her.'

'Surprising, isn't it, when a person changes their appearance? I am her.'

The crowd went nuts.

'She's the real witch. We are all cursed. How can we save ourselves from her curses? She's amongst us.'

Crowd panic began to grow like a voracious fungus. No one present knew how to combat a witch other than burn her at the stake or at the house. It was an historical treatment.

Suddenly, Davidia and Slirander, the scream teenagers, screamed at the top of their voices in a perfectly synchronised duet. The words matched also. It was uncanny. It wasn't rehearsed.

'She is Aunt Mavis and she's not a witch. She's our aunty.'

The strength of their screams stopped the crowd from exiting. They were now stunned. It was a stunning day outside the council building and inside it was happening too.

'Listen to her,' implored Davidia. 'She has a story, just like we all do. Today, she can tell you hers. Please listen. Nobody is cursed. Rumours, misunderstandings and misperceptions abound.'

The crowd glare was everywhere. Mervyn wasn't having his council meeting hijacked by two teenagers and what was at first, a witch's sister. He'd had a gutful. She was proven to be Aunt Mavis, who was well-known in town to be a witch and it was time to end the charade.

'Constable, arrest the witch,' he ordered.

The crowd with the sheep IQ had quietened for a moment. Every word could now be heard.

'Arrest the witch,' said an interjector.

Aunt Mavis turned to Mervyn, took off the shaded sunglasses and shot a thin, red light at his eyes. Did he recognise his missing gems? He baulked momentarily.

'You would have this kind constable arrest your sister?'

'My what?'

'Your sister.'

'I don't have a sister. Isn't that right, Chad?' The truth wand didn't work on Mervyn because he didn't want to tell the truth at any cost.

The truth wand usually worked on those who had doubt, but the truth had a way of being told anyway. Not Mervyn. There was no truth syrup in his body.

Chad responded by saying that they did have a sister once, but she was lost in a dreadful fire.

'Was her name Tabatha?'

Chad and Mervyn almost had coronaries on the spot.

'How in the hell would you know that?' said a belligerent Mervyn.

'I am that sister. My name is Tabatha. I survived that fire. You are my brother, as is Chad, whose real name is Barnaby. Our family name is Bury. Our family once owned a farm that I inherited from our dad, but you led a drunken group of vigilantes with your brother's support and damned me as a witch to perpetrate the excuse to burn down the family farm and me with it. You were all so intoxicated, no one saw me escape, let alone survive. I watched from a safe distance as you destroyed the family home. I left the next day. You then stole the property from me as I was presumed dead. No one questioned it as all those present agreed and then, Mervyn, you cheated your brother out of his share because of his affair with your wife.'

All jaws in the audience represented a sea of open fly-catchers. This was the most exciting event that had happened for years in Humpletoon. Everyone was now paying attention. Merrilyn was suddenly looked on as a scarlet lady, Chad stroked his beard more vigorously and Mervyn was highly embarrassed.

'We have an attempted murderer as mayor,' yelled an audience member. 'Are you one of the curses?'

There was a ground-swell of discontented voices. The councillors stood like a set of ornaments one wouldn't want to adorn their walls with. Tension was felt. Aunt Mavis once again took control. Perhaps she should be mayor?

'All of what I have said is true. I came to your humble town as a refuge from my scarred life. I took up the character of an old hag to avoid personal contact as much as possible. I was afraid, so I hid. The reason I'm here today is to save the quarry from further destruction, not further development. As I own it, the future pottery industry will be properly managed. In doing so, I am being released from a self-imposed curse of an old hag and release all of you from any curse you think you may have suffered.'

She waved her arms as if some magic was in them. The truth this time was to be kept hidden.

'You mean, I'm not cursed,' said a thankful member. 'Wow! There's fresh air inside council rooms as well as outside.'

The crowd became happier with the curses lifted. The title deed to the quarry had lift-off. It floated toward Aunt Mavis like a homing pigeon and returned to its scroll format.

'These will be securely locked away.'

Mervyn was dumbstruck. His career had just been ruined. He'd been outed as an attempted murderer, as was Chad. His office-bearing days were over.

'Excuse me, mayor,' said a serious looking official, 'the cost of the digger you hired needs to be paid in full. It's a write-off.' Add financial ruin as well.

The day couldn't possibly have gotten worse, could it, when Merrilyn fronted her husband and told him their days were over also? The council meeting had certainly provided some entertainment.

'Well, Mervyn, do you have anything to say to your sister? I don't want the farm back or my share, but thanks for not offering it.'

There was no answer. He fled the scene. The audience were amazed that such intrigue existed in their small town.

Mr Hoarse waddled through the door.

'The mayor has disappeared like those tourists do, straight out that end of town.'

His finger couldn't point to exactly which end, but it was the out of town one.

Chad disappeared almost as quickly, to where no one knew. His pottery skills would be all that remained of his residence in town.

Aunt Mavis wasn't going to press any charges for her brothers' past ills so there was no need for them to vamoose.

Merrilyn hoisted her dress mass in both hands. She looked like a porcelain doll at that very moment. She was beautifully dressed with striking red lips, wan complexion, but very fragile. Her world had been twisted in ways she didn't see coming. She confronted Aunt Mavis like a gunfighter at the O.K. Corral. Her facial expressions waxed and waned almost through its complete range of movements. She raised a pointed finger with a death nail on its end. Someone was going to get nailed.

'You witch,' she yelled. The audience were still there experiencing the aftermath of some awful truth. 'You aren't their sister. She's dead. Only zombies return from there.'

'Merrilyn, do you remember the time when we were first introduced? Mervyn brought you out to the farm. You wore a pink twinset and a tartan skirt with slits down each side. Your shoes were brown-tanned leather, shaped like cowboy boots. We sat outside on the veranda sipping a lemon-flavoured soft drink. We were the only two people there.'

Merrilyn was taken aback. That was true.

'Why did you come back? You were better off forgotten. You have destroyed my life.'

The nastiness was continuing.

'You destroyed your own life with your greed and you assisted in the ruination of my life so the farm would become yours and

Mervyn's. I have no sympathy for you. Importantly, look into my eyes.'

Those sunglasses were certainly getting a work-out, on, off, on off. Merrilyn gave Aunt Mavis the death-stare. It possessed a darkness that was endless with no backdrop of goodness. A red flash emanated from Aunt Mavis and scored a direct hit into Merrilyn's brain.

'They look identical to the stolen red rubies,' she said, unintentionally.

No one knew anything about stolen red rubies. She realised her error too late and shut her mouth clamp tight to ensure nothing else incriminating escaped.

'Yes, they are,' replied Aunt Mavis.

The stare stopped, the red flash faded and the scene of two sparring women would be a town memory forever. Merrilyn turned to leave.

'What red rubies?' asked an onlooker.

That was the beginning of the town harassment for Merrilyn which eventually encouraged her to leave.

There was no further point in staying. None of the audience was upset at not being able to confront the council with their extensive list of questions. Entertainment had already been provided. The crowd dissipated.

The council meeting closed.

The town had a spring in its step once again.

14 END OF THE HOLIDAYS

'Are you still really my Aunt Mavis?' asked Davidia, concerned that the discovery of her history may mean that she isn't still her real aunty.

'When I was young, I was involved with your family as I have previously mentioned and my name Tabatha wasn't well-known or accepted. My middle name was Mavis which I began to go by. So, that is how I'm known as Aunt Mavis from all those years ago. My brothers hated the name and always called me Tabatha. Since I was presumed dead, there was no reason for them to remember from so long ago the name they disliked and especially of someone who presumably didn't exist any longer. They would never have matched my name with their thoughts. Anyone can have the same name. It was that then and now wasn't connected. Time can dim many thoughts and they don't have to be attached to a light bulb.'

Aunt Mavis smiled at her mild attempt at humour. She was returning to her original ordinary but special self.

'What will happen now that you have revealed who you really are?' asked Slirander, wondering if Aunt Mavis will continue living in the area or move on.

'I have decided to remain here. My house is suitable. I can continue to work at the pottery with this wonderful special clay and manage the quarry on behalf of the Scrollingers. I don't feel that I am cursed any longer by living the life I have for years. It's a fresh start for me.'

'What about all those curses?' asked Davidia.

'Let's hope that the townspeople no longer relive any of them because that old hag, the perceived cause of every curse, no longer exists. They won't be so eager in future to believe Mr Hoarse and his readings from inside a discarded bottle. I think he'll continue his imaginings.'

The telephone rang. It was Davidia's mother.

'How are the holidays? When will you be coming home? Say hello to Aunt Mavis for me.'

'Tomorrow we leave. It has been a great holiday. Aunt Mavis is really cool. It's been fun, so like never before.'

'Enjoy your time. We'll catch up at home.'

'You can visit us if you like when you have a holiday. Mum says hello to you too,' said Davidia.

'Where's Milo Mac?' said Slirander, almost forgetting her mug buddy.

A muffled sound filtered from Slirander's handbag.

'It's stifling in there. Did I miss anything? I heard a lot of noises but had trouble making any sense of them,' said Milo Mac.

'So did we.'

'Where am I?'

'In Aunt Mavis' home, but you don't belong here. You should be with your caring owners, Eleanor and her grandma. We'll take you there to enjoy your time as a Milo mug. You have found yourself and now your proper owners. The quarry and your clod family clays are to be protected and worked by the pottery under the management of Aunt Mavis. It's been a big day.'

Mac didn't need to be aware of the political nonsense at council. It would be more than a mug could bear.

'Aunt Mavis, we are going into town to meet Beau and say goodbye. The holidays are nearly over.'

'It's only one more sleep before the train departs. See you shortly.'

*   *   *

'Hello, Davidia,' said a passer-by.

'Hello, Slirander,' said her companion.

It felt as if the curtain of doom had been lifted. The town and its people were identical to yesterday, but a fresh attitude had pervaded into their conversations.

It was rumoured that Aunt Mavis, now Tabatha, was going to run for mayoral office. At least this time that official position won't be cursed.

The girls made it to the backpackers hostel. They entered expecting to see Beau with his spaghetti dance moves. Instead, a young girl with a foreign accent greeted them.

'What is it for you I can be doing?' She was of Indian extraction.

'Where is Beau?' asked Davidia.

'He is being gone. His girlfriend took him to her homing.'

'We didn't know he had a girlfriend. The flirt,' said Slirander, somewhat disappointed.

She had enjoyed the flirting and it could have lasted another day. Oh, well! Life moves on.

'Is there any wanting you want to be telling him?'

'Do you have a forwarding address or any contact details?'

'No. He is not wanting to be founded. He said if two girls coming to look at him, he had gone. He was holidaying here. Are you the two flirty girls who were chasing him?'

'His ego was certainly far larger than his holiday pay. Thanks, there's no message.'

'So, you are not wanting him? He is a very wanted young man then.'

The girls left. Holiday romances, especially the ones that don't occur, can certainly be short.

*   *   *

The doorbell said, "Push and ye shall ring".

Davidia did as suggested. There was a musical ring and a short-sighted grandma, brandishing a well-worn walking stick doubling as a defensive weapon, answered. The musty smell of her old home escaped relishing a fresh mix of atmosphere. She was visiting it for the last time after having recently moved out.

'What are you hawking? Can't you read the sign? It's not a trick-or-treat, is it?' she said, squinting to see what shapes were at her door. They were two shapely outlines like perfectly drawn shadows.

'It's Davidia and Slirander. We are returning your Milo mug which we found at the mayor's house where Eleanor had visited with it. He had no further reason to keep it there. It's a beautiful mug. Here,' said Davidia, handing over the precious mug.

Slirander bent over and whispered to Milo Mac thanking him for his help and the pleasure it had been to meet a real mug that wasn't a mug. Milo Mac said thanks for returning him to his nice, future home. Grandma ran her fingers over his fine features and was so delighted to have it back. Her Milo evenings will be a source of future continual pleasure.

'Please let Eleanor know.'

The girls departed with a spring in their step and they weren't even on a trampoline.

They passed by the hotel where Mr Hoarse continued his daily readings.

It was time to leave town.

Next morning at the station, the station-master recognised the two young women from their first visit. He doffed his hat as a gentleman does. He had heard all sorts of weird and wonderful stories that had occurred during their stay with their Aunt Mavis.

'May I assist you with your luggage, ladies?'

'Thank you.'

'Did you meet your aunt? How was your holiday?'

'It was the best experience. We may holiday here again,' said Davidia.

A tall lady strode purposefully toward them along the station platform with flowing hair, dangling arms and each hand holding a small parcel that had been wrapped by royal wrappers. She was dressed in modern clothing. The old coats that once shrouded her body in secrecy had been ditched. Her smiling face had a new confidence. She waved. The girls waved back. It was Aunt Mavis, or was it a reclaimed Tabatha?

'I have a small gift for each of you,' she said, and handed them each a small parcel. 'Open them up when you return home. It's a thank-you gift for finding out who I really am. You did come and save me.'

Davidia thought that was a familiar phrase. Now where had she heard it before? Before she discovered that source, the train tooted and chugged into the station huffing and puffing like an uphill marathon runner with a grimace, not a smile. An expression of steam hid the station in a steamy mist. After it had cleared, Aunt Mavis was nowhere to be seen. They hoped the mist hadn't taken her and if it had, what did it mean?

'Where did she go?' asked a surprised Davidia.

'Home, probably,' said Slirander.

Both girls boarded the train for home. A gentle toot, a hiss of steam, a chug of steel wheels pushed by a steam-making boiler and the lurch of movement, and the train had left the station. The journey home was a contemplative experience about meeting Aunt Mavis and her curse. The girls nodded off. Davidia heard the phrase, 'Come and save me' or was it, 'You have come and saved me'. Her face registered a sleep smile as she dozed.

The train came to an abrupt halt. Was there an obstruction on the track? Had a rail lost its grip with its sleeper mates? Had they shunted up the rear of another train? The girls awoke. We're home.

Davidia's mum was there to greet them with arms open wide for a hugging embrace.

'Hi, mum.'

'Hi,' said Slirander also.

'How was the holiday?'

'We'll tell you all about it at home.'

Davidia said goodbye to her friend, Slirander, when she was dropped off at her home.

'See you at school next week,' said Davidia.

'Thanks for the great holiday,' replied Slirander. 'See you next week.'

Once at home, Davidia explained in detail about their strange aunt and the changes that had taken place.

'It was the best holiday,' said Davidia. 'I'll go to bed early. I'm tired.'

'See you in the morning.'

Davidia retreated to her bedroom, her palace of privacy. She sat on her bed on the soft doona furnishings and remembered the small parcel that she had been given as a gift. She wondered what it was. Cautiously, she opened the parcel and to her surprise gasped with excitement. She immediately rang Slirander who was simultaneously experiencing the same euphoria.

'Oh, my God,' exclaimed Davidia. 'Did you get the same gift as me?'

'Isn't it fantastic? I'm over the moon or any other planet with this,' replied Slirander.

'We can't tell anyone. It's beautiful.'

Each of the girls had been given one of a set of fabulous red rubies that were Aunt Mavis' eyes.

Was she really a witch?